Whispers

of Secrets Past

Book 4 of the Amulet Series

By Julie Pope Petrou

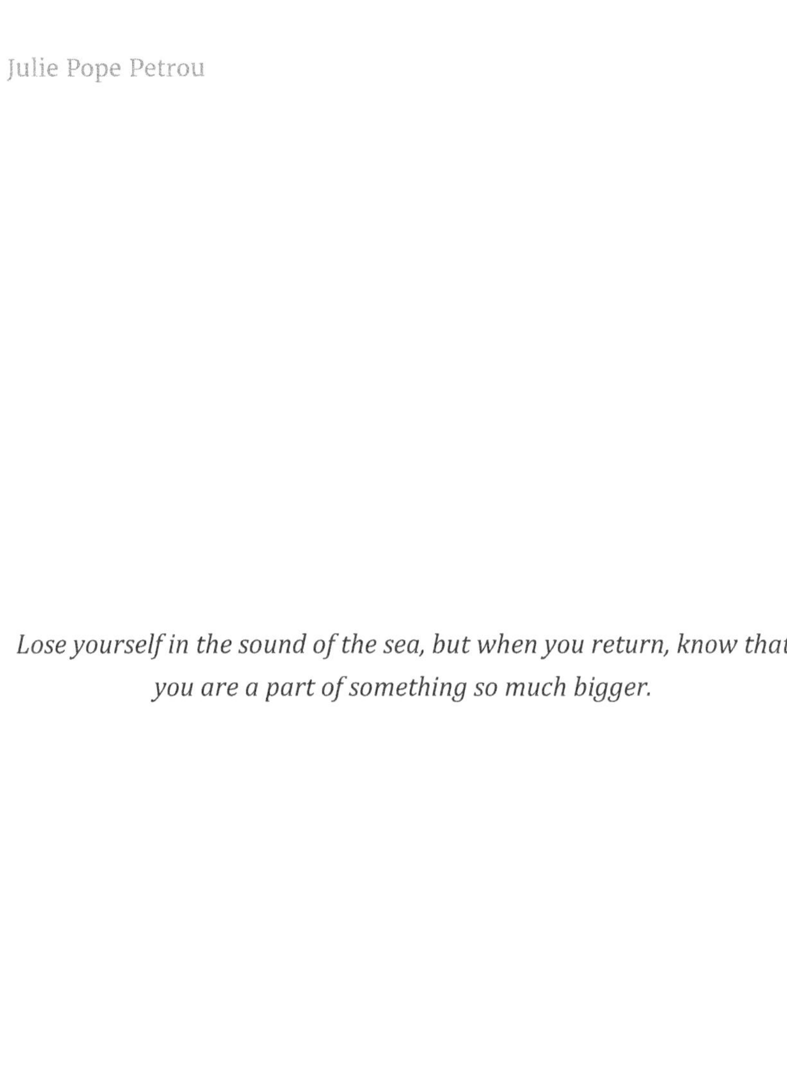

Lose yourself in the sound of the sea, but when you return, know that you are a part of something so much bigger.

WHISPERS OF SECRETS PAST

General Delivery Box
Missoula, MT 59808

This book, Whispers of Secrets Past, is a work of fiction. Any of the names, characters, places, and/or occurrences within are imagined by the author. Any similarity to any person, living or dead is purely coincidental.

ISBN: 979-8-9961754-0-6 Paperback

ISBN: 979-8-9961754-1-3 E-book

Cover Designer: Karen Mitchell, KM Design

Website: Julieuncharted.com

Table of Contents

Prelude

Pirates were terrifying. Some acted on their own, intimidating and threatening, while others, such as privateers, were hired by order of their respective governments. Many would have a "Letter of Marque" granting them the right to confiscate ships laden with valuables on behalf of the throne. Any vessels known to have such valuable cargo were at risk.

After the Spanish laid claim to Central and South America (and parts of North America), several other countries launched campaigns to seize a share of the wealth generated by the raiding, looting, and attacks on these cargo ships. English, Dutch, French, and Portuguese were in the game, many of which were even more cunning and ruthless than the Spanish.

The amulet had its path in the Caribbean as well, exuding life, as though it had a mind of its own. It survives in this story and continues to protect the people of the original bloodline and those they love from the evils they encounter.

Amy and her friends encountered pirates, experiencing a mix of terror and joy, as we now understand that all pirates were thieves, but not all of them were bad people.

The true bloods, now crossing many generations, continue to do right by themselves and the amulet. This story is about discovery, truth, and a love that surpassed the barriers of time.

This fictitious story is written through the eyes of someone who might have been captured and sold as a commodity. Amy ends up being the bravest of the bunch, leading her friends to safety, including one of her ancestors, thus securing her own future.

Whispers of Secrets Past picks up the trail of the amulet after it reaches the Caribbean, only to find it in the pirates' hands (via Isabella), who wore it at the time of her capture. The "Golden Age of Piracy" was a tumultuous era, and most merchant ships feared being attacked by privateers who ranged across the Barbary Coast and beyond. Our main character is victimized, sold, and rescued, and her emotions reach farther and settle deeper than she ever thought possible.

1. Fortunate Find - Pensacola, 1971

Amy Bishop stood, suddenly overwhelmed with emotion, as she wiped away a tear from high on her cheekbone. She had been wandering through her grandmother's house for hours, sorting her things. She felt guilty about not spending enough time with her grandmother, Izzy, over the last couple of years. She had a good excuse, as everyone does, but not one good enough to justify the lack of time she'd spent with her. Now she's gone.

It was only a few days ago when Amy learned the news of her grandmother's passing and left her home to attend Izzy's funeral and wrap up her affairs. The funeral was still a couple of days away, but Amy needed to conjure a few memories in a place where she could feel close to her. She had now padded barefoot into the bedroom, the place where Izzy died.

Amy picked through her grandmother's drawers. She held the blouse Izzy had worn during her last visit. Familiar with it, she found the fabric soft in her hands, which is why her grandmother liked to wear it. Amy held it up to her nose to breathe in her scent, a remnant memory, and the trickle of another tear streaked down her face.

She was in her grandmother's room for a long time, sifting through the clothing in the drawers and lotions that Izzy liked sitting on the dresser. Almost every item she touched ruffled a memory or two.

Her eyes caught sight of the jewelry box, which adorned the space below the round mirror for as long as she could remember. It was a slow process, picking through the years of Izzy's keepsakes. Amy remembered days and events when Izzy would wear some of her jewelry, always with a specific color or on a particular day.

There were many things in that box that Amy didn't remember. Necklaces and bracelets that she had not seen. Her eyes landed on a shallow drawer at the bottom of the box that she had never recalled ever being there. She slid it open and found a small parcel wrapped in brown paper and bound with a jute string. Curious, Amy untied the string around the small bundle and unfolded the paper. She saw the most beautiful stone in an ancient setting. When she picked it up from the paper, it warmed slightly in her hand. Amy cocked her head, a little bewildered, but continued her assessment. There was no chain, only a thin, tan, well-worn leather thong knotted to keep it together.

The stone was a brilliant, mesmerizing blue with tiny streaks of silver and little black spots throughout. The setting was ancient and supported a small piece that appeared to be bone or ivory. It was striking. Amy allowed a glint of a smile as she put it around her neck. She never remembered her grandmother wearing it, but she could feel her now. It must have been something extraordinary for Izzy to hide it like that.

The amulet made Amy feel warm inside as if this fortunate find was meant solely for her. Still perplexed, she looked around the room for other mysteries that Izzy kept secret. Her eyes browsed over the brown paper she found it wrapped in, which now lay on the bed. Curiously, she saw writing on the back side of it. Amy picked it up and read the words Izzy had penned.

> *Amy,*
> *It is special to be chosen by the stone. I knew it would belong to you one day, as the amulet told me so. There is safety, love, and an abundance of knowledge within this amazing stone. Wear it, knowing it will shelter you and give you visions of things not yet seen. These are the most wonderful gifts–things I wish for you.*
> *All my love, Izzy*

Amy was in shock. In a shaky voice, she said, "How did she know I would find it?" It was dumb luck that she happened upon the stone at all. It could have very easily ended up with her cousin, Jennie. But it didn't. Amy looked again at the words on the paper. *I knew it would belong to you one day, as the amulet told me so.* Those were haunting words, and Amy realized just how true they were. It felt like a long-lost friend when she put it on and would likely not take it off.

Jennie was pushy and, from what Amy remembered, very unpleasant. She was tall and clumsy, and although she was only a few years older than Amy, she had wrinkles between her eyebrows from frowning so much.

Like herself, she was very fond of Izzy, and Amy couldn't fault her for that. Her cousin, Jennie, lived much closer to Pensacola than Aunt Jackie, so it made sense for Jennie to make the trip to Izzy's to help clean the house and lay claim to many things that roused her fondest memories. Amy knew she was in town but hadn't seen her yet, and was not unhappy about that fact, either.

She suddenly became overcome with contentment. There was a connection between her, Izzy, and this stone that would keep her close forever. She let a smile spread across her face—*this is something I share with Izzy that no one else ever would.* Amy had lost her mother to cancer a couple of years previously and had since strengthened her relationship with Izzy; another unbreakable connection between them.

Amy and Izzy had talked weekly, sometimes more often when Amy needed the advice of a loved one. She was devastated when Irene, the neighbor who would shop for Izzy and look in on her, called with the unhappy news of her passing.

As if she had nothing else to do, recalling these thoughts slowed her down tremendously, and she found that she had gotten little to nothing done in the last hour. The woman at the funeral home asked her to find something she considered appropriate to bury her grandmother in, and that was Amy's chief duty. However, she had been sidetracked by the memories and trinkets that captured her attention.

Finally, Amy shook herself from the dabbling and gawking and picked a light blue dress with daisies that she remembered Izzy would wear to church. It was nice and fit her well, but Izzy would not wear it for more formal occasions. *It was just right*, Amy thought to herself. She found a pair of white slip-on shoes she remembered and put them in the bag with the dress, a cross, and her pearl earrings.

Amy picked up the bag with the articles in it and left through the front door, turning the deadbolt with her grandmother's key. She got into her car and went directly to the funeral home.

Once she had delivered the bag of clothing, she could make her way to the hotel and get cleaned up. Amy was due for a bit of rest and wished for a shower and a drink.

She popped the cork on a bottle of red wine, filled the tub with bubbles, and lay there soaking. She ruminated on the day's events, then held up the amulet by its leather cord, staring at the rare piece of stone. She began to wonder how her grandmother had gotten that amulet in the first place and couldn't help but feel a sense of mystique surrounding it. Amy wanted to know more.

2. Deep Dive - 1971

Amy got out of bed early, as usual, throwing open the curtain and letting the morning sun splash the pale walls with its warming glow. As her day started, she ran a comb through her loose red ringlets to smooth them, then pulled her hair back with a large clip. She slipped on a baby blue T-shirt, pulled her favorite slides out of her suitcase, and slipped them onto her feet.

She chose to take the stairs rather than the elevator, which smelled like stale beer and old man sweat. As she descended the stairway, Amy couldn't wait to wrap her hands around her morning cup of coffee. It wasn't because she was a slow starter so much as she just wanted a kick. She slowly sipped the hot beverage and pondered the questions that ping-ponged in her mind. "Where did Izzy get this amulet, and why me?" Amy wanted to return to her grandmother's house again and dig around to see if any evidence might provide a lead.

Cautiously, she unlocked the door and heard the distinct "click. "Pushing the door open slowly. The familiar scent of her grandmother's home brought her comfort, as it still made her reminisce about Izzy all over again. It saddened her not to see

Izzy smiling at her as she got herself fully into the room. She slipped in unassumingly and put her purse and keys on the counter.

Walking through the house as quietly as possible, she halted at Izzy's bedroom door, staring at the wallpapered walls. Her first instinct was to rummage through the closet. *Everyone always seems to have a stash in the closet*, Amy thought, using herself as an example. *Some people call them skeletons*. This phrase she said aloud, and it made her smile. It was a statement her mother would use when she had gone to her closet to dig for something on more than one occasion. *Was it a hint?* That thought made her more determined than ever to uncover the layers of the onion that may reveal the secret behind the mysterious stone amulet.

Only a few boxes were behind the area where Izzy's shoes were kept. She opened them one by one and found many treasures, but nothing that jumped out at her. Amy sat on the floor beside the open door and pulled out artifacts. Some were meaningful, and some were unknown, but all the pieces woven together gave her a much clearer picture of the world that her grandmother lived in. A dried-up corsage had a rose-colored ribbon tucked into its cluster. There were a few photographs of Izzy, Aunt Jackie, and her mother, Sophia. Amy stared at one of the pictures for some time. She could see her resemblance staring back at her from the photo.

Two of the women in the picture had dark hair, but Izzy had generous red waves, curls, in fact. They all had very dark, mysterious-looking brown eyes and were hauntingly beautiful.

Amy looked intently at a picture among the others of Izzy with a man and a woman whom she didn't know. Amy knew she had no relatives in Florida, but was unsure about any that might still be in Puerto Rico.

She put the picture down and walked over to the round mirror that hung over the dresser. Amy looked at her reflection now through a different pair of eyes. The furrows on her brow deepened as the thought came to her: *Who am I?* It was the first time she'd ever questioned it. Unlike her mother's and aunt's hair, Amy's was a deep, rich red, with waves and curls rather than the smooth texture of theirs, very similar to Izzy's.
She wondered why. *Why am I different?* She picked up the picture again and looked at it, then refocused on her reflection, batting the long lashes of her deep brown eyes. Amy was now determined to discover more in that closet than just the identity of the amulet; she was looking for a connection, looking to find herself.

Amy sat down again and pulled more things out of the box: a vase, an old wallet, empty, of course, and a couple of books with titles she had never heard of. There was nothing else in this box, but other treasures still hidden in the shadows of the closet held secrets of Izzy's past.

She reached for another box and opened it. There was clothing and a pair of baby booties with blue laces. Amy wondered if they'd ever been worn. She picked through the odd combination of other things, but nothing was special about them. Moving a handful of birthday cards, she found a key at the bottom of the box. It was a single key with no other markings.

The skeleton key was ancient and appeared to open something older than old. "This is interesting," Amy said to herself, tucking the cold medal passkey into her pocket for safekeeping, then she placed the removed articles back into the box.

Amy got up, looking for refreshment. The closet was dusty, and her throat and eyes were scratchy, so a cold beverage was in order. She went into the kitchen and opened the refrigerator. Not much was interesting in the old fridge, but she did find an unopened bottle of iced tea. Popping the top, Amy took a drink. It was certainly cold and refreshing. She took a minute to wipe her eyes and opened the window nearest her to let in some fresh air.

Her expression changed quickly as a flash of something she had seen in the box woke up in her mind. She put down the bottle of tea, ran back into Izzy's bedroom, and opened the box she had just filled. Amy pulled out the two books with titles she didn't recognize and examined them. A smile broke out on her face. "Isabella Rosa Delgado" was the author's name.

"That's Izzy! Now there was a hidden treasure, all right." Amy spoke aloud with no one but the walls and dust to hear. It completely took her by surprise. She decided the books would come with her as well. She had to read them.

Her head was buried again in the closet's depths, and she pulled out yet another box. This one held a treasure trove of photos and scrapbooks. Amy remembered Izzy and her mother looking through these old books when she was young. The pictures contained within showed her ancestors.

On her mother's side, they were a mix of Native American and Puerto Rican; on her father's side, they were very Puerto Rican. There was nothing unusual about it, but it did make it easier to recognize her mother's relatives.

Amy flipped through the pages, and memories swept over her like a splash of cold water. She remembered many of the faces in the pictures or had heard the names spoken of fondly.

She pulled another photo album out of the box and saw the still image of a baby boy. The title under the picture said, "Jorge." There were other keepsakes on the next page, including the baby's picture, cards of congratulations, and a newspaper announcement, "Baby boy Delgado." He was born on October

10, 1921. Amy flipped another page in the book and saw the death announcement: "Died November 2, 1921."

"Poor thing lived 25 days," Amy said in a whisper. Something else she didn't know about her grandmother.

She consciously decided to stop counting the unknowns about Izzy and see if she could find what she started looking for in the first place, what the amulet was all about. As she visualized that thought, her hand found its way to the stone around her neck, and she touched it, carefully memorizing how the stone and its enhancements felt on her fingertips. She touched the piece of bone fragment, wondering where it came from. *Or was it ivory?* She thought intently about how old the amulet might be and wasn't sure exactly what the whitish item was.

Moving on to another scrapbook in the box, Amy found one with preserved images of her and her cousin Jennie. Next, she pulled out a couple of handmade cards with cutout hearts and crayon flowers. She smiled to herself, recalling the misfit memories held within the pages.

There were only a few photographs of Izzy among the scraps and memories. Amy began to turn the pages more fervently, looking for Izzy amongst the images. She found one of her eating ice cream with her Mother and Aunt, but there was little else within the book. At the very back of this dark blue-covered book, Amy found a map. Although it was pretty simple, it was important enough that Izzy wanted it as a keepsake, so she gave it the attention it deserved.

Amy carefully opened the yellowed sheet of heavy paper, revealing a simple map with no real point of reference. Studying the sheet for a long time, she found simple directions like, *Once past the old oak tree, look for a black boulder.* It was descriptive, but it didn't specify a starting point. Amy tucked this into one of the books she planned to take, leaving no trace in the scrapbook from whence it came.

Just as she closed the scrapbook, she heard the front door open. "Hello?" Amy recognized the voice.

"Back here," she said in acknowledgment. Jennie breached the bedroom doorway, leading with her head, as she always did. "Hey," she said to her cousin.

"Hey, to you too," Jennie responded with her usual arrogant tone. "I thought I would come and see if I could help get things packed up. I'm not sure what can be done with all this stuff." Amy looked down at the boxes on the floor around her.

"Yeah, well, I've been digging around to see if there is anything of value in these boxes. This one can probably go, but you'll want to see this one." She put both hands on the box she had just closed and pushed it gently toward Jennie. "It is scrapbooks, pictures, and stuff." Making very spare eye contact with her cousin, Amy was very matter-of-fact up front, but her heart was beating out of her chest. She did not want her cousin to know of the stone amulet or of her quest to find the story behind it.

They looked at each other momentarily, and Jennie said, "This was where she took her last breath."

Amy nodded. "It's hard to believe she's gone." She felt a tear welling up in the corner of her eye. There was obvious tension between Jennie and her, but they shared the same sentiment about Izzy.

Jennie poked around Izzy's bedroom for a while, then decided to go to the kitchen to see if there were any mementos worth keeping. She, too, was searching for memories.

Amy continued in the bedroom. She began piling things on the bed that could be donated to the local charity or to Izzy's church. The stinging fact hit her that in a few short days, the remaining items would be picked up by the auction house and gone for good. She had spotted one more box in the closet and pulled it out, hoping for another lead.

Pulling the items out one by one, Amy made mental notes of each thing she placed on the ground beside her. There was a book of drawings. Most of them were charcoal and quite detailed. She looked them over one at a time, fondly examining the intricate lines, contrasting them with the not-so-white paper. She recalled her grandmother drawing them when she visited.

Still, the memory persisted as Izzy moved on to another artistic outlet. These pages were precious. As she leafed through the numerous works of art, Amy found a drawing of the amulet. It was exact. Izzy's hand had traced every detail of the stone so perfectly that it took her breath away. She folded this gently and tucked it into one of the books. She thought the drawings might also be something Jennie would cherish, so she left the book out of the box and continued.

Digging deeper, Amy pulled out a baby's baptism dress. It was so tiny. She thought it belonged to her Aunt Jackie or her mother. It was an heirloom, nonetheless. Other things in this box belonged to a child, and Amy did not think it was right to part with any of them.

Reaching into the bottom of the box, she found a neatly folded piece of paper with nothing more than an address. 161 Elm St. This address was unfamiliar to her, but she slipped the paper into one of her pockets and decided she would make time to investigate it later. For now, her "deep dive" into the closet was complete.

She walked down the hall into the kitchen and found Jennie doing the same thing she had done the day before. Everything touched brought a wave of memories.

Amy picked up her bottle of tea and took another swig. "There is another one of these in the fridge if you want it." Jennie nodded, wiping away the tear stains left on her cheek. Amy pulled the bottle out of the fridge, popped the top, and handed it to Jennie.

"It's hard. But death is as much a part of life as living is. I learned that when Mom passed. You know you can talk to her whenever you want. She's here with us now." Amy's words were a comfort. In her soul, she never felt that her mother was gone forever, just in a place where she couldn't see her anymore.

Amy's words sounded almost cold and uncaring, but she had undoubtedly wrestled with emotions over the last couple of years. It was her way of coping.

"Remembering them will keep them with us, and the stories *we* tell will pass from us to our kids and our grandkids. They are never really gone." Amy placed her hand on her cousin's shoulder in a gesture of kindness.

The two girls spent hours touching and examining everything they could, and boxing up the items that needed to be taken. Jennie helped Amy load the boxes into the side door of her Volkswagen van so she could deliver them to the donation warehouse. They agreed to meet there again the next day.

After dropping off the boxes, she was anxious to investigate the address. She hoped it was an actual address in this town, as nothing else was on the paper.

Amy finally found Elm and drove slowly, looking at mailboxes for the address. She saw the exact address that had been penned on the paper and stopped her car. It appeared to have been abandoned for years. The house was small and white, with a broken-down porch. Vines dribbled over it, almost hiding the entryway from the street.

It looked creepy and gave Amy the chills when she stepped onto the porch. She tried the door, and it was locked. When she looked at the keyhole, it appeared to require a skeleton key. "Well, I'll be damned," Amy muttered to herself. She pulled the key out of her pocket and slipped it into the lock. Twisting it, the door opened with a click. Moving the vines to the side, she stepped into the old, decrepit house.

As she expected, it was musty and dark, as the ivy on the outside blocked the daylight from the picture window. Amy wandered around, honestly not seeing much but trying to understand why Izzy would have a key to this place. She walked slowly, listening to the floorboards creak and moan. There was a short hall to a bedroom. The bathroom had a pull-chain toilet, a feature that had been absent from homes for many years.

Nothing was remarkable about this house except that it was old. She made it to another bedroom, painted a light blue. She looked up and saw a hole in the ceiling, proof that the only inhabitant was a wayward squirrel. There was a door in the ceiling at the far corner of the bedroom. Amy looked up at it curiously. It had a piece of rope attached, and she instinctively tugged at it. The door opened with a thud, and a ladder flopped down. It was still folded up and unreachable, but it was undoubtedly a ladder. Amy found a rickety wooden stool in the corner and used it to reach the ladder, pulling it the rest of the way down.

"This is cool." She said to herself. Of course, Amy didn't come this far to discontinue her investigation. She climbed the ladder slowly, not knowing if it was strong enough to hold her. One step at a time, she ascended, making prints in the disgusting layer of dust.

When she reached the floor above, Amy stood on the dusty ladder, awestruck. There were many things, all covered with years of dust and filth. She pulled herself to standing in the tiny attic. A small window at the peak gave off just enough light for Amy to see. Under a looking glass near the base of the window, Amy saw a wooden plaque that said "Delgado." This house must have belonged to Izzy once; she guessed it could have been Izzy's mother's home.

The discomfort she felt from sneaking around someone else's place and the fear of what she might find had left her now filled with anxiety.

Amy carefully made her way around this place, but took some time poking and digging through the artifacts within.

These items were incredibly old. Exceeding a hundred years for sure. Amy was as careful as possible, but wanted to look at everything. The more she looked, the more relics she wanted to find. Near another window on the opposite side of the attic was a Mahogany box. It was a replica of a sewing box she had seen in a museum in St. Louis. She was astonished at how old it was. There was a little round metal handle she used to lift the lid, revealing the contents. She opened it slowly, unsure yet eager to see what was held within.

There was a spool of thread and a pair of knitting needles in the top tray. Amy lifted this tray and found another one nestled below it. This was full of papers. It looked like a deed to this house, and the plat description matched what it would have looked like 100 years ago. She found letters. Love letters between "My Love" and "Juan" were folded neatly amid the other papers. There was a fold of paper that looked different than the others. Her first thought was that it appeared to be parchment. But it was not a letter. It was fashioned into an envelope with yet another piece of paper tucked inside. She carefully pulled the guarded message from the envelope and read it.

Spirit of the mountain – I call, asking for the
empowerment of this piece of you. Give this fragment
the power to heal and the power to destroy evil.
Ruler of wisdom - Gather in this amulet and hold
wisdom that it will be part of this soul's future.
Spirit of all-seeing – wrap the wearer of this stone in a
cloak of security, that they may know peace of heart in
the depths of their soul.
Moon goddess– Shine in this stone as the moon shines

upon the Earth. Enlighten the heart and bestow happiness upon the soul of the possessor.

Amy's jaw dropped. It spoke of the stone amulet that holds wisdom. *Is the stone blessed? Enchanted?* she thought, feeling a little lightheaded. The meaning and secrecy of the hiding place became clear to Amy now. It likely wouldn't mean anything to anyone without finding the stone first.

She stood there bewildered and yet more curious. These pieces were not far apart, but she could see how they would be overlooked if not together. And the fact that they were all meant for Amy to find was mind-blowing. Could the stone itself draw her to this place? She shook her head in disbelief. *It couldn't be.* Her heart was all in, but her mind still didn’t trust it.

Putting all the treasured items back into the box, she paused at the tray holding all the papers. As she put them back, she slowly looked each item over, thinking this box might hold more secrets and other treasures among the faded pages, yellowed leaves tinged with age. Her eyes glanced over the one that said "DEED" in graphic letters across the top.

Unfolding the paper to read it, she heard a "plop" sound in the room below. It startled her, but she thought she would be better off not moving if it were a person. *If I don't move, they won't know I'm here.* Quiet and as still as the dust on the attic antiques, she waited. Nearly ten minutes had passed in silence before she continued her quest for knowledge.

Amy picked up the DEED again and saw her name on the line that said, "Granted to." It had been signed and notarized on June 5, 1955, which was Izzy's birthday. "Humph," a huffing noise came out in the calm of the attic. “I was only 13 years old in 1955." Amy smiled, speaking the uttered words. "She knew."

Amy closed the sewing box and held out the parchment envelope, wanting to do more research. When she tried to shove the box back, it was heavier than it should have been.

Giving it a shove, the box tipped onto its back, revealing that the bottom was fake, or at least not like the rest of the box. Amy picked up a crochet hook that had fallen onto the floor and used it to pry the bottom of the box loose. Suddenly, a waterfall of gold coins fell onto the dusty floor.

Suddenly, her eyes opened as wide as they could go, and she slapped a hand over her mouth. "Treasure?" she whispered as if it were a secret.

Amy guessed the coins were Spanish gold and hundreds of years old. Picking one of the heavy, tarnished coins, she examined it closely. Muttering to herself, doing her best to squelch her excitement, she said, "This is better than buried treasure!"

On the verge of crying, Amy laughed when she thought of how Izzy had left these breadcrumbs for her to find. She stuffed some coins into her pocket, returning the rest right where she had found them.

Descending the ladder, she closed everything up as if she had never been there. When she treaded lightly out onto the porch, Amy carefully looked in all directions before stepping off of it and onto the street, not wishing to be seen. The sun was going down now, and she was genuinely famished. She hadn't eaten all day.

The young St. Louis woman stopped for a sandwich and a cup of soup at the diner just down the street from the hotel. She ate and thought deeply about the trail of evidence, pieces left for her to follow. Pondering and taking another bite, Amy thought, *Izzy knew I would believe her. Maybe that's why she picked me.* Taking her time eating, she planned the next day, adding a trip to the library among all the other duties.

3. Generations - 1971

It was Thursday, the last day for her or Jennie to lay claim to Izzy's more personal items. Amy arrived at Izzy's house as early as possible to beat her cousin, Jennie. She was intent on exploring nooks like the basement or attic for those special items meant only for her to find.

She opened the door to Izzy's house and was surprisingly astonished by the smell of her beloved grandmother. It hit her; the distinctive scent she immediately associated with her beloved grandmother. It was as clear to her as a birthmark, but it was all that remained. This morning, the smell of this house brought Amy a host of memories. She smiled, remembering when she was just a child, breaking through the door as fast as possible to be the first to embrace her grandmother. *She had the most loving hugs*, Amy recalled with fondness.

She put down her purse and keys and began poking and prodding, seeking the unknown. She looked for a trap door to a basement. She never remembered one but looked nonetheless. "Leave no stone unturned." She chanted to herself. Amy paused momentarily to take a sip of coffee that she'd stopped to get on the way. Then, she began searching for the attic.

Amy wandered around her grandmother's house, looking up. She did not find a door like the one at Elm Street, but there was a small door in the hallway just in front of the bathroom door. Amy got a stool and climbed on it, teetering as she moved the square piece of wood to the side so she could see. It was an attic crawl space, but what Amy could see was nothing unusual; just insulation and wooden beams.

She returned the stool to the kitchen corner, where she found it, and went back into the bedroom. It was looking pretty sparse now as she and Jennie had managed to box up a lot of not-so-personal items for the charity to come pick up.

Again, she went to the closet and was scouring for anything Izzy might have left for her to find. A shelf, high above the clothing, held only a few miscellaneous items. She knew something too high was difficult to reach, so Amy thought Izzy wouldn't store many things there.

She went into the kitchen to retrieve the stool to see if anything of value was left on the high shelf. She pulled down a couple of smaller boxes and a set of neatly folded curtains, which were not in boxes. Dust flew from them as they dropped onto the closet floor.

Once the dust had settled, Amy saw an article that looked like paper revealed from under the folds of paisley print.

She scrambled down off the stool and pulled out the paper. It was old, like the parchment envelope, but it looked more delicate. The folds were nearly worn clear through by both age and use.

She cleared a place on the bed so she could unfold it. Slowly, carefully, she opened it and revealed a family tree. It was handwritten and started with Izzy, down what appeared to be ten generations or more. From what Amy gathered, this was Izzy's doing. She had begun an investigation into her family tree. Below the last set of names, Izzy noted, *"Incan heritage*."

Her eyes got big with excitement. *Really? Were our ancestors Incan?* Amy never thought their bloodline extended beyond Puerto Rico, but she realized it was only the last hundred years or so that she was familiar with.

With one more artifact neatly tucked away, Amy was satisfied that her search had revealed another clue. Whether it was relevant to the amulet or not, she came away from the treasure hunt with a trail of interesting family facts.

Jennie showed up about an hour later, and the two girls decided to box up some things for themselves. Jennie had driven her car and could load up things she planned to keep for both her and her mother, but Amy struggled to decide what she wanted to keep and what she didn't need.

For Amy, the choices were random, just as the memories that tugged at her heart were. The assorted items she kept were meant to commemorate Izzy's life and character, but just about everything she touched did the same. She wanted the photo albums, but Jennie did too, so they decided to share the pictures as evenly as possible and agreed to get copies made of the others.

Jennie packed a box for her mother, as she did one for herself. It contained some items she had explicitly requested, as well as some random choices that Jennie liked. Overall, the particulars that meant the most to the girls were safely packaged and would likely become heirlooms, living the rest of their days in the boxes they were now packed in.

By afternoon, the room was bare, and designated heirlooms were packed away for Aunt Jackie. Boxes and bags were stacked for the local charity, and a handful of books would be donated to the library. Jennie had spent the morning cleaning out the refrigerator, packing any unopened, frozen items into a box for the homeless shelter. It was sad how little of it they took. Amy could not believe they would turn down free food.

"Well, looks like we're done with all the major stuff," Amy said, looking at her cousin.

Jennie gave her a nod. "Gonna be hard not coming back to this place." Her callous features softened suddenly as she thought of her grandmother.

"I miss her too," Amy remarked, putting her arm around her cousin's shoulder. "I'll be here in the morning, just a bit before nine, for the auction house people. You comin'?"

Jennie answered quietly, "Uh, huh." Then she threw her purse strap over her shoulder and headed out the door.

"See ya." Amy's words trailed off as her cousin let the door close behind her.

They never spent any time together, except for the time they spent at Izzy's. Amy wondered as she drove away if they would ever spend time together again. *They were family*, she thought. She always had mixed feelings about her own; as most people do, she thought about her own existence and connection to Izzy. She did not want to change that.

Rather than head back to the hotel, Amy went straight to the local library. She wanted to research some of the names on the *family tree* document she had found.

There was a large, unoccupied table in the farthest corner of the library, so Amy decided to set up camp there. She pulled out a chair for herself and flopped the rather large shoulder bag on the table, reaching inside to pull out the parchment. She pulled open the folds as carefully as she could, minding that the paper was ancient. Amy took some time to get it laid flat, then pulled out a tablet and a pen to make notes.

She remembered Izzy talking of her great-grandmother, who had died when Izzy was young. She had only heard little bits and pieces about her great-grandfather, a jolly man that her grandmother had spoken so fondly of. But there had to be fourteen or fifteen generations on this tree, and she was determined to investigate as many as possible.

She scoured cemetery directories throughout Florida and birth records, both within county clerk and recorder offices and churches across the state. It was a maze, but she was able to find bits and pieces of the last four generations.

Amy learned that Izzy had a cousin named Angel, who died at eighteen in the First World War. She also learned that Izzy's husband, Juan Delgado, was arrested and spent nearly a month in the local jail for starting a brawl with four of his friends. Getting down to the nitty-gritty was where the interesting stuff happened.

One of her great-great-grandfathers fought in the Spanish-American War, and his grandmother and her family lived with the Seminoles. The history dive was interesting and fun, but none of the information mentioned the amulet or where it was from. She suspected it was of Incan origin, but a theoretical brick wall existed between the US records and those of Puerto Rico. Amy thought deeply about how to get past this.

She found some ship manifests from the late 1700s that included both passenger names and lists of cargo. These records might reveal something about the immigrants. After all, they had to have boarded a boat. She had only begun diving into the records of ships that stopped in Puerto Rico en route to Florida when the library monitor informed her that they would be closing in five minutes, and she would need to leave.

Amy reluctantly got up and stowed her special items back in her bag. Off she went, disappointed that she hadn't even touched on the history of the coins. What she learned gave her many facts to ponder, but it was like peeling back the layers of an onion. She knew there was still more to come—a lot more.

Taking the library's front steps slowly and steadily, Amy nearly walked past the van. Still, deep in thought, she backtracked, climbed behind the wheel, and drove to her hotel. She didn't think she would be able to sleep, as her mind raced, digging for facts just out of reach.

Knowing what the next few hours would look like, she pulled into the parking lot at a store and bought herself a bottle of wine to calm her restless mind.

Amy had the family tree parchment open and spread across the hotel bed as she examined the names. Fernando Juan Paolo and Catherine O'Malley. She never knew she had Irish blood. None of her known relatives had blonde hair or light skin. A smile began to grow on Amy's face. Red hair. Irish blood. Now that began to clarify her thoughts. It gave her a sense of relief that she didn't belong to the Gypsies.

Immersed in research, she stayed up much later than she should have, knowing she needed to be there for the auction house the next morning. Folding the paper carefully, she put it away and prepared herself for bed. Glancing in the mirror at her reflection as she passed by it, she half expected to see someone else. *It's funny,* she thought. *Something that offers a glimpse of your past can alter how you see yourself.*

Amy yawned generously and climbed into bed, wrapping her fingers around the amulet, as if holding onto a stuffed animal that comforts. She fell quickly asleep.

***

Many faces emerged in her dream. She saw Izzy in the blue dress with daisies. She saw her mother laughing, her hair blowing in the wind. She saw her amulet around the neck of a younger girl with thick, wavy red hair, just like hers. She saw falcons and large birds drifting in the wind. They were breathtakingly beautiful.

Not wanting to wake and give up the friendly faces, Amy's eyes flew open wildly, and she drew a deep breath. It was a dream. But this felt different than a dream. She couldn't quite describe it, but it was–something. She realized then that she had a death grip on the stone amulet around her neck and slowly loosened her grip.

Amy was a writer and knew that many good stories came from dreams, so she always had a pad and paper near her to write them down before they were forgotten. She jotted down the dream's details, carefully mentioning the faces she'd seen, both known and unknown. Her journaling complete, she lay back down and closed her eyes, tossing and turning before allowing herself to relax enough to fall asleep again.

4. The Auction House - 1971

It was well past eight before Amy woke up enough to check the clock in the room. "Oh my God!" she exclaimed, jumping out of bed. There was no time for a shower, so brushing through her thick red hair and wrapping it up in a tidy bun was her best option. She blew through the lobby, stopping for a moment to pour a cup of coffee to take with her on the way to Izzy's to meet the auction house people.

She made it with only minutes to spare, breaking as few traffic rules as possible. Amy unlocked the doors and waited for Cameron. He was the person she'd spoken to and the one who would come to assess the values of the items, mostly furniture, and take them to be auctioned. She was alone in the house for only a few minutes, but could swear she wasn't the only one there.

As she slowly meandered through the empty rooms and hallways, Amy felt a presence. It was a strange feeling, but not creepy. She was only beginning to take measure of her company when there was a rap on the front door. She peeked around the corner and saw a shadow on the stoop. "Coming," she said loud enough for the auction house manager to hear her. She glanced casually over her shoulder before heading to the entry to let him in.

Cameron Moreau was a tall man with a commanding stature. His shadow seemed to fill a room before he was even in it. The friendly smile on this striking man's face dispelled any apprehensions she might have had about leaving her grandmother's household items in the hands of strangers. It made her happy. She had a good feeling about him.

The process was quick and relatively painless, given that she was saying goodbye to what was left of the memories of Izzy's home. She was sure Cam (as he preferred to be called) had done this repeatedly, and his actions were careful and courteous to help lessen the blow. She watched him work and admired his keen organizational skills. He had a way of giving orders without being bossy or condescending, and also diligently pitched in to help. He never asked others to perform anything he wouldn't do himself.

The auction house manager had been working for a while before he noticed her watching him. When their eyes met, the corner of his mouth turned up into a smile.

He slowly approached her and said, "I hope this process isn't too painful for you." She knew immediately that he meant what he said.

"Thank you for your concern, but I'm fine." He tipped his head forward, nodded his understanding, and then went back to work. Cam was tall with dark-brown wavy hair and baby-blue eyes. When he looked at her, his eyes were nearly translucent, and she could see a kind brightness in his expression. He seemed truly genuine.

Amy tried to remain expressionless, but the fact that she was taken with him was difficult to hide. She needed to divert her attention elsewhere, so she turned and went into the kitchen to polish off the hotel coffee in the styrofoam cup. Taking a swig, she found it cold and disagreeable, so she washed what was left down the sink and threw the cup in the trash. This day would be riddled with emotion, and this was just the beginning.

The crew loading her grandmother's belongings into a truck worked swiftly, and within an hour and a half, the house was empty. Cam approached her to recite the final value of the items. The auction house would purchase the items outright and then sell or auction them to earn its profit.

He pushed the necessary paperwork toward Amy, giving her a chance to view and sign. "A check will be ready for you at the main office in about an hour. Would you like to come pick it up?" Cam's tone was courteous. Their hands touched when he handed her the clipboard and pen, and Amy looked up at him. She smiled, surprised at just how simple the auction house's process was, and of course, was utterly drawn in by his gaze.

"Thank you, Cam. I can be there."

She handed the clipboard back to him, and he looked at her with his dazzling smile. He asked, "Has anyone ever told you you have the most incredible eyes?"

Amy blushed slightly. "No, not really." Her eyes were a deep brown, darker than brown eyes typically are, and her left eye had a streak of gray that stood out, almost shimmering against the dark chocolate background.

"They are breathtaking," Cam said to her with a wink. "We'll see you in an hour then." He turned to leave and glanced back a second time, seeing the smile on her face.

***

Amy was now showered and snacked on crackers she bought from the convenience store. She had dressed for the funeral before going to the auction house, knowing she was limited on time and didn't fancy running back and forth to the hotel. Her dress was a classic, solid dark blue with a straight-line skirt and a short slit up the back. It was stunning, with a square neckline, and the color contrasted beautifully with her hair and complexion.

It gave Amy a certain amount of satisfaction when she looked at herself in the mirror. The only jewelry she wore was the amulet. It was not as appealing as a string of pearls, but it would do. She was unwilling to part with it just yet. And besides, it made her feel closer to Izzy.

Pausing for a moment, Amy looked around the room again, checking to be sure she hadn't forgotten anything, then slowly closed the door as she left.

Cam was waiting for her in the office and saw her pull into the parking lot. He greeted her at the door, holding it open like a gentleman. "Hello," Amy said, making contact with those beautiful eyes that shone like crystals in the sun.

"And hello to you, too." His warm, welcoming smile made Amy think he was more than happy to see her.

Cam invited her to sit down and offered her water or coffee, the only choices in the office unless he went to the warehouse to get a soda from the machine.

"No, thank you. Amy said delicately.

"You look beautiful," Cam said, the tips of his ears tinged with pink. Amy just smiled. She knew she did. This dress was not only appropriate for the funeral but looked as though it had been made just for her.

Cam had the check ready, and he strode over to the file cabinet behind her to get it, silently admiring her graceful features. Her wavy hair was casually pulled back in a loose ponytail, wisps of shorter, twisty hair falling out around her face, softening her appearance. Amy's shoulders were delicate but presented as firm and straight. He marveled at her, not only at how she looked, but also at how she carried herself, proud and determined. There was a great deal of detail packed into such a small package.

"Here you go," He said, putting a cheerful tone to his words. He reached over Amy's shapely shoulder from behind and handed her the check. She took it from his hand, brushing his knuckle lightly in one smooth motion. With her eyes diverted downward, her delicate features pulled into a bashful smile.

"Thank you, Cam."

He couldn't just let her go, as this might be the last chance he would have to see her. The tall, handsome man took a deep breath and hesitated a minute, wishing to continue the brief contact.

"Look, I know this is a tough day for you, but I want to see you again." He was intent but a little nervous as he seemed to stumble over the words. "Would you possibly like to have dinner with me? Maybe tomorrow?"

Although Amy had a lot on her mind, she hoped to make this kind of connection with him and was delighted when he said the words. "That would be very nice, Cam." Her eyes met his and sparkled brightly, then she deliberately looked away. Her intention was not to be too forward but to let him know she admired him, too.

His eyes lit up when he heard his name flow so naturally from her lips. She looked at him and smiled. There was a moment of awkward silence between them, then Cam softly broke the quietness. "We'll talk tomorrow. I'll call you."

Still looking at him, Amy smiled with her deep brown eyes, saying, "That would be perfect." Then she stood, holding the check up, batting her eyes, and said, "Thank you, I look forward to the call." She gave him a casual wink as she walked out of the office.

He watched her leave, still admiring the confident aura around her, and was surprised by the emotions that stirred when he thought about it. Then he shook his head slightly. He was thinking how very different Amy was from his ex-wife. He closed the cabinet door, went to the warehouse, and returned to work.

Amy could feel his eyes on her when she walked out, and took great care to be sure they stayed that way. Walking tall and queenly, she emphasized her steps with just enough swing to hold his gaze. Gracefully getting into her car, she backed out of the parking spot, gave a finger-wave to him out her car window, and left, smiling.

5. Greetings and Goodbyes - 1971

Driving down the boulevard, Amy thought about fate and how it seemed to work. She wasn't sure if she could have a relationship with this man but thought about having a nice dinner and another chance to look into those eyes.

Amy tried to remain composed, but her mind drifted in and out of a desirous dream state. *If only*, she thought again. Finding someone so perfect wasn't her luck, and she doubted the match would become anything. She tried to pull her thoughts together as she turned the van into the parking lot of the funeral home.

It was the last time she would say goodbye to Izzy. The idea struck a melancholy chord. *Greetings to some old friends and goodbyes to others*, Amy thought as she looked down at the toe of her shoe. Izzy made the connection between herself and some of the people who would be attending today, and she might never see them again now that Izzy is gone.

Amy walked into the chapel and saw Jennie with her Aunt Jackie sitting next to people she didn't know. Amy walked up to her Aunt and smiled. They hugged hard and long.

"Hello, Auntie. It's wonderful to see you."

Jackie smiled. "You too, dear. Thank you for being so helpful and attentive these last few days. Jennie needed company, and I truly needed the help." She reached out and grabbed both girls' hands as she spoke. "I just can't do what I used to, and I am so grateful I have you two girls. Don't know what I would have done without you."

She seemed exceedingly feeble today. Amy knew she'd had arthritis issues and was now walking with a cane. She looked at her Aunt warmly. The Spanish accent in her voice brought back to Amy's mind the vision of her mother and Izzy, warming her heart. Jackie's eyes filled with moisture as she reviewed all the things she knew the two cousins handled.

"It was important to me, Auntie. Don't worry about it. Jennie and I worked it out just fine."

Jackie nodded. "Grateful," she said in a meek tone, and then she wiped away the tear that welled up in the corner of her eye.

Right behind her Aunt was her cousin Anna. Amy smiled and took her cousin’s hand, pulling her closer for a kiss on the cheek.

"I will miss Aunty Izzy with all my heart. It is wonderful how you both tended to her needs," Anna said with an appreciative nod. Amy returned the smile, rubbing the back of Anna's hand warmly.

"It is wonderful that you came. It'll give us some time to catch up." Amy said to her, then took a second to point out where her Aunt Jackie was sitting.

As the funeral home filled, the two cousins greeted and met the eyes of the many friends who had known their grandmother over the years—old, young, friendly, and forlorn. Amy thought of the tales they all could tell.

A frail older gentleman that Amy didn't recognize approached her. "I see you have the stone now." Amy looked at him curiously. "I knew she would pass it to you." Amy held his hand and had the other on the stone.

She asked, "How do you know about this?" Her voice was barely more than a whisper.

"It is a legend. The great protector." Then he gently pulled his hand away from hers and went to sit down at the back of the chapel.

Amy was astonished. She'd been searching for days, trying to find information about the amulet, but it was still such a mystery. She would try to find this gentleman at the reception after the funeral and ask him to tell her more. *Who was he anyway? I've never met him before.* She struggled, searching her mind for an inkling of recognition. *What a strange thing.* Amy's thoughts were so clear, she felt as though she'd said them out loud. Then she recalled the events of the last week and decided that this was NOT the strangest thing she'd encountered recently.

After the service and her grandmother's interment, many gathered in the reception hall for cookies and coffee. Amy frantically looked around for the feeble older man, who wasn't there. She should have known and was sure the investigation would continue without help. As the crowd thinned and the stress of all the "goodbyes" for Izzy had dissipated, Amy and Jennie cleaned up what they could and parted ways.

"Well, I'm sorry we couldn't have spent more time together; maybe do things that were more recreational."

Jennie smiled. "I agree. It was still nice to spend time with you, Amy. It's been a long time." Then Amy hugged Jennie and her Aunt Jackie before Jennie assisted her out the door and into her car.

As Amy headed back to her hotel, she drove down the avenue between the funeral home and the inn. There, walking down the sidewalk, was the man from the funeral. He was quite feeble in appearance but had been moving along at a fair pace.

Amy pulled her car over. "Hello again." It was awkward, given that she'd only met this gentleman once, but she felt compelled to at least talk to him. "Is there somewhere I can take you?"

He looked at her for a moment, unsure if he recognized her. Then, a smile broke out on his face. "Hello. Yes, a ride would be nice." He opened the car door and got into the passenger seat, sitting down with a *humph*.

Once he was settled, Amy put her hand out and said, "I'm Amy; Izzy was my grandmother."

The man nodded and said, "I know. I'm Tino." He had a thick Puerto Rican accent, and Tino was a name her grandmother never mentioned.

Amy said, "Nice to meet you."

She got directions from him and headed out. "I was wondering how you knew about the amulet," Amy said, blurting out her question.

"Izzy and I are from the same tribe." He said very matter-of-factly.

The thought wrinkles appeared on Amy's forehead again. "Tribe? What tribe?"

Tino showed little expression and kept his eyes forward. "Well, you must know that many Puerto Ricans have Incan ancestors. Our ancestors came from the same tribe. The same region in Peru." Amy's face looked shocked, as though she'd just received a slap. She never knew that fact, except for a single mention on the family tree document Izzy left for her to find.

"So, what tribe is that?" Amy said anxiously.

Tino smiled. "Chachapo. It was one of the oldest and most respected villages in Peru." He hesitated momentarily, then added, "And you have the same hair as the 'blessed one'—the first holder of the stone." Tino smiled. I knew it was you."

Amy was surprised at the bits of knowledge Tino knew. "How do you know all of this?"

The man nodded. "Some information was given to me, just like it was given to you. I searched for some of it. Izzy and I did a lot of research to find out what we know." He had a smile and a far-off look in his eye. Amy now had more questions than she had before her conversation with Tino.

"Where do you start? There is so little documented about the Incas."

Tino nodded. "You have to walk the path of the ancestors." Then he signaled to her where he wanted to get out.

Amy pulled the car over, and Tino opened the door, stepping onto the curb. "Thank you for telling me about the amulet," she said, putting her hand on the mysterious stone.

Tino smiled at her and blinked his eyes, adding an obvious pause to the conversation. He said, "many of your questions can be answered by consulting the stone." Gently, Tino closed the door and hobbled away.

Amy sat for a minute, thinking about how little she knew. Deep in thought, she drove back to her hotel, realizing that all the digging and pondering didn't matter. She had the amulet and hoped it would enchant her with the same gifts it had given to the previous owners, including Izzy.

When she returned to her hotel room, Amy slipped out of her dress and opted for shorts and a T-shirt instead. The day had been trying, and Amy wanted to relax and think about something else. She clicked on the TV and flipped through the channels, then flopped onto the bed, and with minimal effort, dozed off.

***

Waking abruptly, Amy tried to focus. It was dark outside, but her vision was crystal clear; she suddenly found herself in a strange place, watching falcons.

She could feel the wind blasting up the side of the mountain. She could hear the whishing of their wings as they flapped against the wind. The view from the ledge where she stood was breathtaking. But it was only a dream.

Taking a deep breath, Amy woke, startled by the screech of the birds. She blinked the sleep out of her eyes, then clicked on a lamp. As was her habit, she found a pen and began writing down what she had observed in her dream.

It was the falcons again. Amy's heart skipped a beat as she watched them, experiencing the freedom of their flight. She could see the creatures move their wings to catch the wind, and she felt the exhilaration they felt. She saw a tall, dark-skinned man who was stern, but she also saw the love and turmoil in his eyes. The emotions shown on his face were so pronounced that it scared her.

In a prior vision, she'd seen the young girl who held out the amulet to her. The stone was the same one Amy had. She whispered, *Huk sasan regalo*. That was twice she'd heard it in a dream and had written it down as best she could. The words were not in a language she was familiar with. She'd have to research that.

That was exhilarating! Amy thought to herself. Her mind raced through the faces in the dream. They were not familiar to her, but it was apparent that the representation she'd seen was of a previous possessor of the amulet who was passing it to her. The room was quiet and lonely. She sat up for a moment and just looked at the stone. It was rare. She knew that. But what power did it have, and why? Amy was determined to discover the gifts this amulet had to offer, whatever they may be.

She drifted off to sleep again about an hour later, but did not sleep well for the rest of the night. When the first light of the new day shone in the sky, Amy was up and out. She looked forward to an early morning run on the beach to help clear her mind. *"Just breathe,"* she thought, walking down the steps and out the door.

6. Gifted? - 1971

Amy clambered into her van and just drove, leaving the window open. This morning, she felt it necessary to blow away the cobwebs and wake up her mind. She felt an urge to write the dream on paper to create a story or, at the very least, record these very vivid dreams. The thought of it was far-fetched, but the nighttime encounter seemed so real.

The air was dense with moisture, and her clothes and hair felt damp, but it wasn't hot yet, and she knew the beach run would be pleasant.

She pulled into a convenience store to fill her thermos, sure she would need refreshment after her run. Amy strolled into the store, pushing the heavy front door with her shoulder, spotting an older woman with a labored expression at the front counter. Amy nodded politely and continued to the back of the store to the fountain to fill her container. As she approached the beer coolers, she caught a reflection that stopped her in her tracks. *Was that a gun?* she thought. Before continuing past the door, her eyes swiftly scanned the store aisles, feeling a stranger's gaze upon her.

Amy stopped and gasped. Right in front of her was a younger-looking man holding a long-barreled gun, with his nose and the gun barrel focused on her. Amy's eyes opened wide with surprise, and her heart pounded hard in her chest.

The man brandishing the weapon was tall and blonde, his face framed by a rusty-colored beard. He told her, "I think you need to come up front with me, lady." Amy stepped backward to avoid the end of the gun and slowly walked to the front of the store, scared about what this man could do. When she turned away from the armed fellow, the not-so-shy St. Louis woman whispered a prayer, fearing he could have shot her in the back. Even though he was armed, she sensed that he had no intention of hurting anyone.

He held the gun, and Amy knew the best decision would be to avoid confrontation altogether, but she felt as though she knew him; at least she could sense what he was all about. When she and the gunman approached the front of the store, Amy's eyes met with those of the lady at the counter, and she moved her eyes in a way that might signal the woman to move aside. Amy wanted the clerk to be separated from where she and the attacker stood. The woman took a few small, quiet steps to the right, out of the way of the gunman and his captive.

The young man waving the gun wanted her to go behind the counter as well, but instead, Amy turned to look at him, swallowing hard. She asked, "What is your name?" The bearded man looked at her as if she were sprouting another head and didn't say anything. Amy insisted. "What is your name? If I am to die today, I need to know the name of the man who killed me so I can haunt him in his dreams." She scowled at the man haughtily, her brows pressed together.

The gunman loosened his grip on the gun just a little. His blue eyes looked at her and said, "Curt. My name is Curt, and I don't want to kill you."

Amy smiled and said, "Well, want or not, we both could easily die here. Why don't you tell us what you want so we can help you?" Then Amy glanced at the cashier to have her at least acknowledge what she had just said. The woman nodded, still silent.

Amy's voice was calm as she talked to the man. "My guess is that you have someone waiting on the money from this register, and they put you up to it, right?"

Curt looked at her intently and said, "How do you know that? What makes you think you know anything about me?"

She glanced at his hand on the trigger of the gun. "I bet you need money desperately, and your wife doesn't know anything about your visit here or that you'd ever hold a gun up to an unarmed woman."

Curt looked at her, pain showing in his eyes. "I can't feed my family. I don't have the money for rent. I have to do something."

Amy took a step closer to him. "Violence doesn't get it done, Curt. There are people out there who can help you, and you won't have to use violence." He looked her in the eye once more and lowered the gun, slumping to the ground. She walked over to him and put a hand on his shoulder, squatting beside him. He was so tense that she didn't think he could feel her touch.

"So, Curt, what happened that keeps you from feeding your family?" Slowly, he relaxed enough to tell Amy why he was so desperate.

She asked the cashier for her name. "Louann," the woman said to Amy, trying not to embellish her name.

Amy looked at her calmly. "Would you mind locking the door and putting up the closed sign so Curt and I could have a little peace?" Louann nodded and grabbed her keys. She smoothly walked to the door and followed Amy's instructions to the letter.

Amy focused on Curt, letting him pour his heart out to her, and suggested where he could get help and possibly work. Since Amy was in the news business, she had written articles about homeless people and the organizations that helped them. She made a couple of phone calls to those places to inquire. He seemed so much more human now. He was calm and almost embarrassed about his behavior.

Amy got his address from him so she could bring groceries to his family to help out. Curt left the store discreetly, and Amy turned to Louann with a smile.

Louann was in shock. "How did you know he wouldn't hurt you? It's a gift. How you handled that, I mean."

Amy reached over and touched Louann's hand. "He was married, and his hands were shaking. I could see in his eyes that he was desperate, not a criminal. It could have gone wrong in a bazillion ways, but he just needed to be heard. I hope I helped him."

Louann came around the counter and hugged Amy, still trembling. Amy took it gladly. "I'm glad you're ok," she said to her. Amy returned to the coffee pots, filled her thermos with water, and left the store, giving Louann a wink on the way out.

With the ordeal over, Amy got back into her car and drove to the beach, reflecting on the incident. *How did I know?* She thought to herself. Amy never considered herself brave, but since she'd arrived in Florida, she'd begun to see a different side of herself.

A few minutes later, she pulled into the parking lot of a grocery store, filling a cart with staples for Curt's family. She was not extravagant in her choices and stuck to practical things. Compelled to do the right thing for him, Amy recalled the desperation in his eyes. She couldn't imagine what it would be like to be stripped of a means to provide for a family, those at home that counted on him.

Loading the groceries into her car, she found his address and delivered the sacks to his front porch. She rang the doorbell, then turned to leave, seeing Curt through the window with a baby in his arms. It was a relief that giving the man a break was the most helpful thing she could do.

***

Turning the wheel, she pulled her van into the lot near the beach overlooking the gulf. The sea air was dense and smelled of fish. The waves were murky and dull-colored, and Amy couldn't help but think that each wave was a new surprise, or at least an opportunity for it. She sighed deeply as she relished the sun's touch. Getting out of the van, she stretched, then began her exercise.

Amy jogged down the beach, letting her thoughts dissipate and fade, making way for new ideas and happy thoughts to take hold. Breathing in the ocean breeze was medicinal, as she felt herself rapidly overwhelmed with appreciation for so many things. A new perspective was one of the significant side effects of jogging on the beach, which ordinarily allowed the mind to relax.

When she was finished, she walked back to the parking lot instead of jogging, scanning the sand as she went along, looking for interesting things. Seashells, in general, fascinated her, with their varied sizes and colors. There were not many of them on the beach that hadn't been destroyed by the seagulls, but she found a few. Amy thought, *If Izzy were here, she would draw this*. She fondled the beautiful, sculpted shell in her hand.

Reflecting for just a moment, it saddened Amy to think her grandmother was gone. Then, as if to wrangle the bravery in her soul, she thought, *everyone deserves to rest. It was Izzy's time.* She flung the shell back out into the sea and began walking again.

The beach was relatively empty, which surprised Amy. It was such a peaceful place. She continued her walk, looking down the whole time as she searched for trinkets. The tip of something brown caught her eye, and she kicked at it with the toe of her tennis shoe. It barely moved. With a little more effort, Amy kicked again. She finally stooped down to pull whatever it was out of the ground. Her efforts revealed an ancient bottle.

Her eyes got big with surprise, and she began to smile. Amy loved to see old things. When she held the bottle up in the sunlight, she could see it was plugged with what looked like wax, and something was safe inside it.

"A message in a bottle!" Amy said aloud to no one as she stood alone on the beach. She took the bottle with her and began to double-step towards the car. Amy wanted to get inside the bottle very badly to see the message.

Feeling as though she'd stolen something, she looked over her shoulder, scanning the area for other prying eyes. There were none, of course, and if others were around, they clearly wouldn't care about someone finding a bottle on the beach.

Amy climbed into her car and drove directly to her hotel room. Once there, she found a letter opener—a sharp instrument that would break the bottle's seal. She worked at it for some time before it finally gave way, and she cleared its throat. Once she did, getting her fingers in there to pull out the paper was another thing. She tried multiple times and failed. Then she remembered the pair of tweezers she had in her toiletry bag. They were small but long enough to reach a corner of the paper. "Finally!" Amy whispered to herself.

She had gotten just a corner exposed and carefully pulled the paper out. It was thick, like parchment, and had yellowed with age. Amy thought that paper from a hundred years ago was probably not white like paper is now.

Sitting cross-legged on the bed, she handled the paper delicately to avoid tearing or damaging it. The words were in Spanish and appeared to have been written with something messy, like charcoal. A smile spread on her face in awe of this rare find.

Amy jotted down the words. She knew some Spanish but had been taught to speak it, not read it. She scribbled, sounding out the words, producing prose on paper.

Estamos varados porque nuestro barco ha sido tomado por piratas. Por favor ayudanos. Al norte de la Española dos días en el mar. Al Norte de Nevis por dos días en el mar. La flora es densa. Por favor ven pronto! Maria, Isabella, Carmen Louisa

Sighing deeply, Amy put down the pencil and recited the words. Unsure she was reading them correctly, she scribbled the exact words on the hotel notepad and took it to the front desk, hoping a person there could help her translate. After all, most of the service workers were Spanish or Puerto Rican.

There was a woman at the front desk whom Amy had overheard speaking Spanish to another. She just happened to be there today. "Good morning, Ma'am. Could I trouble you for a moment to help me translate this?" Amy's voice was hopeful, and she looked at the woman who greeted her pleasantly, hoping to gain her favor.

The woman looked at her momentarily and responded with a friendly voice. "Of course. What have we here?" The woman’s name tag said "Roz," and she politely reached for the paper Amy handed her. The clerk looked at it for a minute, struggling to read it as Amy had truly scribbled it. Roz tipped her head, thinking the words and the request were peculiar, but she translated them for Amy.

We are stranded as our ship has been wrecked in a storm. Please help us. North of Nevis, two days at sea. If you get this, please come soon. Maria, Isabella, and Carmen Luisa."

In one smooth motion, Roz handed back the paper and said, "That's weird. Where did you get that?"

Amy looked down at her feet, hiding her expression from the clerk. "Oh, uh—it was in a book I was reading, and I don't understand much Spanish. I just needed a little help. Thank you so much!" Then Amy took back the paper and headed to her room. Roz watched her as she walked away, then shook her head and returned to work.

Amy took the stairs two at a time to the second floor. *This was a plea for help!* It was mind-boggling to her that someone would reach out in such a way. "They must be desperate, and desperation makes people do desperate things," she murmured as she traipsed up the steps.

When she found the paper again on her bed, she looked hard at it. Touching it now, she could sense the aura of the hands that had last held it. Amy tried, without success, to put faces to the names that appeared there. She went to the table and picked up the bottle to examine it. It was crude and dirty.

There was no way its mouth could hold anything other than a cork. She tried to find a mark on it, but found nothing except the scratches made by the sand. Amy decided to try to find an antique dealer who might know its origin.

The telephone interrupted her thoughts. The ring was a blasting sound that could wake the dead. "Hello?" Amy took the receiver, wondering who might call.

"Well, hello to you, too. It's Cam."

A smile broke out on her face. "Oh, so glad it's you. How are you?" Amy was genuinely happy to hear his voice.

"Pretty good." She smiled and batted her eyes, hearing his smile over the phone. "Wondering if tonight might be a good night for dinner?"

Her heart began to beat faster. "Yes, I would love to! Where and when?"

Cam's voice was steady and oh-so-sexy. "How about I pick you up at seven? Do you like Italian?" Amy said, "Yes, to seven and yes to Italian.

I look forward to it."

Cam answered her. "Me too. So, I'll pick you up. I'm in a silver Ford pickup."

Amy nodded to herself. "Perfect. See you then." She heard Cam say "Bye," and she hung up the phone. Her next thought was what to wear to dinner. She had only packed one dress for the funeral and thought she needed to be somewhat formal for the night out, the date.

"Looks like I'm going shopping," she said as she rifled through her suitcase again. She showered, pulled on shorts and a T-shirt, and then walked down the street to the strip mall she'd seen that morning.

Amy was not one for shopping, but had to come up with something. She perused the racks and shelves for a suitable dress, looking for something simple and classic. Settling on a yellow sundress and a pair of slip-on sandals that suited her, she was delighted, finding the price was within her budget.

She purchased the dress and began her walk back to the hotel, thinking how grateful she was to have found something so quickly. Amy immensely enjoyed the walk, as the sun was warm and cheery, and the sky was crystal clear, evoking a grin as she squinted against the sun's rays. Then she remembered the bottle and the message, which reminded her of the investigation of the newly acquired amulet, and she quickened her pace.

It was nearing afternoon, and Amy climbed into her car to head to the library again. Today, she wanted to learn more about the stone itself. She needed to investigate the type of mineral it was and determine whether it was precious or at least had been precious a long time ago.

Geology. Amy thought. That was where she could begin her research.

She had spent a lot of time in libraries and had been to many different sections, but never to the "Geology" section.

Where to start? Her mind was racing from one subject to another. She needed to identify the stone and its origin before digging into anything else. Amy wanted to know why this stone was so unique. *Was it special to everyone?*

She picked a few books off the shelves and leafed through them, looking for something that spoke to her. There were many minerals and their classifications; however, the first book she looked at was about how minerals formed. Opening the second one, Amy saw a chapter about *South American Minerals and their Classes* that drew her full attention. She scoured the pages and examined the descriptions closely.

Finally, her investigation came across something similar to her amulet. She studied the words, looked at her amulet, and then re-examined the picture on the page. The description read:

> *"This special stone was thought to have mystical powers. Protection and future visions have been experienced, but reports have not been proven. It is only found in two regions on Earth, the Siberian peninsula, and the Peruvian Andes."*

Amy thought to herself, *so, the Peruvian Andes, huh?* It was right in the middle of the Incan Empire and had powers or expected powers that would speak to her fascinating dreams. She slowly closed the book and thought, *who made the amulet? Who was it made for? And how did it get into Izzy's hands?*

Something like a magical stone amulet was likely passed down from generation to generation, but it could be stolen or lost. Looking down at the stone, Amy decided that tracing this amulet's path would be painstaking. Maybe digging into her genealogy would be the shortest route from A to Z rather than tracking the stone itself.

Every trip she'd taken to the library taught her something, so her quest was not lost. She sat and pondered for a moment about which direction to take in her research, making some notes in her notebook. Looking up, she caught sight of the clock on the wall. It was five minutes to five. "Oh crap, I've got to go get ready!" Amy reshelved the books and headed out the door with her notes in hand.

7. Flutters - 1971

Amy cleaned herself up, donned the new yellow dress, and put on the flats she'd just purchased. She chose a more conservative look with her makeup because, for some reason, she felt that too much was overkill. The climate was warm and humid enough that she would probably sweat it off anyway.

It was a quarter of seven, and Amy grasped the leather strap of her purse and her white sweater, just in case, then headed to the lobby to wait for Cam. She was nervous, as she hadn't been on a date with such an attractive guy in a long time. Admittedly, she had butterflies and secretly hoped it wouldn't affect her appetite for dinner. The pretty young woman reached the lobby, catching the eyes of onlookers with her striking yellow sundress and beautiful head of deep red hair.

Standing at the window, she watched for his truck. Little birds darted between the shrubs and kept her entertained while she waited. Amy looked for a nest, but the dense bush didn't allow her to see its depths. She could hear the tiny wings of birds flutter and subtle "peeps" as they spoke to each other. She was momentarily lost, staring into the branches, focusing on the activity behind the scenes.

Out of the corner of her eye, she saw Cam sitting in his truck in the hotel's front entryway. "Oh my God," Amy uttered, grabbed her things, and headed to the door. She was mildly embarrassed over the fact that she had been so easily distracted.

Smiling, she walked out the heavy glass door, grasped the handle of the pickup, and climbed in beside him.

"Well, hello there." Cam's voice was clear and deep, and his light blue eyes reflected his mood.

"Hi," Amy said as she settled herself on the seat. Her curly red hair was bouncy and shining, reflecting the warm colors of the evening sun.

"So, how was the rest of your day?"

Amy was cheerful but not quite willing to share too much of her adventures with him. "It was good. I took a jog on the beach and did a little shopping."

A warm smile appeared on his face. "What?" Amy said back at him, wondering what he found funny in her statement.

"Sounds like a typical girl's day."

Amy shook her head. "That sounds like a very male thing to say." They both chuckled. Cam was chatty, wanting to know more about Amy, and she promptly answered his questions.

"You were close with your grandma then?"

Amy nodded. "I truly don't have much family, at least not many that I am close to, neither geographically nor emotionally. My cousin Jennie and my Aunt Jackie are all that's left. My Aunt treats me as if I were her child, and my cousin, well–she's another thing."

"Family, right? Can't live with 'em, and you can't kill 'em." Amy opened her mouth with an expression of shock, then shook her head.

Cam giggled. "Well, I really wouldn't do that. Just putting a little emphasis on how difficult family is sometimes."

Amy nodded hesitantly, wondering what this guy was all about. "I wish I had the chance to have a family to complain about." Amy dropped her eyes. She didn't want to ruin the conversation with her lonely response, but neither did she want to keep the same conversation path.

Cam realized he struck a nerve. "I'm sorry. I wasn't thinking."

Amy's eyes still did not meet him when she chirped, trying to change the subject, "So, where are you taking me?"

Cam smiled. "You're gonna like it. Luigi's. It's probably the oldest Italian restaurant in Pensacola, but it is the best." Amy looked up at him then, and his expression held the excitement of a little boy. *He must really like the place*, she thought.

"I've heard of that place before, but I've never been." Cam smiled shyly. He was glad his unorthodox comments didn't completely ruin the evening.

"Here we are, " Cam said lightheartedly, pulling into the famed restaurant's parking lot.

He jumped out of the truck first, running around it to open the door for his date. Cordiality was becoming increasingly rare; however, Cam seemed genuinely interested in treating her with respect and courtesy.

"Thank you," Amy said as he took her hand and helped her out of the truck. His warm touch stirred a deep fervor within her, leaving her bewildered. Her intuition told her that this person was special, that this relationship was almost magical. How could she walk away from that?

Cam had made a reservation, and a table was waiting for them. He looked at Amy and asked, "Red wine?"

Amy nodded her head and said, "Yes, thank you." Then Cam waved the waiter over and ordered a bottle of wine. She liked this royal attention. He was quite old-fashioned for being a young man in the 1970s.

She waited for the wine to be poured before asking, "So, can I ask how old you are?"

Cam smiled. "Of course, I'm 32. How about you?"

Amy blinked. He was older than she had thought, but not by much. Then she responded. "29."

Cam replied very nonchalantly, "That's about what I'd guessed, you, having a career and all."

Amy's eyes shone in surprise. "You have a career too, don't you?"

"Yeah, it was my family heirloom. However, I sit here, single, with no attachment to anything but my work."

She giggled. "Well, I hope so!" Then he realized how his words sounded. He rolled his eyes and gave her a half-cocked smile.

"Guess I'm nervous. I keep putting my foot in my mouth."

Amy held up her wine glass to his and tapped it, hearing the little "ting" of the glass against another. "Cheers," she said, smiling back at him.

***

"The food and company were delicious," she said, slurring her S's. Amy had indulged a bit more than she had planned, and Cam found her liberation amusing. They walked along the sidewalk, and she held her shoes in her hand, loving her freedom and the awe of the concrete's cleanliness. Maybe getting drunk was in the plan from the beginning, or perhaps she wanted to drown her sorrows. Either way, Amy needed to let her hair down.

Cam held her hand to both support her and be near her. It had been a long time since he'd spent time with someone, nearly giving up hope of finding that special relationship. Lynae broke his heart, plain and simple. He wasn't sure where Amy was in her life right now, whether or not she was looking for someone, but he hoped to be the next Mr. Right. Amy was adorable, both in her petiteness and her intoxicating brown eyes. She swayed and fell against him. He breathed in deeply, taking in the scent of her. Catching her around the waist, he pulled her in close.

"Do you mind if I kiss you?" Cam asked gently.

Amy smiled. "Sure," she said as she looked up at him. Cam reached down and kissed her softly, his lips meeting hers with intent. As he pulled back, Amy let out a muffled "Mmm." Cam smiled. "Let's get you home."

He helped her out of his truck again and assisted her into the lobby. "You got it from here?"

Amy said, "Heck yeah, I'm fine. Will I see you tomorrow?" A playful smile developed on his lips, glad she said it first.

"Yeah, how about I pick you up for lunch? Do you have any plans?" Amy scrunched up her brow in thought. "I just have to meet a lawyer tomorrow around 3:00. Lunch would be great."

Cam reached down and kissed her again. "See you tomorrow." Then he turned and headed out the hotel's large, glass entry door.

Amy smiled to herself as she headed up the stairs to her room. She didn't expect her heart to flutter the way it did when he kissed her. *His kiss was so soft,* she thought as she ascended.

Her thoughts returned to what they had discussed over dinner. It was not a traditional way to meet someone. After all, what reason would she have had otherwise to run into him? She had determined it was either kismet or divine intervention, but either way, she was happy about it.

Opening the door to her room, she fiddled with the lock, distracted by the cursing heard down the hall. She flopped the key down on the dresser, kicked off her shoes, then crashed into her bed and didn't move till morning.

***

Amy's eyes blinked rapidly before finally realizing it was dawn. She had slept fully dressed from the night before. The daylight was inching into her room, but it wasn't full-out sunlight yet. *What time is it?* she thought to herself. Blinking to focus, she looked at the alarm clock, and it was 5:15.

"Hmm." She let out the sound, blinking curiously, reliving the events from the night before. She smiled to herself and then made her way over to the window to greet the day.

She brought a typewriter from St. Louis with her. It was old and clunky, but it worked, and she wanted to write down her thoughts. She began typing an account of the last few days, feeling all the emotions of those experiences as she wrote. Amy worked for well over an hour. Down deep, she needed this reflection to unburden herself and organize her thoughts.

The last week had been a whirlwind, with sorting out Izzy's house, attending the funeral, a close call at the convenience store, and now her inner response to a new relationship.

When she finished, she had nearly ten pages. She shook her head when she realized just how much had happened in the last week.

Amy made her way down to the lobby and poured a cup of coffee, suddenly needing the company of others. There were only two people in the lobby area: one behind the desk, doing whatever desk clerks do to keep themselves busy, and another man sitting quietly reading a book.

Flopping down in a chair near the window, she caught sight of the same little birds she had watched the night before. Thinking then of how dedicated they were, fussing over their home, she observed them constantly trying to make it perfect. She didn't see any chicks and thought about how the little birds were obsessed.

In another second, she thought about how these tiny birds had been given by nature this one thing to do. Their duty was to have babies and teach them how to be in the world.

She watched for a minute or two, then rose, and went to the carafe around the corner, and filled her cup again, then slowly climbed the stairs to her room.

8. Discoveries - 1971

Amy showered and dressed, knowing it would be hours before lunch. She had some time to begin the research she wanted to conduct regarding both the amulet and the mysterious message in the bottle. She needed to wait by the phone long enough to get Cam's call before she went back to the library.

Having previously checked out a book about "Ancient Incas and their Peruvian History," Amy would see if anything was recorded about the amulet, its unique attributes, or stories of the special powers the stone was said to have, desperately looking for hints about its mystique.

She knew that throughout the centuries, many tribal groups had believed in and held tight to myths and legends, and she felt she would find references to them if she studied the history of the Incan culture. Amy read and took notes on the leads she thought would be worth following up on.

It was an interesting read, and she thought that if it hadn't been for the stone, she would never have read a book like this. Flipping the pages, Amy saw references to mining in the mountains and how dangerous it was. Within the references listed on the page, she saw "mining deaths" and "devastation of families due to mining." She made notes about the books mentioned there so she could dig deeper.

Amy began to understand the lifestyle in the Peruvian Andes, but didn't quite understand how the culture collapsed relatively quickly. The rarity of her lineage made her feel even more special, as she was now the torchbearer for those unsure about whether their bloodline would continue.

Amy's thoughts were interrupted by the phone's loud ring. She startled and then raised herself off the bed to answer it.

"Good morning, sunshine. How are you feeling today?" Cam's cheerful voice answered the other end of the phone.

"Well, better than you'd think." Amy was smiling as she spoke to him, and he knew it. "I was up with the sun, had my coffee, and dove into a good book. How about you?"

Cam sounded a little surprised. "I wasn't sure what state you would be in today. I'm glad you're not hungover."

Amy defended herself. "Well, I don't drink very often, and a little bit will go a long way with me."

Cam gave a small chuckle. He paused for a moment and asked her, "So, are you up for lunch today?"

She fidgeted with the phone cord as he spoke. "Of course. What did you have in mind?"

Cam's smile could be heard in his voice. "It's a surprise. I'll pick you up around 1:00. Will that work?" She let go of the cord and watched it bounce on top of the desk.

"Perfect. I'll see you then."

Cam responded," Okay, see you then. By the way, I had a great time last night."

Her last words were, "me too." As Amy hung up the phone, her heart fluttered again, and she thought about how she was completely falling for him, and doubted she deserved it.

Once she calmed down, Amy settled into her book again and pulled out the map and the family tree she'd found. She spread these documents again and studied them, reviewing the names and the jotted notes on the outer edges of the paper. It was a long shot, but Amy hoped to find, amid all this jostled information, a reference to any of the names in the family tree. Maybe there's a hint about a particular location or event that could bring the scribbles on the map to life.

Although her investigation was fruitless, the book provided valuable information and gave her a thorough understanding of Peruvian culture and life in the Andes Mountains. It also contained references to locations of lost cities and old mines, which she had also jotted down on the notepad, expecting to find a connection to the bits and pieces she already knew.

The morning hours had flown by, and before she knew it, the clock read noon. Closing the book, Amy decided that after lunch, she would head back to the library and investigate some of the notes and citations she'd written. She quickened her steps, needing to reach the lobby before Cam showed up.

She donned a pair of white capris and a dark blue blouse. Amy wasn't sure where Cam was taking her, but thought the look was casual enough to suit many different atmospheres, except formal. Amy was skilled at braiding her masses of thick, wavy hair and created a French braid down her back, finishing it with a dark blue ribbon. Adding a pair of silver hoops, she finished her look, deciding the whole ensemble complemented the bulky amulet.

Standing back now, she studied her reflection, seeing something different. She had never spent much time looking at herself, but was seeing a different person. These eyes had more depth. Amy liked how she looked and felt. She had never given much thought to her family's heritage and had certainly never delved into their history as deeply as she had in the past week. Knowing more about them would help her to see the steps her ancestors had taken long before her.

Amy's original leave of absence from work was two weeks, enough time to wrap things up and get home. She still needed to meet with the lawyer to discuss the details of Izzy's will, since she was the executor of her grandmother's estate.

Amy thought it best to sell the property, but right now it was more than she wanted to deal with. Selling was the obvious choice, but it would sever her connection to her grandmother, and her heart was not ready to let go.

She finished her mascara and added lip gloss, then decided she was satisfied. Wrapping her fingers around the strap of her purse, she headed down the stairs to await Cam's arrival. Just thinking of him and imagining his face made her smile. He had such a twinkle in his eye. She only scratched the surface of this man's tough outer shell and was determined to soften him up.

Amy rounded the corner to the hallway leading to the lobby and saw her reflection in a glass pane. Her appearance made her feel quite confident about the impression she would make on Cam and others she would meet. It would take a lot to rattle her confidence today.

Glancing at the clock, Amy saw she was a few minutes early and chose a chair in a quiet corner from where she could still see the entrance. A local newspaper sat on the table next to her, and she picked it up, immediately turning to the obituary section. The newspaper had scheduled to print Izzy's obit only days ago, but Amy couldn't remember exactly when.

She flipped through the pages and looked at the faces on the paper, abruptly stopping when she found Izzy. There she was. *What a vibrant woman!* Amy wrestled again with the thought that Izzy was gone, but what a life she had! She was proud of her granny and even prouder of the bloodline that continued with her. As she stared at the picture, she promised herself that her future would give a reality to Izzy's dreams–and her own. Her gifts would continue to live because Amy wouldn't let them die.

She saw Cam's truck pull into the hotel parking lot a moment later. Amy rose and headed for the door, her smile growing. She flung open the door just as he pulled his truck to a stop. She clicked the knob and opened the pickup door before Cam could get out of the cab.

"I got it," Amy said brightly and sat down, tugging the handle to shut the door.

"You look amazing!" Cam took her hand and pulled her close, giving her a soft, passionate kiss.

Slowly, they pulled away from the kiss, and Amy looked up with her smiling eyes and said in a flirty voice, "Well, a girl just can't resist such an ambitious greeting."

If it were possible, Cam smiled even more than before. "Shall we?"

Amy nodded enthusiastically. "We shall." And off they went.

She curiously batted her eyes and glanced over as Cam turned the truck onto the main road. “So, where are you taking me today?”

Cam smiled. "I thought we'd have a picnic on the beach. I know a great place that is somewhat private." Amy was happy to hear this. Being from St. Louis, a trip to the beach didn't happen often enough.

"Fantastic idea," Amy said, touching his hand again. Looking closely at it, she couldn't help but wonder about the many tasks those hands had taken on and how many more were to come. She wished to know more, much more.

It was quite a drive to the barrier island, and after nearly an hour, Cam pulled into a parking lot marked Opal Beach. He jumped out of the truck and quickly moved to the passenger side to assist Amy, behaving in a gentlemanly manner. "You don't have to do that, you know," Amy said, in a voice that reflected her happy mood.

"I like taking care of you," he responded, making her statement sound almost silly. He closed the door behind her and opened his tailgate, grabbing a picnic basket and a small cooler out of the back, then, with the tip of his head, showed Amy where he was headed.

They walked for a few minutes and arrived at a bluff with a few low-growing trees, which still allowed for a shoreline view. Cam pulled out a blue plaid blanket, big enough for both of them, and spread a picnic fare between them. He brought red wine, crackers, cheese, prosciutto, and sliced melon. He'd packed a couple of wine glasses and plates for the food, along with cocktail forks and napkins.

It was a spectacular day with a light breeze coming off the ocean and the bluest sky spattered with fluffy white clouds, revealing such beauty that it should have been the subject of a painting. Amy turned her face toward the breeze, letting it waft across her cheeks and caress her lashes, her eyes closed as she absorbed every moment of this day.

Cam was fussing over the food and watched her with one eye, squinting against the sunlight. She was exotic to him. Her beautiful, wavy red hair was pulled back, and a few pieces of it wisped around her face. Her eyes were deep brown, round, and bright. Full of passion and anticipation of what might lie around the next corner.

Without speaking, he poured her a glass of wine and touched her hand so she could open her eyes and see him holding it out. Looking at her hand, she smiled. Holding on to him with one hand, she took the glass in the other, admiring it as the sunlight shone through it. "This is perfect, Cam. Just perfect."

He smiled, reached over, and kissed her as if he planned it. "Now it's perfect."

They ate their food, discussing the dinner from the night before, the waiter, and the bread basket, which was quite generous by anyone's standards. "I want to know more about what makes Amy tick," Cam said to her seriously. "We've done a lot of talking, but you haven't shown me your poker hand yet."

She raised one eyebrow at his comment. "Well, if I showed it to you, then I wouldn't be much of a poker player now, would I?"

Cam laughed openly. She had a way of painting her words with color. "You know what I mean. I want to know more about you."

Amy paused for a moment, put down her cracker, and took a sip of wine. "I'm a deep thinker." Amy started with what was the most obvious to her. "I give things a lot of thought before I draw conclusions. I'm selfish with my soda; I don't like to be woken up by anything except daylight. I read and write whenever the mood strikes me, sometimes in the middle of the night."

Cam nodded his head. "That's what I'm talking about."

Amy took a piece of melon and said to him, "What about you? There has to be more to Cameron Moreau than a silver pickup and pushing papers in the auction house office. What things do you like to do that are not work-related?" She held up her finger to stop him before he opened his mouth with the warning, knowing how a man might answer that question.

Cam made a man sound like "humph," and then he took a second to clear his throat. A person could tell he didn't like to talk about himself. "I, uh–well, I like to fish, and I like the beach a lot. I love watching old reruns, like *Mister Ed* and *The Three Stooges*. I play softball in the summer and watch sunsets every chance I get." Amy smiled at him. She was happy he told her, even though she'd guessed about everything except the old TV shows.

"Well, from my perspective, that makes you a pretty good guy."

Amy began cleaning up the food scraps and repacking the items. Cam put the wine back in the cooler and the meat and cheese in their containers.

"Let's walk, shall we?" Amy got to her feet and held her hand out to Cam. He smiled and took it, and then they made their way down the path to the beach, never letting go of each other the whole time. The ocean waves crashed gently against the shore, leaving bits of kelp and small creatures along the way. It was mesmerizing and relaxing, even more so after a glass of wine. Their conversation morphed slightly, moving to the next level, disclosing items of a more personal nature now that the ice had been broken.

They strolled, talking, hand in hand and eventually, arm in arm. They turned back after walking for a while, hoping what was left of the picnic hadn't been carried off by strangers. Cam slowed to a stop and turned to Amy. "I've never met anyone like you before. You are so easy for me to talk to. It means a lot."

A smile grew on Amy's face. "Ditto," she said, tightening her embrace around him. Keeping his gaze, she moved in slowly for a kiss, this time with much more passion than any of the kisses before. Cam's heart began to beat faster. *Was it fear?* He thought to himself. She felt so good in his arms that he doubted that was the issue.

He breathed deeply, slowing the anxious feeling, and looked deeply into her eyes. He knew that would tell him what he needed to know. He saw kindness, intensity, and caring that you don't see in many people these days. "You are a beautiful individual, you know that?"

Amy didn't expect to hear such an observation from him, but was happy he thought so. "I'm pretty taken with you, too." Then she turned away, keeping hold of his arm, and they continued their walk back to the picnic place.

The ride home was quiet and content, and Amy sat as close to Cam as possible. She was only a child the last time someone's arms comforted her, and she thought it was high time.

The truck pulled up in front of the hotel, and she reached over for a goodbye kiss. It was soft and full of meaning. "Thank you. I had a wonderful time."

Cam smiled, his eyes twinkling as always. "I did, too. I'll call you later." She slid out of the truck and gave a flirty smile as she closed the door.

Amy practically floated as she ascended the stairs, relishing the day's events. She had always kept men at arm's length for a long time, never quite finding the "Mr. Right" of her dreams. Cam was different. Or maybe she was different. Her life had taken a few turns in the last couple of weeks. Perhaps she saw things differently than before.

Still light on her feet and brimming from the day's events, she flung open the door of her room and saw the map and family tree spread out on the bed. "Oh crap," she said to herself, and rather than flop on the bed and dream of the sparkling eyes and firm chin of the man she had just spent the day with, she grabbed her tablet with the notes and spun on her heels, exiting the room once more.

***

Amy bolted through the library's main door, anxious to continue the historic journey she'd begun when she found the amulet. Heading directly to the History section, she looked for the books referenced in the previous examination of "History of Lost Incas in Peru," which she had already checked out. One was on the shelf, but the other was not. She held tight to the one she'd found to check it out as well. She'd made notes on the tablet using specific words that might aid her in the search.

There was a reference section just around the corner from History, and Amy rifled through it. One thing she found particularly interesting was the Ship Manifests. She saw a mention of South America and Puerto Rico, then found the date range inscribed at the bottom of each large leather-bound book. This section was divided by the shipping companies that frequented the area. The more she found, the more excited she got.

Amy flipped through the documents with an intent scowl. She could visualize the ship as it was described. The cargo, the crew, and the slaves all had faces to her. After completing one book, she dove into another. She found a manifest book titled "The King's Trading Company, Jamaica – 1621." It was the oldest one she'd viewed so far. She carefully opened the book and leafed through dozens of different Caribbean trading records.

So many of these ships are hauling the same things, Amy thought to herself, then, rethinking, she realized these ships might have been sent to South America for specific items. "Ah, here is one." Amy held up a parchment, yellowed with age, that carried more than just coffee, iron, and spices. She saw the names and ages of several girls. At least, she thought the names belonged to girls. Names like this stood out on the paper, as the recording of people was quite different from the products. Amy saw:

Jami – 16 – good teeth – strong
Kobu – 21 – foot injury – no lice

Awana– 17 – evil eye – clean

And so on. There were nearly fifty names with similar descriptions. *Slaves!* Amy thought. These identifiers must be how they would sell them. She shook her head, unaware that she was doing it, shocked by what she had seen. The hand that wrote the words was steady, and each letter was a work of art. Some pages had smears and water stains but were in perfect shape.

Amy turned yet another page, seeing even more numbered names. This page had names that were more Spanish than African. These were similar to the others; she mentally noted their names and ages. Then she saw writing on the page that jumped out at her. It was a letter from Isabella De Cabrillo to her father, Cayo De Cabrillo. The letter was brief, stating she was well and working beside some wonderful people in Hispaniola. She was safe and missed them very much.

Amy stared at the yellowed parchment page, feeling a stirring deep inside that was hard to describe. Her hands tingled, and she realized the amulet around her neck was warm and reacting to her emotions.

She sat back, feeling her heartbeat quicken. *There is something about this Isabella and this stone,* she thought. It was such an odd feeling. Empowering. She decisively jumped up, took the book to the front desk, and asked if she could get a copy of it. The woman nodded and turned to go into a back room to make the copy Amy requested. She appeared once more and handed a white sheet to Amy, along with the book pages she'd found it in. The walk back to the table was slow as she thought about where the ship came from and where it was going.

She found another book, *"The History of Ships that Sailed the Caribbean."* Sitting down, Amy scoured the pages for records of the merchant ships and their cargo. The information that graced the pages was fascinating to her. She anxiously jotted down the names of ships, the ports from which they sailed, and where they were destined. She found a reference to a vessel named *Belladonna* in the book, and she felt a jolt as the amulet began to warm. *What is it about this ship?* she thought. The manifest stated that it sailed from the Caribbean to Africa, then along South America, and back to the Caribbean, without traveling to Spain.

In another paragraph, she saw that many ships had been pirated or traded, sometimes even lost on a bet. Nothing indicated what had happened with the *Belladonna*, but Amy guessed it was one of the reasons she had just read.

She had been at it for several hours, only realizing it when she looked at the clock on the wall. Amy gathered the books on the table, intent on checking them out.

She got behind the wheel of her car and drove directly to the hotel. When she arrived at her room, the papers and books scattered over her bed made her smile, reminding her of her college years and her irregular study routine. Amy opened the tablet and looked at the notes she'd written at the library, then followed up with the book she'd brought back about the Caribbean ships. She continued reading about the *Belladonna* and found that it had been lost at sea in 1589, with a suspected cargo of slaves.

She continued reading, learning how the trade in the Caribbean changed after the Spanish invasion, forcing many from South America to scatter across the islands like cockroaches. They'd left all they knew behind to escape tyranny. Instead of finding a way out, they were trapped like wild animals and traded, sold, or killed. After the conquistadors ravaged South America in search of gold and riches, little remained of the indigenous tribes that had once flourished there.

Amy tried to imagine what it would be like to have all you know and love ripped from your grasp, and a cold chill ran down her spine. She knew there was no discrepancy regarding young men and women, and they'd have no control over what would happen to them.

Interrupted by the loud ringing of the phone, Amy's research was put on hold. Before she picked up the receiver, she looked at the clock. *Hmm, it's nine.* She thought the only person who would call her was Cam.

She picked up the phone, not saying a word. She loved to hear his calm and resonant voice. "Hello? Are you there?" Then Amy started to giggle. She couldn't help it.

"Of course I am. Who do you think picked up the phone?"

Then he laughed. "I was afraid I might have called the wrong room."

"So, how are you?"

Their conversation flowed from there, and ten minutes later, Cam said, "I'm taking the day off tomorrow. Let's spend it together."

Amy suddenly remembered her missed appointment. "Oh crap!" she exclaimed. "I forgot the lawyer!"

Cam's bewilderment came through in his words over the phone. "So, is that a yes?"

9. Surprises All Around - 1971

Amy yawned and stretched, finally getting out of bed to peek through the curtains. Low, gray clouds hung in the sky, moving so slowly that the movement was barely discernible. She was bewildered and hadn't noticed the weather forecast in the last week, never imagining there was anything but sunshine in Florida.

She glanced over at the clock. It was nearly eight, and she needed to kiss the lawyer's ass for missing her appointment the day before. She dialed the number. A very polite, nasally sounding woman answered the phone. "I'm sorry, I missed my appointment with Mr. Andrews yesterday. May I please reschedule?" Amy was unknowingly biting her lip, anxious about what kind of response she would get.

"Oh, hello, Miss Bishop. Yes, I do have an opening today around 10 a.m. Would that work?" Amy was relieved.

"Absolutely. I will see you at ten. Thank you." As she hung up the phone, she let out the air she had been holding and muttered, *What am I thinking? What is the worst thing they could tell me?*

After getting herself ready for the day, Amy called Cam. They had planned lunch, a walk on the beach, and other entertaining activities. The couple wanted to spend more time together, and today was the perfect opportunity.

"Hello, beautiful." His bright and pleasant voice came through the phone. She thought he sounded sexy, but consciously erased it from her mind. It was probably just her, but she noticed her heart was pounding harder just hearing his voice.

Amy filled him in about her appointment, and they agreed he would pick her up at the hotel at noon. She hung up the phone and smiled. Reflecting on her other relationships, it was clear that this one was different.

The appointment went much as Amy expected; details of reviewing Izzy's will and subsequent property would be finalized within the next week, and she would be free to wrap up and go home. She felt uneasy leaving the office and returned to the hotel. *What would happen to her and Cam when it was time to go back to St. Louis?* She considered seriously how that would shake out. She has no real reason to hesitate, as her life is settled in St. Louis, but Cam has made that much more complicated to consider.

Amy took one last look in the mirror before she headed out of the hotel room to meet him. She wanted to be perfect, but was aware that her imperfections would still show through, no matter what.

She stood outside the hotel in the breezeway, watching the cars go by and listening to the low-pitched rush of the ever-present, subtle sounds. Amy smiled as she could hear and feel the heartbeat of a city. One advantage of being a writer is that it makes a person more observant. She considered for a moment that it was her nature and might be a disadvantage, but she couldn't change. Amy turned slowly and noticed her reflection in the window, suddenly wondering what Cam saw. His impression of her was probably very different from her impression of him. She pondered whether it was the amulet that brought them together or a natural attraction.

Closing her eyes, Amy felt the sun and alternate shade touch her skin, as the warmth was interrupted by fluffy clouds passing by. It was a very pleasant day, and she responded to the sun's soothing warmth on her skin. She rubbed her arm right where the sun caressed it and wished the warmth would sink in so she could save it for a rainy day. St. Louis was not always as sunny as Florida, but spending time in Pensacola helped her memorize the feel of the sun, even though it didn’t appear as often at home.

Amy heard Cam's truck coming from half a mile away. She had become familiar with the sound and began to smile when she thought of how proud he was of it. A couple of blocks up, she watched him turn onto the boulevard and approach, one block at a time. He pulled up under the hotel's overhang and looked in her direction, then smiled a flirty smile. She opened the door and gracefully slid her backside onto the seat beside him, stretching in his direction to steal a kiss.

"Hey." Amy was the first to speak.

"Hey," he said right back. They drove off, glowing.

Cam pulled up in front of the café, with quaint little tables under umbrellas and charming violin music playing softly in the background. They were shown to a table outside, where a gentle breeze occasionally wafted through, creating a casual, relaxed atmosphere. Various types of bread accompanied the wine as an appetizer. They ordered light meals, ate, laughed, and enjoyed each other's company.

Before ending such a lovely day, Cam drove along the highway that led to the beach. He went a different direction, this time to *Castaway Beach,* a place Amy hadn't been before.

Standing in the parking lot, she looked both ways and saw nothing but the beach and water. There was a constant breeze that was almost too cool for her, but at least it wasn't stifling heat.

"So, what other secrets do you have that you haven't shared with me yet?"

Cam smiled mischievously and touted, "I'll never tell." Amy reached for his hand and gave it a swat. He gathered her close and kissed her, nearly lifting her feet off the ground. He pulled away, taking a moment to look into her eyes. She wasn't sure whether she recognized the man in front of her, as his expression had changed. Even his kiss was different.

They walked and talked about childhood dreams and some of their favorite things. Cam was uncomfortable talking about his past, feeling that his college years were a blur.

"I did a lot of drinking throughout college and made a lot of mistakes. I'm thankful my life went in the direction it did. Any other path might have been a disaster." He said it in jest, but Amy knew it was true. One of the gifts of the amulet was being able to smell bullshit a mile away. She had also spent enough time with Cam to know his truth, but he was clueless about how it didn't matter to her. She would take him, flaws and all. They had a connection, plain and simple.

The couple had walked about half a mile and picked a spot on the beach to sit in the sand. It was warm and had such fine granules that it felt silky. Sitting quietly and listening to the waves felt like a form of meditation. It was breathtaking.

Cam put his arm around her and kissed her forehead. "I want you," he said, quietly guiding her head up so he could see her eyes, then finished his sentence with a soft kiss.

"I want you too." Amy couldn't believe she said it, but she wanted to be closer to him if possible. Cam pulled Amy to her feet, grasping her waist with his strong arm.

"Is my place ok?" Amy nodded, swooning so that she could have fallen over with the next breeze.

The two of them spoke but a few words as they made their way back to the truck and went to Cam's house. He lived in a white, one-level house only a block from the city beach. A large deck on the front that met the steps from the sidewalk, and a few chairs occupied the space. Amy thought about his craving for sunsets and realized this house suited him perfectly.

He held her hand firmly as if she would escape any minute, but Amy's only plan was to be with him. He opened the door and, like a gentleman, guided her through it first.

The second the door closed behind him, he wrapped her in his big arms and kissed her passionately. He kissed her neck slowly, the warmth of his breath sending shivers down her spine. Her heartbeat began to speed up, and her legs went soft. Still locked in a kiss, she had no objection when he walked with her backward, staggering into the bedroom, his left arm around her while his right hand fumbled with the button on his pants.

Amy pulled away and caught his gaze. "Here, let me."

Slowing the pace, she calmly undid the button on his pants and unzipped them. It was obvious that he was aroused, as she could feel his hardness when he drew her close. In one motion, she pulled off her shirt, and Cam's hand went smoothly to the small of her back, pulling her to him with urgency. Amy wanted nothing more than to feel his skin against her, the softness of his lips, warm and inviting. The clothes hit the floor, and they fell onto the bed a moment later.

Amy touched everything she could, feeling and sensing their togetherness. Unable to wait any longer, Cam moved to her, their bodies flawlessly melded into one, lifting each other into a lust-filled fury. Amy let out a low, slow, pleasure-filled moan as Cam kissed her passionately. He was emotionally all in and wanted nothing more than to please her.

Cam held her close when they'd finished, not wanting it to end. Their hearts were beating rapidly, now sharing something between them that no one else could. He felt the curve of her back and buttocks, and she gracefully fingered his well-muscled shoulders and chest.

She kissed his neck gently, then his chin and his lips. "I don't want it to end," she whispered.

Cam said. "Me neither." Amy was nearly breathless as he caressed her breast softly. Then he drew her in again, and like the waves crashing on the shore, they were joined, wanting to drink in the other's soul, to be one.

Amy's hair was disheveled and messy, and tiny ringlets fell around her face. Cam was breathless as he lay facing her, watching her exposed chest rise and fall with each breath.

"You're so–perfect." Then, he reached over and kissed her breast, pulling her closer as he did.

Amy let out a quiet giggle, still in awe. "This is not how I pictured our afternoon."

Cam smiled. "I didn't either, but I'm really happy about how it turned out."

The two got up and dressed, and Amy took a moment to look around, surprised at how tidy the house was for a single guy. Cam entered the kitchen to get some beers and then led her onto the oversized deck. They lounged in the deck chairs, watching the sunset.

"It's the perfect end to a perfect day," Cam said, unable to stop smiling. They spent the evening engaging in small talk, sharing flirtatious smiles, and sipping beer.

Cam suddenly scrunched his forehead and gasped. "Crap, I gotta go check on Nick's place."

Amy remembered that Cam was house-sitting for his buddy, who was away on a research project for a while.

She nodded as he continued. "I gotta stop by the office. I think I left Nick's keychain there on my desk. Will you come with me?"

Both the statement and the question made her smile. "Of course I will."

The auction house was about halfway between Cam's house and Nick's, so it was easy to swing by on the way. Cam and Amy pulled into the lot and parked sideways across the painted yellow lines since no customers would be there after hours.

He grabbed Amy's hand, making her look up at him. Bringing it to his lips, he kissed it gently. "I'll be right back." She smiled and winked as he climbed out of the truck and hurried up the steps.

Cam rummaged around the office for the keys to Nick's place, not finding them where he thought he'd put them. Finally, they gave up their location in the lower drawer as he slammed the drawer above and heard a clinking noise. "God damn things," he muttered, slipping the key ring into his pocket.

Amy was twittering her thumbs in the truck, waiting for Cam to return, when she saw movement in the alleyway behind the warehouse. She sat statue-still, watching the activity, unsure of what to make of it. There was an old blue pickup truck with the tailgate down. She saw two men dressed alike, or at least the same color, loading crates into it. The suspicious movement appeared strange to her. Nothing should be going on at this time of night, and certainly no one is loading any outgoing freight.

Cam reached the front door, turned and locked it on his way out, ambling down the steps, and opened the truck door in one motion. He flopped down on the seat with a broad smile on his face.

When he looked at Amy's bewildered expression, his smile changed to a question. "What?" He sounded genuinely concerned.

She spoke to him in a faint voice, wanting to remain invisible. "There were two guys in the back with a blue pickup truck, and they were loading stuff into it. That's not normal, is it?"

Cam's expression darkened like clouds blocking the sun on a summer day. "No, it's not."

He reached for the door handle, and Amy stopped him. "Don't put yourself in danger. We should get the police."

Amy watched Cam as he tiptoed around the building to see without being heard. He was gone for what seemed like forever, and then, as smoothly as he left, he got back in the truck, pulling the door shut softly. He started it and drove off before saying a word.

"It's Rick and Danny. They're two of the three guys who work for me. From what I could hear, they had a buyer for their goods."

Amy shook her head when she heard that. "They're stealing and selling your auction items. It's part of the inventory. They can't do that."

Cam nodded, almost doubting. "Well, yes, that's right. Tomorrow, I will demand an inventory and oversee it myself. I'll come back to the warehouse later to see if I can find what they're selling."

Amy saw the irritation on his face and decided she didn't have much else to say. *No reason to poke at the beehive*, she thought, keeping her lips pressed together.

They arrived at Nick's place and went inside. Cam turned on a couple of lights, and Amy went around to water the plants, which were dying of thirst. He picked up the mail that had been dropped through the slot and set it neatly on the kitchen counter. Amy could see the steady control that Cam constantly had slowly breaking down after experiencing anger and disappointment.

She approached him and softly touched his arm, gaining his attention. "It's going to be just fine,"

Cam huffed. He appreciated her kindness and thought she probably was right, but now he was angry and wanted to stay that way.

Appearing desperate to find out what was happening at his warehouse, Cam found it difficult to wait. "A couple of hours should be good, right?" He looked at Amy for encouragement. She nodded.

"I think so," Amy responded, unsure if she answered a rhetorical question.

It was a long two hours. The two new lovers waited at Nick's, then went to Cam's and waited some more. He thought he should take her back to her hotel and investigate the warehouse alone, but Amy would have none of it.

“Two heads are better than one. We can do this together." Without much of a reaction, Cam silently agreed. It would be a good idea to have moral support.

They found two flashlights, and soon after midnight, Cam and Amy went to the warehouse to examine evidence of the recent suspicious activity. Cam parked the silver truck across the street, and hand in hand, they crept up to the back drive, looking for signs of any lingering movement. It looked like his two criminal sidekicks were gone, and the warehouse was locked up tight.

"Thank God for that," Cam thought, feeling his anger subside a bit. He fumbled for his keys and unlocked the side door, pulling it open very slowly, careful not to make a sound.

Once satisfied that nobody else was lurking, Cam entered the building and turned on the floodlights. It was such a sudden burst of brightness that neither could see for a few seconds. Their vision settled in, and they each went down separate aisles, looking for anything suspicious. Many crates looked similar to the ones that Amy saw being hoisted into the truck, but there had to be something about them that stood out.

Often, markings would be put there for inventory and identification, but those marks wouldn't help them now.

Enough time had passed, and Cam was unsure whether there was any proof of items the two mongrels could have taken. They both continued their search, looking in, on, around, and below the crates, boxes, and odd-shaped wrapped items in the neat rows on the warehouse floor. Amy turned her flashlight on the floor between two crates and saw a single swirl of wood wool on the ground. It just seemed out of place.

"Cam?" she said hesitantly. "Is this normal?" He came over to the row of crates by her. He shone his flashlight on the solitary twist on the floor.

"No, it's not. We don't use that for packaging."

He stared at it as though it had teeth. He looked closely, examining the whole area around the line of shipping items under which Amy found the strange packing material. Using his flashlight, he could see scuff marks in the micro-thin layer of dust on the floor.

"There was undoubtedly something that was moved from here." Cam's voice was now filled with determination. His focus then turned to the crates and containers themselves. His mind ran an inventory of what should be on the floor and what was out of place. Without interrupting him, Amy watched, careful to stay out of Cam's way and zoning in on what he was doing.

She continued searching for out-of-place items while he matched the crates in the aisle against an inventory list, hoping something might stand out to him. He was tenacious, to say the least, and found two other crates with numbers that weren't on the list. Amy watched him as he used a short crowbar to pry open one of the crates.

She stopped what she was doing and went over to him, unsure what to expect when he pulled off the lid. "Did you find one?" Amy asked.

"I think so." She made a mental note of the marking on the crate, D-Pen-11, which would have fit into the inventory list if it hadn't been auctioned off the day before. He rested the lid of the box alongside the same crate and removed the wood wool to have a look.

Cam's eyes got as big as baseballs. A couple of geodes were sitting neatly in the middle of the container alongside what appeared to be bricks of cocaine.

"Those bastards," Cam said, loud and clear. "My business–my life is now all fucked up because of those bastards."

Amy approached and looked into the crate. "The surprises just keep coming," she muttered under her breath.

She wanted to offer comfort, but this struck her too. "How dare they?" She was suddenly affected by a mischievous look that might provide a satisfying resolution.

Looking up at him, she said, "What if we set them up, trap them in the act?" Her heart began to beat faster with the thought of a sting that could not only catch the crooks but simultaneously prove Cam's innocence during the undercover operation.

She explained her idea to Cam, and the morsel of hope made him smile at the grand idea. He closed the crate, making it appear untouched, but marked it with a lengthy line of red to quickly identify it amongst similar crates. Cam found one other crate clear across the warehouse with the same appearance and had the same bricks of cocaine in it, stashed among other objects.

He marked that crate the same, satisfied they had done what they could. Then, the two worked together to create a map, which they would hand over to the police so that the boxes could be clearly identified when the time came.

Cam's temper calmed, and he was much more amiable during their ride back to the hotel. It was nearly 2 a.m. when Amy finished the evening with a soft, warm kiss, making Cam smile. "I'll come back for more of that tomorrow."

Amy smiled. "I look forward to it." She pushed through the hotel door, throwing a final glance over her shoulder at him.

Just for the fun of it, she gave him a wink, then watched him as he smiled and slowly drove away.

10. No Small Dream - 1971

All at once, Amy sat upright in bed. The room was completely dark, except for a single line of light from the streetlight on the corner, reflecting on the wall from behind the curtains. She gasped for air, truly scared of the dream that had woken her so violently.

It was Cam, blood pouring out of his chest, his limbs limp and lifeless. And those damn lights! Endless flashing lights made her even more uneasy. She saw men in black scurry all around her. Some were frantic, others were determined, but none had discernible faces as their identities blurred. She saw herself standing over Cam, wanting to reach out to him, but she couldn't. What helplessness. The worst part was that she knew to be wary of these dreams. This one was no small dream. Amy got out of bed, feeling weak. She found a towel, wet it with cool water, and then wiped the sweat from her face and neck.

She went over to the window and pulled back the curtain; the brightness of the streetlight against the room's darkness made her squint. Dropping the curtain, Amy looked at the clock. There was an hour or more before the sun would rise, and she hoped to get a little more sleep before it did, as she was not a very nice person when she was sleep-deprived. She lay back down on top of the bed covers, flopping the pillow over her head to hide her eyes from the slim glint of light against the wall.

Amy was able to doze but didn't sleep well for the rest of the night. When she finally began her day, she started with a long, hot shower, unable to shake the fear she felt from the very real dream.

She was meticulous in preparing for her day, which helped her make sense of what was hard to understand. Since she'd adorned herself with the amulet, her dreams were no longer just dreams; they were windows to places and things that foretold future events. This one scared her. Running the events of her dream through her mind repeatedly, she could not see the beginning or the end, but she could see the blood! There was so much blood. She couldn't get that out of her mind.

Amy made her way downstairs and poured a cup of fresh coffee. It helped her shake off the cobwebs and smooth out her thoughts. Rather than sitting, she chose to stand and watch the morning activity begin to hum all around her. The little birds had also started their day, twitting from here to there, entertaining her among other onlookers. It was easy to become mesmerized by their constant busyness, and it was a welcome distraction.

She slowly made her way back to her room and sat down at the typewriter, expressing and processing her thoughts, some good and some bad. She and Cam had a beautiful day yesterday, and it ended very nicely when she recalled the last kiss of the night.

Amy began forming a plan for the evening, knowing that the back-stabbing employees would have their final moments of freedom with absolute prosecution, which was a no-brainer. The phone rang abruptly, making her jump. "That thing is so darn loud," she exclaimed as she walked over to the obnoxious noisemaker on the nightstand.

"Hello, beautiful," Cam's voice said in a low, sexy tone. She wasn't sure whether he was doing that on purpose or if it was indeed his phone voice. Either way, she liked it, softening when she heard him speak.

"I was just thinking about you," Amy said, smiling as she spoke. She continued. "I had a horrible dream about you last night–I hope tonight goes well."

Cam envisioned her expression and was pleased by it, but was a little troubled about how Amy put those two sentences together. "I went to the police station this morning and explained it to the detectives, who said they would devise a plan. I just don't know when anything will happen next, and the only way to be sure I'm not a suspect is to catch them in the act."

Amy heard his concern. She listened carefully but hadn't told him, or anybody, about the "gifted amulet" and was not ready to tell Cam how sure she was that her dream was a vision of the future. "I'm sure they've had to deal with this sort of thing before, being a city so close to the ocean. Smuggling probably happens more often than we know."

Cam agreed. "Sometimes, ignorance is bliss." Amy chuckled at that. What a cliché!

"I've been thinking about you all morning. I can't wait to wrap my arms around you again." His voice was much softer and throatier than before.

"Well, if you didn't have to work, we'd have all day." Cam chuckled this time. "Okay, then, now you're asking for it."

Cam would come to pick her up after five and take her to dinner. Then, they would stake out the warehouse using Amy's car, as it would be less conspicuous. "Should I pick you up at your house?" She'd never driven to his house, but getting there from the hotel would be simple, taking major roads in the area.

"Sure, that is a good idea. I'm usually home by 5:15, then I grab a shower, and I should be ready to go by 5:45."

Amy hesitated. "Would you like some company?" She wasn't sure he would get what she was insinuating, but he did almost as quickly as she said it. "Oh, sure. I could use some help washing my back."

She smiled again, thinking about the previous evening at his house. "I'll see you then," she said.

There were hours to kill, and Amy despised shopping, but she went anyway. She had packed for a week and was halfway through week two, feeling the need to add variety. She also wanted to look fantastic. The trip to the store wasn't long, and she found a beige pleated mini skirt and a turquoise-blue cap-sleeved blouse with a Queen Ann collar. She was busty enough that a dipping neckline would show off her cleavage. Not too short or too revealing. She finished off the look with a sensible beige-colored slip-on sandal. "Perfect." She thought to herself.

Amy took the long way back to the hotel. It would be days before she would wrap things up with the lawyer and head back to the city with the Gateway Arch, but she now considered whether that was the future she wanted. The beach was a major attraction, and Amy knew she could freelance here and likely make more money than she could back in St. Louis.

Her grandmother's house also needed to be part of the equation, as someone would have to handle its sale after the will was read and the paperwork was completed. Then there was Cam. *Was it a fling?* she thought to herself. Amy knew her heart was all in, but did not know enough about Cam to guess his feelings about their relationship. It made her nervous to think about it. Once the bust was over, she would have a heart-to-heart with Cam to clear the air. It might help her make up her mind about the future.

Then, the frantic, larger-than-life dream came to mind. *What if it did come true? What then?* Her heart began beating faster as she tried to recall more details of the dream.

***

The day dragged on, but between frets of fear and the research she was doing on her family history, her scattered thoughts kept returning to Cam. Amy shut her eyes and remembered the walk on the beach—the time he told her, "I want you," and the confident way he led her up the steps and held the door for her. She wondered if this was what love was, pausing to take another sip of tea.

After floundering most of the afternoon, it was finally nearing 5:00, and Amy put herself together, picking out the most intriguing lingerie she'd packed in her suitcase. She pulled her hair up provocatively and glanced once more in the mirror at herself, then headed out the door to Cam's. Driving to his house was strange, as she'd only been there once and had been a passenger, but she navigated the boulevards perfectly and pulled into his house only minutes before he did.

With his eyes focused on Amy, Cam slammed the door to the silver pickup truck. She looked flirty and adorable, and a broad smile spread across his face. He sauntered up to her.

"What a welcome sight on such a stressful day," Cam said, one eyebrow raised and waiting for a reaction.

She took a few steps toward him, meeting his stare and putting her arms around his waist. She reached up and kissed him, searching out his soft lips. "Well, so far, you are the best part of my day." Then she smiled her very feminine smile as she turned to maneuver up his front steps. They ascended hand in hand until Cam had to stop and fumble with his house keys.

He stooped to pick up his mail and tossed it on the kitchen counter. Kicking off his shoes, he walked back to the bedroom sock-footed, holding Amy's hand as though she didn't know the way. He pulled off his shirt; she pulled off hers. He dropped his pants in a pile on the floor, and her new skirt lay on the floor next to his attire. He stood, staring for a minute, noticing her tantalizing undergarments, suddenly anxious to take them off.

Knowing he could now have her touching him, he pulled her in close and kissed her. Amy had nothing to say, but she let out a "mmm" when his lips moved down and kissed the soft place below her ear, then slid slowly to her shoulder. It aroused him knowing she was enjoying him as much as he was enjoying her.

His bathroom and shower were just feet away, and he reached in and turned on the faucet to warm the water. Now Cam wanted to remove her beautiful lingerie, even though she looked fantastic. As he did, she could see it was getting to him, so she put her arms around his neck and pushed up against him, teasingly. He pulled off his jockeys quickly, and they moved into the water, letting it sweep over them as they poked and played with each other. They enjoyed more than just the shower and had finally been wet long enough. Cam shut off the water, reached for a towel to dry off, and continued admiring the view.

Their physical attraction was alluring, and although they had accomplished what they'd set out to do in the shower, they flopped onto the bed, still wet, and began round two. Amy's deep red hair was quite curly and out of control, aggressively wetting down the pillow where she lay her head.

The little spare curls of Cam's chest hair were still wet from the shower, tickling Amy's chest as he moved.

Drinking up all they could of each other, they remained in his bed, touching and fondling, giggling and kissing. It was a release for sure; they both knew the night would be a long one if they caught the smuggling buggers red-handed.

After the two lovers dressed again, Amy was famished. "There is a place just down the way that delivers pizza. Will that be okay with you?" Cam said politely. "Sure. That would be great." Cam got the phone number, and Amy made the call. They sat on the generously sized deck, drinking beer and watching the sun slowly set in the western sky, waiting for pizza.

Cam agreed to meet with Detective Macy and other officers at 9:00, about a block from the warehouse. When he and Amy pulled up in the lot, there were a couple of unmarked cars, a flatbed truck, and a van. Cam was curious about what James Macy had in mind, and when he asked, the detective said, "Leave it to me." Cam didn't question him, but down deep, he needed to know, and he insisted.

"We will send around a couple of officers undercover, one from the front and one from the back. They will have backups in case we have runners. The trucks are to block their ability to take off with the goods and allow us to get another couple of officers on the scene. If you've marked the boxes and they're taken, our exterior-mounted cameras should pick them up. Once we have confirmation, we can move in."

Cam was impressed by the team's relaxed, confident attitude. "I want to see you guys at work. Can I be a passenger in one of the trucks?" Although Macy was not thrilled with the idea, he thought Cam would be the kind of person who would follow his instructions in the letter.

"Jackson!" The detective waved his arm, signaling Jace Jackson to approach him. "Mister Moreau here wants a front-row seat. He's with you."

Jackson nodded his head and said, "The flatbed."

Macy sent the two street-dressed officers out to conduct walking reconnaissance and see if there was any activity yet.

Teddy Ames came back on his radio, "Nothing yet." Macy and Cam looked at each other, waiting impatiently for the other officer to report.

It had been more than a minute when they heard Tom Petraski's voice: "A van just pulled up. Black, I think." Cam's heart began to beat faster. Jackson looked at Cam and motioned for him to head for the truck. He glanced over at Macy, who was reviewing the map of the warehouse floor and the locations of the marked crates.

Amy was in her car in the staging parking lot and finally got out when she heard the sounds of action on the radio. She stayed distant, just within earshot of the voices transmitting. There were long periods of unnerving silence, and she quickly realized that waiting was the worst part. She began to bite her pinky fingernail, and her wrist bumped into the amulet on her neck. She was reminded that no matter what happened, everything would be okay. She closed her eyes and felt the amulet warm reactively. It was an amazing feeling that brought her calm. "It's all gonna be okay," she whispered to herself and began listening again to what she could hear on the broadcasts.

Once it could be confirmed that the boxes loaded into the van held the drugs, the gaggle of officers moved in. They came from all directions, ears alert and their guns pointed at the van, intensely aware of any movement. It was a block away, but

Amy could hear, "Don't move, we gotcha' covered." Then there were gunshots.

Not once did she think those dumbshits would be shooting back at the officers. "Guns," she said out loud, and one of the officers holding the radio looked over at her blankly. There were loud shouts and indistinguishable yelps, and the radio traffic clearly seemed panicked. Amy felt a blanket of dread when she thought about what they might find when they were finally allowed to go to the sting site. She gripped the amulet tightly in one hand and closed her eyes. "Keep him safe," she muttered under her breath. It felt strange asking the stone to help her protect her loved one. *Wow, there it is.* Her mind suddenly became distracted by intrusive thoughts. *I'm in love with him.*

It was only a few minutes before the gunfire ceased, and the voices calmed, but it seemed like hours. One of the officers said, "Let's move in." That was all Amy needed to hear. She was on her way. It wasn't very comforting to think about what she would see, but she needed to know Cam was alright.

They jogged the distance to the warehouse, the men in black armed to the teeth. As soon as the building came into sight, she saw men on the ground breathing hard, while others looked through the van. An officer was questioning another, and someone was writing down the sequence of events. Amy tried desperately to discern Cam's face among the blur of strangers, but he was nowhere to be seen.

"Where is he?" She said this indirectly to anyone who could hear or might give her an answer. Amy's eye caught sight of Jackson squatting on the ground. "Finally, a face I recognize." She headed over to him; the question in her mind was cocked and ready for her to release it. "Where's …" was all she said as she realized the man next to Jackson on the ground was Cam.

"Oh, my God!" Amy blurted loudly, her eyes now focused on Cam. She darted past various activities, unable to see anything except him. In a split second, she was on the ground next to him, crying and caressing his face. "What happened? Why you?"

The questions came one after the other, succinctly. Cam writhed with discomfort. Jackson had a hand towel-sized white cloth and bandages nearby. He had the towel in his hand, applying pressure to the wound. "You were shot?"

Cam's eyes were closed, and sweat had broken out on his face as he required effort to abate the pain. "I'm fine. Jace said the bullet went clean through my shoulder." Amy kissed his forehead, and tears filled her beautiful brown eyes.

"It's awful, Cam. You could have been killed!" Cam loved that she cared so much but was sorry to see her distress. He opened his eyes to look at her.

"It will take more than a bullet to stop me. Besides, we got the bastards. "That's good, right?" Then, just to be sly, he smiled at her. Amy was too worried to be pissed off, but his nonchalant display angered her. *How dare he?*

When Jace had moved the towel enough for her to see the gunshot, she was surprised at the amount of blood that stained his shirt. The officer perked up, "We have an ambulance on the way."

Amy saw someone giving aid to another officer, and Cam's employees sprawled out on the asphalt drive. "Are they dead?" she asked Jace.

"Rick Armstrong is dead. He shot at us and emptied his clip, so we fired back. Danny took one in the arm but fell back and knocked himself out. He'll go to the hospital, and Rick will go to the morgue."

Jace seemed very matter-of-fact about the whole thing while Amy was shaking and disturbed by the sight of the man she loved on the ground, watching his blood spill from him.

The ambulances arrived, and Cam was loaded into one, secured, and sent to Pensacola General. Once the ambulance left, Amy, accompanied by officers, returned to her car at the law enforcement staging area.

She silently remembered her disturbing dream. *It was a warning*. She blinked hard, wishing it were not the case. She didn't want that kind of gift—that power. Knowing and understanding the picture it paints has its benefits and its downfalls.

11. Sifting Through Debris - 1971

Popping her head through the door of room 228, Amy smiled brightly, holding a fruit smoothie in her hand.

"Hey, baby," she said. Approaching the bed, Amy softly sat down beside Cam. He had been sleeping but roused to life when he saw her and returned a drowsy smile.

“Hey." He said with sleepy eyes, yawning big, then wiping the hand of his good arm over his face. Amy moved closer and kissed him sweetly.

"How ya' doin' today?"

Cam nodded. "Feeling like I got a hole in me, but seeing you made me forget about it."

Amy brushed her hand along his bristly chin, then kissed him again. "Here, I brought this for you." She rolled the serving table over and placed the smoothie on it. "It's strawberry."

Cam smiled and took a drink. Sweet and cold, it was refreshing, unlike the bland hospital food. He'd just pulled the drink up for another sip when he heard a light tapping at the door. Cam and Amy looked up and saw a man in a dark blue shirt wearing a badge on his belt.

"Cameron Moreau?" Cam glanced at Amy and then back at the man at the door.

"Yeah, that's me."

"Hello, Mr. Moreau. I'm Allen Marshall with the Pensacola Police Investigations Unit. I have a couple of questions if you're up to it."

"Sure, c'mon in."

Amy got up and politely moved behind Cam's bed, leaving the chair available for Officer Marshall.

"This is a bit of a private matter," Allen said, shooting a look at Amy.

"Naw, she's good. She knows all about it." Allen nodded and took a seat.

"We need to get as much detail from you about your warehouse's recent involvement regarding the massive amount of drugs being moved through it. Can you tell me when you suspected the illegal activity?"

"Well, Amy and I swung by the warehouse this last Saturday evening to pick up my keys. She was waiting in my truck, saw my employees doing something suspicious, and told me about it."

"So, Saturday evening?"

"Yes."

"Thanks, Mr. Moreau. Tell me, what did you do then?"

"I waited until they were gone and checked the warehouse floor for anything suspicious. We package and ship sold items daily, so it's not unusual to see new crates next to old ones on the warehouse floor. I would know if something was there that shouldn't be."

"And when was the activity reported?"

“After I confirmed some crates shouldn't be there."

"Did you open the crates?"

"Yes, just to be sure they weren’t part of our inventory."

Sighing heavily, the tone in Allen's voice changed slightly. "Mr. Moreau, have you ever been charged with any drug-related crime?"

Cam swallowed hard, taking a second to respond. "Yes, when I was seventeen, a buddy and I got caught with pot."

"What was your charge?"

"Minor in possession. I had to pay some fees and was on probation for a year."

"Where did you get those drugs?"

Cam began to feel accused. He looked down at the smoothie in his hand, scrunching his eyebrows. "There was a guy who hung out at our school. Everyone knew him."

"So you got them from a dealer at school?"

"Yeah."

"Are you still in contact with that dealer?"

"No, I'm not. Never have been, just found the dealer on the street."

"How about now, Mr. Moreau, do you use drugs?"

"No. Why are you questioning me like this? I reported the drugs." His voice was insistent and defensive.

"You understand that we have to flesh out any involvement. It was your warehouse, and you located the crates with the drugs. Maybe you know more than you're letting on."

Officer Marshall asked questions for another twenty minutes before he felt he had enough information to leave Cam and Amy to their own devices. He left a card and asked Cam to call if he thought of anything else that may be helpful to the case.

Once Officer Marshall left, Amy commented in a low voice. "That was intense," she said, touching Cam's hand.

"Yeah, it was. I hope my questionable behavior as a kid won't screw this up for me. That would suck."

***

The next day, they let Cam go home, his arm strapped to his body to limit the movement. Cam was told it would have to be immobilized for ten days to two weeks, and then his successful recovery would require assigned exercise therapy after that.

His warehouse remained locked up for a week after the bust, and a section of the floor had been roped off until the investigation wrapped up, but as soon as he could, Cam was back to work. His first order of business was to get two more warehousemen hired to handle the crates. He needed to move the goods in the warehouse so he could start getting paid again.

Amy extended her leave from her job to help Cam until he got back on his feet. She now had so much here: Izzy's house, her house on Elm Street, and, of course, her growing love for Cam.

He received a subpoena by certified mail the next day, upon his return home, requiring him to give a deposition. The official paper mentioned possible international activity. He wasn't happy about it, but he knew that recording the incident was for his own good, as it would protect him and his property.

That evening, Amy went to Cam's with dinner and a bottle of red wine in hand. She served him the meal on a TV tray and then picked out some music to listen to. She wanted him to relax a bit before she dug into a conversation about what her and Cam's future looked like. An hour later, she finally worked up the courage to bring it up.

"I extended my stay in Florida for another month."

Cam looked up and smiled. "Good." She watched his reaction but couldn't read it.

"I still need to deal with Izzy's house, and I found out she left me some property. I gotta decide what to do with it."

Cam watched her talk, nodded politely, but didn't speak. He felt that it was her decision, not his. Besides, it was none of his business.

She continued nervously. "Do you know how long it might take to sell property in Pensacola?" Cam shook his head. "Well, do you know how much I should ask for the property?" Cam shook his head again. "Cam, I need a little help here." He put his good arm around her shoulder and reached over to kiss her. His soft lips delicately brushed her eyebrow.

"I don't know much about real estate. I bought my house almost seven years ago. I'm sure a lot has changed. You'll have to speak to a realtor. But as for you ..." He hesitated long enough to bend forward and look her in the eye. "I want you to stay forever." There was a twinkle in his eyes when he spoke to her. "I'm not ready for anything permanent, but I want more time with you. I want to see you when I go to sleep and when I wake up. I've never felt like this with anyone before."

Amy kissed him and gently hugged him. "That answers that. You're not the only reason, but you're a big one. I'm deciding whether or not to stay here."

They sat side by side quietly as the night gathered around them, finally migrating to the deck to take in the sunset, sharing the close of another day.

***

It was a Wednesday when Amy finally called a realtor who was able to meet her at Izzy's that morning. The house was no longer the same without her grandmother to greet her, but when she flung open the door, a flood of memories washed over her, making it hard for her to hold back the tears.

Gaining her composure, she escorted the realtor through the home, pointing out a few details that might be important to the sale. Just like that, the house was listed.

She mentally checked this one thing off her list, noting that tomorrow was the day the lawyer would read the will. As far as she knew, neither her Aunt Jackie nor Jennie would be there as they had returned to their homes the prior week. Amy was trustworthy enough to see her grandmother's wishes carried out to the letter. Besides, she was the executor and very capable.

After she met with the realtor, Amy headed back to the library. It was time for her to research the gold coins Izzy had left her. She might have found details about the amulet and even the house, but the gold was undoubtedly another thing, and right now, there were more questions than answers.

The book was titled "Coins: World Currency History." Amy planned to check it out to examine the pictures and compare them to the real gold she now had in abundance. She wondered whether the coins and the amulet shared a common story or had separate, equally curious histories.

She flopped down on the hotel bed, holding the book, and leafed through it. Continuing her research, Amy still found only a small amount of information about the gold pieces in the attic.

They were Spanish Escudos, dated from 1598 to 1621, stamped with King Phillip III's mark. At a rough guess, each coin, just in gold weight alone, was probably 0.80 to 2.0 ounces, and if she only went by today's gold price, not counting the coin's rarity, she guessed its worth to be anywhere from $90,000 to $200,000. The thought of this made her smile. She could get badly needed repairs to her car, remodel the Elm Street house, and put some away for a rainy day—possibly multiple rainy days.

Amy continued searching for a couple of hours, learning more about ancient coins than she ever wanted to know. She closed the book and then took a shower. Cam would be home soon, and she wanted to be there when he arrived.

After deciding to stay in Florida, it felt like her life was splitting in two, and half of that equation made her feel like she was teetering at the edge of a cliff. She hadn't informed anyone of her plans, partly because she hadn't made a decision yet, but either she would get back to work or submit a formal notice to her employer. Sitting down at the desk, a clean sheet of paper in her hand, she wrote her resignation letter.

When the letter was complete, she embellished it with her signature and the address of the Elm Street house. Then, folding it neatly, Amy slid it into an envelope. Printing her name in the top left corner, she stopped abruptly. Something inside her just didn't feel right about finalizing this just yet. Staring at the envelope for some time, she slipped it into the desk drawer, deciding it wasn't a battle she was ready to take on yet.

She hadn't shared any of the mysterious information she'd learned from the library with Cam, afraid he'd think her to be wacko. She was determined to tell him, but not quite yet. Something was nagging at her that kept reminding her it wasn’t right. She still needed time to process it and was anxious to find clues, or at least answers, to the mystery of the stone's existence.

Amy looked at the leather lace and blue stone staring back at her from the dark brown Formica-covered countertop. She contemplated wearing it, but decided to leave it behind. *Just one more day,* she thought, grabbing her keys and walking out the door.

12. Odds and Ends - 1971

Amy scrubbed her lathered head for the second time in the shower, her mind twirling through many thoughts and memories. She didn't know what the day would hold, but she put on a brave face, dressed like she meant business, then headed out the door to Izzy's lawyer's office.

Andrews, Jones, and Smyth - Wills - Probate - Property Law. As usual, the heavy oak door bore a brass-plated sign listing the occupants and their competencies. Amy pushed through the door and walked up to the receptionist's desk, politely reciting, "I have a 9:00 appointment with Mr. Andrews."

She was escorted to a waiting room and offered coffee by a petite blonde receptionist with a friendly smile. Asking frivolous questions to maintain a light conversation, Amy nodded, smiled, and sipped the coffee from a styrofoam cup. Within a few minutes, Mr. Andrews himself came and introduced himself. "Hello, Miss Bishop. Right this way."

With a polite smile, Mr. Andrews was a man of medium build, with short, neatly groomed gray hair and a goatee. She followed the man to his office and sat respectfully in a large brown leather chair opposite the attorney.

Nodding, the man seated himself behind the desk, then remarked, "Your grandmother was quite a gal," he said, with a bright smile that pierced his expression. “I was quite fond of her."

"So was I," Amy replied politely, then sighed deeply. She fidgeted and pressed her hand to the amulet for emotional support.

"Isabella has a will that clearly spells things out. Your grandmother has a daughter who is still living, and you and a cousin. Is that right?"

"Yes." Amy swallowed and gave a slight nod.

He asked a few questions and took notes, ensuring he had current and accurate information before proceeding. "Isabella wished for her house and contents to go to her daughter, Jacqueline Foster."

Amy nodded to him each time something was read, indicating her understanding. She knew about these things but was anxious to know if Izzy had anything else that remained a mystery.

"A house, 161 Elm Street, and all its contents are given in its entirety to Amy Bishop." Amy knew this as well, and she nodded again.

"And finally, the contents of her bank account of roughly $761,000 will be divided equally between the three of you." The money was something that caught her by surprise. She had no idea that Izzy had that kind of money. At this, Amy nodded, choking back her surprise.

"She asked that I hand you this in person. It is the key to a safe deposit box. Her instructions were that the items contained be left to your discretion." Amy shook her head, unable to process the news. From this day forward, she would be wealthy.

Amy thanked the lawyer for his diligence and kind words, then immediately headed to the safe deposit box to survey its contents. It was on the opposite side of town, but the drive gave her a few minutes to process the astounding news.

In the past few weeks, she'd lost her grandmother, planned a funeral, emptied a house, been given a home, gold, and other treasures, put a house up for sale, fallen in love, and witnessed a drug bust. Her mind was reeling from all she'd endured, and having the time to think about it overwhelmed her. Making an effort to divert her thoughts, Amy drove to the beach to step back for just a few minutes instead of heading directly to the bank. Taking the break offered her escape from the real world and a moment to center herself.

She removed her shoes and began to walk, first with the wind in her face, then right along the water's edge, letting the waves carry her worries away. This meditation suddenly brought her to another place. She faced a stranger with the bluest eyes she'd ever seen, dusty brown hair, and a smile that warmed her heart. She'd never seen this man before, yet he was familiar. His hand gently rested on the small of her back, and although she'd never seen him, she felt she knew him.

Her eyes fluttered, and she stopped. Looking around the beach, she saw no one except a mother and a toddler almost 100 yards away. She realized then the amulet was speaking to her. Amy had been so wrapped up lately that she hadn't been listening to it, and now, in the peace of the beach and ocean breezes, she understood that she needed the calm to hear it.

Her face flushed with the realization, and she smiled, understanding her relationship with the stone, and knew she needed to trust it. Suddenly satisfied with her unforeseen maturity, she strolled back to her car, empowered enough to conquer the world.

Mindlessly steering her van to the bank, Amy met a banker who led her to Izzy's safe-deposit box. Thanking the woman, she stood there, momentarily looking at it, knowing Izzy was the last person to touch the hidden contents. Gathering the strength to see the treasures within, she finally opened it, finding only a few items in the box. She pulled them out one by one.

Eight savings bonds totaling around $4,000.00 were included, along with a duplicate key to 161 Elm Street, a copy of her marriage license, and a map. Amy unrolled the map and laid it on the table in the center of the room. She scooted the box over to one side and silently slipped the key into the outer pocket of her purse.

Examining the few details, Amy's eyes opened wide with intense curiosity. She smiled as she realized the map was what she lived for, what Izzy lived for. Silently, she understood why it was tucked away in a safe deposit box. Among all the gifts Izzy left her, this was the one thing that held the most value.

The paper the map was on was yellowed and old, but surprisingly durable. Amy smiled inconspicuously as she recognized a few familiar landmarks, including San Juan and Guadeloupe. She recognized the reference to the black boulder, realizing that the map she had found in the closet was a small copy of a portion of this one, depicting a specific point in Guadalupe.

Now, contemplating why it was in the box, she tried to put herself in Izzy's shoes. *Izzy thought it was something of value,* Amy thought deeply, *and this box was its haven.*

Reflecting on the morning's events, Amy was consumed by a whirlwind of emotions, feeling like a tightly wound rubber band on the verge of snapping. The last of her grandmother's wishes was carried out to the letter, and she suddenly felt that her life was different, with a big piece missing in the middle. Would she ever be able to fill in the blanks? Overcome with sadness, she looked at the box. It felt so final.

Leaving the last items in the box, she held out the map, closed the lid, and returned the box. She rolled up the map exactly as she found it and left the building. Feeling almost as connected to the map as she was to the amulet, Amy placed it carefully in the passenger seat, right where she could keep an eye on it, then drove straight to the hotel.

After the door closed behind her, Amy laid out all the information, one clue at a time, on her bed and worked to form a hypothesis, hoping all these separate things would shape into a story.

The best she could tell was that the amulet was from either Peru or Guadeloupe, and from what she had read in the library, the stone was likely from Peru. The part of the map with the most detail was Guadeloupe, so she guessed it was where Izzy's ancestors settled or spent a great deal of time. Lastly, Puerto Rico. Across the center of the picture of the island, she saw the word, *Ch'in wasi*. This reference was unclear, but her research led her to believe they'd left Peru, stayed in Guadeloupe, and ended their travel in Puerto Rico, as her family on her mother's side were all from there.

Amy felt confident enough in the details of her investigation to visit the place where her ancestors came from and try to trace their history. Maybe there was more to it than she thought she knew.

It was late afternoon when Amy wrapped up most of the details, primped herself, and headed to Cam's house. He was feeling better and was scheduled for physical therapy three days a week, today being one of them. She stopped by a food truck on her way to see him and picked up tacos. By the time Amy got back to her car, she had decided to tell him about the stone, the gold, and the inheritance.

Cam was lying on the couch when she opened the door. "Hi, hon. I got us tacos," she said, holding up the bag. When he did not respond, she paused for a minute and asked, "What's wrong?"

He was about as unhappy as she'd ever seen him, and not letting her eyes stray away from his, Amy sat down beside him, waiting to hear his unhappy news.

"The investigators keep coming around and asking questions. I'm sick of them and feeling like they're pointing a finger at me."

She reached over and kissed his cheek, feeling his day-old stubble scratching her lips. "You're innocent. They can't possibly implicate you. Don't worry; it'll be over before you know it." Amy put extra effort into sounding positive, for his sake. Placing the bag of tacos on the coffee table, she went to the refrigerator for a couple of beers, silently wondering what the investigators might be after. *It's been three weeks. Don't they have what they need yet?*

Because he was in such a sour mood, Amy decided to withhold the information she'd been waiting to discuss with him. There was already too much to handle; she didn't want to add stress to an already stressful situation.

As the light outside faded and the room became darker, the shadows danced on the walls, reflecting the activity on the TV. Although she cared deeply for Cam, she was not inclined to stay the night with him as others in her position might have. She knew he tolerated her chatty self and was not afraid to call a spade a spade. Today, he didn't say much, which bothered her. He was never without words.

Switching her mindset to a more positive one, she thought that if all goes well tomorrow, he could remove his brace, which might help him out of his funk. *That might cheer him up,* she thought.

He grabbed her hand and pulled her to him, lying prone and pressed against her. There were only a few words that passed between them, and they cuddled, enjoying the quiet away from life's complications.

***

The alarm blasted, and she watched Cam reach up and

switch it off. He stretched, then turned over and saw her, coaxing a smile. "I could get used to this," he said in a morning-raspy voice, then reached for her, his large hand caressing, running from her shoulder to her hip. Amy's hair was wild, and part of it covered her face. He brushed it out of the way and kissed her cheek, then let his hand wander the curves of her naked body, looking for a reaction. "I'd stay and play, but I have an appointment."

Amy brushed his cheek gently with her hand, blinking slowly, then Cam rolled over and climbed out of bed.

She heard the shower turn on, so she joined him, knowing that this might be the only time today they could spend together. She looked forward to Cam receiving good news from the doctor's office, while she had plans to meet with a contractor to get an estimate for fixing her house. She'd never been a property owner before, and this meeting with Caden O'Keefe Construction gave her an unspoken thrill.

They soaped each other up and rinsed off, completing the morning's routine with shared passion; however, the lovemaking lacked a certain emotional element. It was fun enough and left them both leaving the house with flushed cheeks and smiles.

They kissed again, discussing dinner at their favorite Italian cafe by the sea. Amy needed to stop at the hotel to change clothes and check the return dates for her library books.

Taking care of details before leaving, she was interrupted by the sight of the map spread out on the bed, along with other details of the Caribbean she needed to know. She took the "Do Not Disturb" sign and placed it on the doorknob, deciding that before the end of the day, she would book her excursion to Peru.

Driving down the boulevard toward Elm Street, Amy realized how confident and in control she felt. She never knew where she was going; she just went. There was no starting point or finish line; she just rolled from one thing to another, uninterrupted. Now, suddenly, she was driven to complete her trip, knowing it was what Izzy wanted. Curious about her newfound confidence, she wondered, w*as it Izzy's passing? Was it Cam?* Those ideas swirled around in her head as if stuck in an eddy in a stream.

Sitting at a stoplight, Amy felt the amulet begin to warm. *It's reading my thoughts.* She had never noticed this before, and although she knew her expression had changed repeatedly, she finally smiled, realizing the stone amulet did sync with her in every way. When she thought about it, the stone was most certainly guiding her. The overwhelming feeling of security and knowledge had to come from it, as she knew she wouldn't feel this way without it.

Caden O'Keefe was already parked on the street when she pulled up. "Good morning, sir. It's nice to meet you," Amy said, politely extending her hand. Caden was a rather large man dressed in contractor attire.

"So, this is it, huh? I drove past this place a few months ago when I worked for a guy about a block away. I thought it needed some work. I'm glad you called."

Amy smiled. "It was willed to me. My grandmother just passed, and I decided to move here."

"I'm sorry about your grandmother," Caden said quietly.

"Thanks," Amy replied, then walked up the concrete path to the house with Caden following close behind.

"I can fix this porch and the sidewalk, too."

They walked through the house. Amy asked questions, and Caden wrote down notes regarding the changes she wanted to make. The place was about 1,200 square feet and had three bedrooms and one bathroom.

"Please, don't do anything with this room or the attic." She said pleadingly. "Sentimental value." She did not want to give anyone, even someone trustworthy, access to her secrets. Not yet. At that moment, she decided to install a locking knob on the door to the room with the attic access.

By afternoon, Cam was free of his arm brace, and although his left shoulder was weak, it didn't deter him from getting back to work. Feeling like a butterfly that had just emerged from a cocoon, he immediately went to the warehouse and dove into the mounds of paper and messages that awaited him.

He'd taken a complete inventory and was about to make a couple of sales calls when a man and a woman in Armani suits showed up at the office asking for him.

"Hello, are you Mr. Cameron Moreau?"

"Yes. Who's asking?"

"Our office has been made privy to a delicate situation regarding your, uh, export business."

"What? It's not an export business; it's an auction house. And what delicate situation are you talking about?"

The dark-haired gentleman in the charcoal suit handed him a business card. It read, *"David Harwood, Defense Attorney*."

"I'm sorry, but you're wasting your time. I'm on the other side. Perhaps you need to find Danny Spears. He'll need a Defense Attorney.

The two attorneys exchanged a glance. David, smiling at his cohort, said, "Keep the card. Let us know how we can help." Then they turned and walked out, leaving Cam scratching his head in confusion.

***

Cam was especially quiet during what was supposed to be a romantic dinner. Amy asked several times what was bothering him, but he kept telling her, "It's nothing, just work stuff."

Sipping her glass of wine, she pondered. Aware that some people have reactions to pain meds, Amy searched for a reason why he was acting so weird. She decided just to let it be. She could feel that something was up that he wasn't telling her about, but she couldn't make him share his misery with her against his will.

Slugging down the last bit of wine in her glass, Amy plopped down the empty glass, then said, "I'm planning a trip—something my Izzy started but didn't finish." She paused, waiting for a reaction from him, which never came. *How odd,* she thought. "I'm leaving next Tuesday for Peru."

13. Path Paved in Gold - Peru 1971

The bustling Peruvian city seemed so crowded. Maybe it was just that the streets were narrow and the sidewalks were nonexistent that made Lima seem so, but Amy felt like she couldn't breathe. Hoisting the backpack over her shoulder once more, she chose to walk rather than take public transportation, thinking that cramming herself on a bus with a dozen others would make her feel claustrophobic.

After an hour of wandering and occasionally asking directions from strangers, Amy found her way to the train depot and purchased a ticket. Chachapo was still a long way from Lima, and to get there, she would need to take a 12-hour train ride, then a bus, and then another mile or two to reach the village.

Sitting next to the window, Amy pulled out the notebook, which contained her notes, names, and a map. Chachapo was on the very edge of civilization, high in the remote, rugged Andes Mountains. It was now nothing more than a stop on a tour bus, but Amy knew it was much more than that—certainly much more to her.

An older woman dressed in black sat next to her. She had kind eyes, and thank God, she didn't smell.

"Good day," she said, nodding to Amy.

Amy smiled, "Good day to you." And an awkward silence fell between them once more. It was going to be a long ride, and she knew there were many stops along the way. She silently wondered how long this woman would be with her on this journey.

Once the train was underway, the woman pulled out her embroidery and began sewing. Amy watched her skilled hands create beautiful patterns in bright colors on the pale cream shade of linen.

The woman could feel Amy's eyes on her as she got on with her task. Finally, the woman turned to look Amy in the eye.

"Do you sew?"

Amy shook her head. "I'm afraid not. Your work is beautiful." The woman held the cloth up and saw that it was an apron. She smiled and nodded. "I'm Amy."

The woman nodded. "Nice to meet you, Amy. I'm Irena." Amy stuck out her hand to shake, but the woman took it in one hand and patted it with the other. "Strangers shake."

Amy giggled and decided she liked this woman. As they began to chat about the area, Irena said she was traveling to visit her grandson in Chiclayo, about 8 hours from Lima.

Then, the woman asked Amy about what she was doing on the train. Amy didn't tell her everything, but she did say she was looking for answers. Her mission was clear: she wanted to know more about her family history and had discovered they came from a place called Chachapo.

Irena put down her sewing and stared at Amy. Her eyes examined the girl's features as if she were exploring a map. She smiled gently. "I see it in you. Espíritu de las estrellas."

Amy looked at her, not knowing what the words meant. Irena could see her confusion and smiled kindly. "Spirit of the Stars," she said.

Trying not to be rude, the woman glanced down at the stone Amy wore around her neck. She pointed at the amulet gently, "You see, the Gods speak through you. I feel it." She nodded gently and smiled.

Amy was suddenly dumbstruck. She thought, *" Does everyone know about this stone but me?*

"Can you tell me more? This amulet was a gift from my grandmother. I'm trying to find out how she got it and why it was passed to me."

Irena shrugged her shoulders and went back to her embroidery. "I know it is a very special amulet and has gifts. The bearer has a special pathway. It is truly precious."

Amy held the amulet in her hand, feeling the warmth and security she had grown accustomed to. Smiling graciously, she reached over and patted the woman's hand, then turned her attention to the things outside the window, daydreaming of what this world was like 300 years ago.

Very few comforts were offered on the train, and Amy got off it when Irena did, escorting her to meet her grandson. She watched as Irena's grandson, Luis, greeted his grandmother with such love. Although Amy smiled broadly as she watched, she was suddenly stricken with jealousy. She didn't have her mother, grandmother, or a sibling to greet her; Aunt Jackie and Jennie were all that was left. They were family, but the greetings were never as warm and heartfelt as this.

Cordially receiving a goodbye hug from her new friend and her grandson, Amy was confident that she was leaving Irena in good hands and bade them goodbye.

She used the disgusting restroom at the station and bought a candy bar and a bottle of soda before hopping back on the train to continue her journey. There were far fewer people on the second half of the trip, and she knew she was likely one of a few to continue to Chachapo.

***

With her backpack swung over her shoulder, Amy jumped heavily off the bus's metal step and onto the rich black mud in the empty village. Her eyes fell upon precisely cut stones covered with moss, the skyline shrouded in mist, hiding the sharp, rugged peaks that were among the tour's most sought-after features.

During the village tour, the guide, who also served as the bus driver, discussed a rare occurrence that Amy was most excited about. It required a half-mile hike up a steep trail in the rain, but the rare treat of seeing the falcons fly was worth the work and the wet.

It was a place where the westerly winds would shoot up the side of the cliffs, and the falcons, native to this area, would dive down into the updraft with their wings tucked, then suddenly open them up and let the winds carry them far above the tops of the peaks. The phenomenon was rare because the right geography was required for it to occur.

A younger man spoke over the conversations and chatter, telling the guests that the mountain trek to see the falcons would leave in 5 minutes. Amy asked the bus driver if she could leave her backpack on the bus, then noticed that others' belongings were still occupying their seats. He gave her a slight nod, and Amy took only her camera, leaving the rest behind.

The hike was steep in some places but leveled off in others. As they inched up the ridge, the mist began to clear, and the wind rose, revealing the promised view. The brisk wind whirled around the tourists, encouraging chatter of pleasant surprise among them. Amy felt like she was on top of the world, and watched the falcons from a distance as they suddenly appeared and disappeared off the cliff's edge, giving the visitors a joyous reception.

The rest of the world slipped away as she watched the captivating dance. The birds made her feel so free and light-hearted. She took pictures of so many things that the roll of film was gone before she knew it.

Chachapo was a popular ghost town to visit, and the tour company exploited it, taking measures to keep the tourists away from the nesting area. Those making the trek up the mountain would see something so rare on earth; truly a life-changing experience.

The resident falcons rode the brisk winds that swept up the mountain cliff, rising far above the clusters of people, oblivious to the camera snapshots and the gasps of the crowd watching them.

On the descent down the mountain trail, the guide also bragged about the mining of rare minerals in this region, including gold. The mining of precious stones was mentioned, and she found a reference to Lapis Lazuli in the tour booklet.

She'd seen the falcons in her dreams, and the mystical stone that was once mined from here now hung around her neck. It was becoming impossible to deny the eerie coincidence of her entanglement with this place.

The knowledgeable guide discussed the region and offered a creative description of the village in its heyday. The community was involved in making blankets and hats from alpaca wool and produced its meals from the wonderful, tiered gardens, being completely self-reliant. He mentioned mining, which had proudly produced many tons of gold and precious gems. He also touched on safety concerns, and although the mine was rich in ore, many men lost their lives in prospecting ventures, sacrificing for the wealth it would bring.

Amy asked the guide, "Are there any records of village inhabitants?" Of course, her interest was more in finding her connection to these Incan people than learning about their lifestyles.

The guide replied, shaking his head. "Sadly, very little documentation existed of Chachapo. If there were any records, they'd be enshrined in the museum in Cusco, not hanging around here."

As the bus left the mountain village, Amy felt a sense of dread and sadness. Even knowing what had become of the people there, and feeling her emotions stretched to their thinnest, she felt their prideful resilience. After all, she was an Incan and had been moved by her visit there.

The dilapidated vehicle traveled down the steep, winding road amid the densest forest she'd ever seen. Amy shuffled through her notebook. She'd kept scraps of notes and copies of all the random information Izzy supplied, hoping to wrap up the mystery of her ancestors and the enchanted stone.

There were references to a ship, the São Luis, which eventually wrecked and lost all but a few hired hands. At the time of its undoing, there were no travelers along, only crew members. That information seemed out of place among all the other more personal documents and tidbits. Amy wondered why it was in the stores of information she'd found. What was significant about São Luis?"

14. Chachapo - 1971

Amy sat on a tourist bus, leaving the old village of Chachapo and traveling to the fishing village of Moray.

God, don't these people know how to shower? Amy scrunched her nose and reached into her bag for the scented hand lotion, hoping to rub it long and slow on the back of her hands and close to her nose. She became agitated when the strong body odor woke her from her brief nap.

The bus was crammed with local Peruvians, and only a select few spoke English; however, she was quite comfortable among the Spanish-speaking passengers, as the region's primary language was her family's native tongue.

She felt like the odd man out in this place by herself, but the isolation gave her some time to think and review the details of the hints that Izzy had meticulously left for her.

Amy closed her eyes and reflected on the images of the people she'd met at Izzy's house over the years. She never remembered meeting Tino, but she felt a connection to him as she would to an uncle or another family member. He was quite mysterious about what he knew of the stone, but maybe it was because he didn't know her well. Some people are that way with strangers. *I knew she would pass it to you.* Amy brought Tino's words to mind. *What is it about him?* She thought introspectively, hoping all her sleuthing would reveal the truth about the stone and its mysterious magical powers.

This area of the Andes had recently sustained a torrential downpour, even though the sun was out and the air was thick with moist heat. She could hear the rainwater dripping off the trees and dense brush, so loud it echoed. Amy watched out the window as the flora rushed past the bus, observing the narrow, winding, steep road ahead of the overcrowded vehicle. The mountains here were strangers to her, but the dense landscape and the depth of the shades of green were breathtakingly beautiful.

In her research, she found that this area of the Andes was where her family originated. Searching for tidbits of proof had been a slow and tedious process. However, she remained determined to follow the minuscule traces of her ancestral name, Huapaya. She came across a small tour company that offered day trips to several villages the Conquistadors had ravaged during the Conquest of the Americas. Chachapo appeared on the tour. Only a few such villages were restored years later, but Chachapo remained a ghost town.

The little tourist bus jolted suddenly, and all the passengers leaned heavily to the left, sending Amy into the lap of the tall man sitting next to her. "*Perdon*," she said to the man, grasping the seatback in front of her for support. As the bus came around and corrected itself, the shifting of the passengers threw the little bus heavily in the other direction, now sliding out of control on the muddy road.

An undeniable sense of weightlessness overtook the travelers as the vehicle caught air, leaving the earth, then making contact with the embankment, leaving the road at the wrong place and at the wrong time.

The ordeal was bewildering. There was a moment when the twenty passengers and one driver were suspended, and all were silent, but as the bus encountered bushes, trees, rocks, and water, a cacophony of screams and gasps could be heard collectively. Amy closed her eyes and tried to pull her knees in, feeling the weight of other people and belongings coming down on her. Experiencing the floating sensation again, Amy wondered just how far the bus would go. *Was this the end?*

As the motion began to slow and the floating sensation stopped, something large and heavy toppled and struck her head, sending her into what she thought was the bus's roof, and everything went black.

15. Captive

Somewhere in the Caribbean-1620

As she opened her eyes, Amy couldn't bring anything into focus. She heard a young woman's voice above her, and someone patted her cheek. Amy made out the sound of other women who chattered in the background, and she could tell they were keeping their voices low.

She closed her eyes again, feeling ill, as the woman put a cold compress on her forehead. She was so dizzy that it was preventing her from focusing, or the inability to focus was causing her to feel dizzy. Either way, she thought she'd be better off just keeping her eyes closed.

Another hour had passed, and Amy's eyes fluttered open again. This time, a beautiful young woman fell right into her line of sight. Confused and still reeling from her accident, she blinked several times, trying to recall the pretty face.

"Where am I?" she asked. The woman looked at someone else in the room and jabbered to her in Spanish. Amy tried again, this time in a language they would understand.

"Dónde estoy?" This time, the woman who had been hovering over her nodded.

The words she and the other woman shared now were all in Spanish. "Don't you remember? Those criminals broke into the Concepcion de Medico and kidnapped us. They intend to enslave us!"

Amy gasped and closed her eyes again. *How did I get here?* She thought, her mind flitting through recent memory, but couldn't make a clear picture of why she was there with those women.

Still in pain and disoriented, Amy was sure she was hallucinating. She expected, after the accident, that she should be in some hospital, but this wasn't a hospital. Not even a rudimentary care center, and this was certainly not where she started.

Trying to move her head, she slowly looked around the room for others. *If this isn't a hospital, then what is it?* Surprisingly, as if on cue, she felt the motion of waves and opened her eyes wide as fear shot through her. Looking pleadingly at the woman, she asked, "Are we in a boat?"

The woman looked at her as if she didn't want to tell Amy the truth. She nodded, not saying anything.

"No wonder I feel sick," Amy muttered under her breath. "Who are you?"

The woman partially covered her face and giggled. "It's me, Isabella."

Amy looked around to see the others. Two women were on the floor in the shadows against the wall. The space was very dark, with only a tiny round window to peek out of. "And you?" She waved her hand in the direction of the other girls, wincing at the pain in her head and neck.

"That is Maria and Carmen Louisa. We were all together at the hospital. Don't you remember?"

Amy shook her head, completely frustrated and completely lost. She closed her eyes, trying to recall these women, sure she'd never seen them. There was, however, something about the three names. What was it? Was this a dream? Forcing herself slowly to sit, she looked around the small, dank room. All the girls had pretty, smooth skin and beautiful features, long dark hair, and deep brown eyes. Spanish, for sure.

"How did we get here?" Amy asked, squinting at the pain pounding in her head.

Isabella described the abduction with a scowl on her face. "These pirates burst into the hospital looking for someone to help their crew member with a knife wound. They said he'd picked a fight at the docks. Maria and I went to help him, and you and Carmen Louisa brought water and bandages. We were all there together, and they grabbed us by the hair and led us to this ship, stuffing the four of us into this awful place. You put up a fight, and one of them rapped you on the head with the butt of his knife. You've been unconscious since then." Amy watched as the fear and anger of the encounter painted her face.

With a catch in her penitent voice, Carmen Louisa said, "We were only trying to do the right thing!"

Amy nodded her understanding to Isabella, but still appeared lost in this world. She stood up, trying to walk across the small room, swaying with the boat's movement. "How many do you think are on this ship?" she asked, her eyes seeking out Isabella, who seemed more proactive and less emotional.

"I only saw two others on the deck besides the four that came to the hospital."

Still standing on wobbly legs, Amy went to the door. She tried the latch, half expecting it to be blocked or locked. Her hunch was correct; they were stuck—prisoners. The only thing she could think of was getting the door open, but without a weapon, they couldn't even defend themselves.

***

The jingle of keys clanked behind the door, and all the women jumped up suddenly. When the door creaked open, a dirty, bearded man with a floppy-brimmed hat held a tray, followed by another similar-looking man brandishing two pistols.

"Food and water," was all the server said as he dropped the tray on the ground, and the two men backed out of the room, locking the door behind them. Barely able to see what was on the tray, the women clamored around it, more thirsty than they'd ever been. Finding a flask, they each took a drink, holding back just enough for later.

There was a bowl of slop. It looked like broth and greens, but they needed the food to keep their strength up. The four women passed the bowl around, each taking a turn to slurp the meager meal, ensuring they each got some greens.

Once the soup was gone, the women gathered in one corner, using their aprons and each other as pillows, and fell asleep restlessly. The boat pitched and plunged all night, shifting the room's contents, including the pile of women, who constantly sought comfort where they could find it.

The darkness in the tiny room was enshrouding. Although there was a very small hole high up on the wall, there was not even a glimmer of moonlight to orient oneself in this space. None of the girls moved from their pile until subtle hues of the morning began to show through the porthole. Amy wriggled away, found the flask, and took a drink. She brought it to the other girls, encouraging them to share its contents.

Without speaking, she scrolled through her thoughts, looking for the path that had taken her from one place to another. She hadn't thought about her dress or how the other women dressed until now. They were clothed in long, shapeless brown dresses and simple shoes that resembled slippers. Although they were all beautiful, they wore no makeup or adornments.

"What day is it?" Amy said softly.

Carmen Louisa stared at her for a moment. "I believe it is the Sabbath."

"But what day?" Amy insisted.

Carmen Louisa paused. "I think it is the 23rd of September."

Amy hesitated to ask the next question. "What year?"

The other girls' ears perked up, and looking at one another before Carmen Louisa answered, they all had surprised looks on their faces. Amy needed to know, but was unwilling to share the strange tale of her bewildering appearance.

"The year of our Lord, Sixteen hundred and twenty." Rather than give away her shocked reaction, Amy's eyes went to the wisp of daylight that could be seen from the tiny window. Silence filled the corners of the dank room as the four women avoided eye contact. Maria was quite sure the bump Amy had taken on the head did more to her than knock her out.

Amy kept her eyes on the bit of light that shone through the hole as she fought back tears. All that she knew yesterday was certainly not what she experienced today. Long moments passed, and although she was weak with fear and perplexed beyond explanation, she needed to try to behave as if she belonged there. Resisting the urge to panic, Amy held her breath, letting it out in one big huff.

Abruptly insisting like the ship's captain, Amy said, "Isabella, you're the tallest. Come over here and help me." When Isabella stood, she saw a flash of the same amulet her grandmother had mysteriously given her. Staring at it as it brushed the girl's cleavage, Amy was nearly paralyzed.

Isabella gave her a confused look but stood, taking the two steps needed to reach her. Amy briefly explained what she intended, then crouched down and slipped her head between Isabella's legs, lifting her onto her shoulders. Maria rushed over to help Amy stand, finally understanding what she wanted.

"What do you see?" Amy asked.

"I'm afraid I see nothing but water."

"Hmm …" Amy responded. She thought that at some point, the ship would make a port, and the girls might be able to signal their distress. Now, her mood was dampened. "Where are they taking us?" She said the words, not expecting an answer.

The heat in this subtropical climate climbed as the day wore on, making the room seem close and uncomfortable. The growing discomfort was making the women cranky. Maria began to weep.

"It's not hopeless," Amy said, rolling her eyes at the tender-hearted girl. The harsh words only made Maria cry harder.

By afternoon, the same dirty man who had come before to serve food paid the women another visit. This time, Amy asked before he had a chance to make his announcement.

"Where are you taking us?"

The pirate's dark eyes landed on her, and he began to smile. "Not to worry, lassy. You belong to us now. Relax." He plopped the tray down onto the floor once more, and the clicking of the keys could be heard again in the door lock.

The little morsel of hope Amy had in her heart diminished quickly. *It is impossible; rescue is a dream,* she thought.

The women followed the same routine as before, eating, drinking, and sharing to stay strong. She thought that being locked in this room, at the very least, kept them from being exposed to many more horrible things.

16. Filthy Animals - 1620

The hardest part about being kept in the grim darkness was all the empty time with nothing to do. The inhabitants of this space began making up games to occupy their time, such as word games, rhymes, and songs—anything to help them forget the black misery they had to endure.

There was a clatter at the door, and two other pirates were there; this time, they went after Amy, grabbing her by the wrists and then her hair, and pulled her from the room, locking it after them.

The taller one in front, holding a long, bulky pistol in one hand, had the lantern in the other. The shorter, bearded man kept hold of her hair and jammed the nose of a gun in her back. Although feisty enough to break loose, she wasn't quite willing to die.

The two bastards led her down a ladder to a storage area, where they briefly argued about who would go first. The taller man, with lighter-colored hair and a mustache, seemed younger but was undoubtedly the more menacing of the two.

Without giving any thought to the present company, he pushed her over a barrel, holding her down with one hand as he fussed with his breeches with the other. He was in the process of lifting her skirt when Amy started to scream, then instead of holding her down, he quickly covered her mouth, muffling the fearful cries.

"What the devil!" Amy heard a third, angry voice from the floor above, and both men backed away as a ruckus ensued.

"I'm sure the cap'n will not approve of you damaging his goods!" Amy kept her head down, wriggling so that her skirt would fall to cover her backside. She heard fists and grunts, curses and angry voices, but otherwise kept her eyes closed.

"Come along," the third man said. The middle-aged, clean-shaven man took her arm and led her back to the ladder, as the two moron pirates lay out on the floor. Although he was just another filthy animal doing pirates' work, the man looked at her with pity-filled eyes, softness hid deep within them. He led her back to the prison room, expressing a few words, and shoved her in. Still shocked, Amy wiped away tears from the emotional jolt she'd experienced with the close call, then heard the kinder pirate lock the door behind her.

***

Amy began to cry, dropping to her knees and saying a

prayer there in the tiny, dank room, her womanhood disheveled, but still intact.

Isabella covered her mouth when she saw Amy and grabbed her arm before she collapsed. "What did they do?" She said, almost as distressed as Amy was.

"What do you think? Luckily, there was one among them that stopped it." Amy's words were sharp. Her anger and hurt were apparent.

Maria stood staring at her, shocked, having been raped when she was ten, and knew there was nothing anyone could say to comfort someone who endured such brutality. Silently, she suspected that this would happen to all of them. They were captives and at the captor's mercy. The abuse was something they'd have to duck and dodge like bullets.

***

It was days before Amy began to communicate with the girls normally. She was unable to make sense of the abuse she'd suffered. So scared of being a victim one minute, Amy found herself so angry she could kill the next.

The mundane routine went on day after day, and more than once the women had to fight off the filthy pirates, but screeching and making a racket seemed to draw attention, stopping them. The encounters had come too close for comfort more than once. She noticed, however, that the pirates never reached out for Isabella. Amy knew it had nothing to do with her beauty and everything to do with the amulet. She knew it was the "great protector," which obviously worked in her friend's favor.

Overwhelmed with melancholy, Amy began to wish for a way to end it. She even considered ending her life, but there was nothing in this room except the four of them. During the sleepless nights, Amy occupied her thoughts with revenge. She couldn't believe the things she thought of or how often she hoped to have a chance to get even, wanting to make the bastards pay. *These criminals are worse than animals*, she thought. *They're piles of shit without souls*.

Her eyes scanned the room for the hundredth time, watching how the full moon's light painted the corner and the floor. She stood silently against the wall as far back as she could so she might see a glimpse of it. Catching sight of a tiny sliver of the enchanting moon, she dreamed of it dusting her with magical light, like fairy dust, and taking her away from this place. Sadly, it never did.

Amy sank back down on the floor, now losing sight of the round, bright moon, and gently closed her eyes. She began to imagine being on the beach, running and laughing. No, she was *taunting* someone. At that moment, she felt a surge of happiness.

The dream slowly faded from the glaring sunlight of the pretend place back to the piercing darkness she had grown accustomed to. Refocusing, Amy found the moonlit corner and looked down at the tips of her shoes. Recalling the daydream, she breathed in a sigh, and for that moment, she began to hope. She was trepidatious about it, but that state was the most light-hearted she'd felt in weeks.

Concentrating, she thought about how long she'd been a prisoner, and a month was her best guess. She honestly couldn't remember how long they'd been confined.

Amy wondered about the amulet around Isabella's neck as she sat awake in the quiet darkness. She moved closer to her as she dozed next to the other girls, and her eyes focused on the stone. It spoke to her calmly, like a friend. The little silver streaks sparkled brightly, and Amy felt her heart respond. It was most peculiar because, instead of dread and anger, she felt stronger and more determined to help rescue her friends and end this dreadful circle of sadness and abuse.

She finally gave in to exhaustion and lay beside the other girls. Her eyes closed, and a single tear trickled down her cheek. Why, of all places in the universe, did she end up here, in this hell?

Defiantly, she wiped away the tears of fear and frustration and sighed. When her soul resigned, she almost immediately began to dream.

She saw herself on the beach in Pensacola, where Izzy lived, scavenging for shells and plopping down on a blanket for a picnic lunch. The sun was quite warm, but the wind always blew, making it a perfect day. Then, without warning, the clouds began to gather, and she was suddenly whisked away to a time years later when she received the phone call about Izzy.

17. Island - 1621

A flurry of footsteps could be heard coming from the deck above as the boat made port and tied up to the pier. These noises and thumps were part of the routine the crew members followed when they needed supplies or moved cargo but today was different. There was very little noise coming from the pier. The normal shouts and greetings didn't occur; there were none today. Although the captives were curious, no one said anything to the other for fear of hoping, only to be left with another day of disappointment.

Almost oblivious to the sound of someone at the door, the young women turned their heads when it opened. The squat little man, Pierre, and the tall, skinny man who would sometimes bring the meals were at the door with a few lengths of rope.

"Come along. Wez gonna be ere a while." The girls didn't move, so Pierre reached for Carmen Louisa's arm. He lashed the wrists with the rope and pushed her aside, looking for another victim to bind.

When all four were bound at the wrists, Pierre led the group of women up the ladder one at a time. The tall, skinny man, Jake, followed the close-knit friends until they were all above deck, and the younger, mean one was there to keep an eye on them.

"Weez gonna stay ere until we make a deal to sell ye." The mean-tempered pirate had a subtle glimmer in his eye just then, making Amy wonder what he was up to.

"What is your name?" Amy asked him, wanting to distinguish the kind pirate from the rank one.

Pierre perked up. "Das Jamie Whiles. Wez call im da Wild J," then he laughed deviously.

Jamie looked at her with half-crazed eyes and responded with a growl. "That is none of your concern!"

"Alright, Jamie, where are we then?" Amy asked indignantly. The other girls looked at her, shocked. They didn't expect any of the women to be so direct to the scum.

"That is also not your concern. This island belongs to us, and we'll wait here for the Red. Then we'll be done wit ya'!"

Amy hung her head, discouraged and beleaguered, so smelly she couldn't stand herself. She knew she'd jump in the water, entirely clothed, the first chance she got. She thought about the power the amulet might give her, but then she remembered that Isabella had the stone, not her.

The sun was so bright that it took the women some time to adjust their eyes. Their bound hands could barely offer any protection as they waited for their sight to recover. They all breathed deeply; fresh air at last. Sadly, the women weren't aware that it had been over a month since they'd been in the open air. Without realizing it, a smile began to spread on Amy's face. It was amazing what being outdoors would do to a person's sensibility.

With the assistance of their two guards, the women managed to climb onto the deck and then descend the rope ladder to the pier. Pierre and Jamie marched them down the well-worn wooden landing toward the white sand beach. Amy eyed the water, and when she could see that it was shallow enough, she tipped herself over and fell in. She was an adequate swimmer, but she didn't know how she would manage without using her arms.

The other girls giggled and followed her before either of their guards knew what was happening. Splashing and joyful, the four captives washed the month's worth of filth off their bodies, much to the chagrin of the other two smelly pirates who were forced to jump in after them.

The bath was brief, and slowly but surely, Pierre and Jake pulled them out of the water by their hair. The women wanted nothing more than to be clean, and at the very least, the jump into the ocean washed away a bit of the disagreeable stench. It made them just as happy that the pirates in charge of their confinement smelled better, too.

Now out of the water and walking single file through the deep sand and into the dense brush, Amy thought about who they would end up with now. *At least we have the use of our hands*, she thought, since the bindings slipped off easily after they'd come out of the water. Thinking too deeply about it, perhaps, Amy reasoned as they walked. The mess they were in was terrible, but what if the next wealthier pirate was worse? Surely, a man who would purchase women as a commodity was not a man of morals, and honestly, he would have to be a cruel and heartless individual.

Considering the men who guarded the four women, it was evident that Wild J's job was to break them and make them surrender under any circumstances, but that wasn't what she felt. Her righteous heart was telling her something quite different. It was not vengeance; she just wanted to stop it. Stop the cycle of slavery.

Amy knew about how slavery was and how it turned out for the enslaved for the next 240 years, but this treatment was so demeaning. *What makes them, these insults to humanity, think they're better than other humans?*

She didn't know how to do it, but she would free these women and stop the bastards that held them, no matter what.

***

They came to a clearing with a wide circle, and she saw two tiny huts and a fire pit in its center. She thought it must be a place where pirates met, drank, and made shady deals. "This is where the world changes," she muttered to herself, wavering sharply between bravery and fear.

They encountered two other dirty men dressed as sailors in this encampment, but they all looked similar. Pierre and Jake were cleaner only because the canny women had willfully forced them into the sea.

One of the pirates greeted Jake and asked, "Where do you want 'em?

"Clear that out. That'll do for now." He'd merely nudged his head toward one of the little huts, giving a subtle signal to the other marauder.

Pierre and another man, whom he called Ollie, pitched a couple of boxes out of the bleached box and onto a clump of grass just behind the sunburned hut. One of the boxes seemed heavy, and the two men strained to move it, then plopped it down with a *thunk*. "That'll do," Pierre said, nodding, a scowl gracing his expression. Then Jake poked Amy to go inside the hut, pushing the others to follow.

Now confined yet again, the women sat on the ground and adjusted to their new surroundings. It was sand and a much softer surface than the black-walled room they'd been kept in on the ship.

Amy looked at the girls with a shadow of a wry grin and whispered, "That box is full of treasure, and we're going to steal it when we leave this place."

Carmen Louisa looked at her, cocked her head, and said, "And how are we going to do that?"

Amy blinked, then her eyes darted to the view from the little window in the door of the hut. She answered the statement confidently, "An opportunity will present itself, don't worry."

All three girls now looked down, unable to make eye contact with each other. Maria thought that Amy had finally lost her wits and had gone cuckoo, but they didn't know that her plan involved Isabella and her precious amulet.

The shadows from the trees and shrubs shifted, and soon there was more shade than daylight as dusk approached. Pierre brought each hostage a piece of the rabbit they'd just roasted and a flask of water. It was dreadfully hot in the cramped hut in the full sun of the day, and the thirst was almost too much to bear. Amy realized they had been given just enough food and water to stay alive, all four of them shrinking in size and strength. Ultimately, it made it easier for the pirates to handle them.

As twilight approached, the girls stopped staring at the firelight's reflection and gave in to exhaustion. The weight of it seemed to be brought on by the island's heavy, dense air.

Although the other women had settled down, Amy remained awake for a bit longer, as her restless mind wouldn't subside. She waited until she was sure Maria and Carmen Louisa were asleep, then gently roused Isabella. She whispered close to her, "Wake up, I need to talk to you."

Isabella's eyes fluttered for a moment; then they met Amy's. "What is it?"

"I need to ask you about that amulet. Where did you get it?" Isabella reached for it, then looked toward Amy again, confused.

"My grandmother gave it to me. She promised it would be with me my whole life, and I could count on the magic for protection. I'm afraid a Christian wouldn't understand, so I've not spoken of it."

Amy kept after her, bombarding the girl with questions, as all she could think of was finding out about the amulet's past. "Did your grandmother tell you where she got it? Have you ever had vivid dreams while wearing it? Do you know what she meant by saying the stone would protect you?"

As Isabella spoke, the stone began to warm, and she reached for it, quite surprised. She answered Amy's questions and said, "I can feel it talking to me."

Amy shook her head very slowly. "Do something for me," she said softly. "Close your eyes, hold the stone tightly, and wait for it to show you. You will have a vision; a glimpse of something, but you need to remember all you can of what it shows you."

Isabella did what she'd told her, finally being sucked into the trance-like state that Amy knew all too well. Her engagement with the magic lasted only a few minutes, then the amulet let go, and she gently opened her eyes.

After a few seconds of recovery, Isabella's eyes began to tear, half in fear and half in joy.

"Tell me about your dream," Amy said point-blank. She knew the overwhelming consequence of the amulet's work, unquestionably something she had experienced, too.

Isabella asked, suddenly swayed by the intensity of the otherworldly illumination. "How did you know?"

Amy knew the two women must have a conversation about the encounter Isabella just had, and she did not want what she was about to say to elicit fear or frenzy.

"I know of the power of the stone. I know it gives visions; however, the visions you see will be of things to come, things that haven't happened yet. If you saw something, tell me what it was. I can help you understand it. What did you see?"

Isabella stared at her in awe of her knowledge, but rather than becoming hysterical, she began to speak slowly. "The man they're selling us to is named Red. He will be kind to us but not so kind to our captors." She swallowed hard. “We will sail away on a different boat, but I don't see the end—if we make it to another place."

Amy looked puzzled as she thought. *Kind to us and not kind to our captors.* She had hoped that the stone would give Isabella a way to escape the living hell they faced. However, the news she shared was not all bad. A new master might have them, but she was now assured that their conditions would improve.

"How did you know about this amulet? How did you know what it would do?" Isabella's eyes met Amy's as though she were bewitched, suddenly feeling as though her friend were conjuring evil.

Amy stared into Isabella's eyes and knew that 1620 was not ready to hear about time travel. "I've, uh," Amy hesitated. "I've encountered a jewel before, just like it. I know about the visions. It's almost frightening."

Isabella seemed satisfied with that and reached out to touch Amy's hand. "Thank you for telling me this. I hope that what this stone bestows will be a gift and not a curse."

Amy smiled kindly at her and said, "Let's try to get some sleep." She waited for Isabella to settle down and then lay down, making herself a pillow of sand.

18. Pillage

Toward the evening of the second day at the beach camp, a commotion was heard on the trail leading to the fire circle. The only thing like a window was in the door, which faced the endless brambles and shrubs that covered most of this island. Amy pushed her head up against the wall, peeking through a gap in the wood. She could merely see the flicker of the fire, but was glad to see what the excitement was all about.

From behind the circle where the fire was, she could see the heads of half a dozen more men laughing and holding up bottles or metal that reflected the firelight. She knew these were other pirates, celebrating a successful raid on unsuspecting victims. She was sure the marauders had taken things they didn't need or even want, only to show merchants and sailors they could, just as they did when the women were captured.

She realized that the place they had brought her and her friends to must be an island where this gang of pirates met or hid out. They all acted like they knew each other and bragged about their finds, just as a kid would behave on a playground.

The other women were crabby and uninterested, but Amy wanted to know everything. She watched the new group approach the circle and make fun of Pierre, toting their wine and showing off a new blade or a fancy hat. The fact was that there was little difference between them. They looked so similar to each other. The only distinct difference was the length or color of their hair.

She could, however, make out that the gangly group was a mix of nationalities. She was able to make out the fairer-skinned buccaneers among those with darker, bronze skin. Amy remembered reading stories about Captain Hook and Black Beard, and the chaos they caused and the trouble they got away with. She held back a catch in her throat as she realized that history was unfolding before her. These gnarly misfits were the ones spoken of in history books. It was apparent that you were either on their side or you were sold, killed, or enslaved.

***

Surrounded by all the strangeness, Amy couldn't help but feel that she was here for a reason, unable to piece it all together. *Why me? Why here?* she thought, straining to see the goings-on from the hole in the wall of the tiny hut. The most bizarre thing was that she and the amulet ended up in the same place simultaneously. This occurrence had to be more than just a coincidence.

It struck her that Isabella said she had gotten the amulet from her grandmother. Amy pondered for a minute, wondering if that meant that her grandmother's name appeared on the family tree she found at Izzy's. She closed her eyes and tried to envision the family tree, remembering several Isabellas named over many generations.

Trying her best to organize the tiny bits of information she'd gotten from Isabella, she offhandedly thought of a game they could play that could pull facts from her friends and help her piece together the history she was seeking in Peru to begin with.

"I have an idea." Amy blurted as she turned around swiftly, sporting a wry smile.

"Oh, what is that?" Maria said with a snarky tone. She was one to almost wither in the heat and had been on her last nerve for the past few days.

"Oh, come on, it will be fun!" Amy continued. "Each of us will give three simple facts about ourselves; one will be a lie, and two will be truths. The game is called Two Truths and a Lie." Amy secretly hoped Isabella would reveal something about her family that would help connect the amulet's history and its curious magic.

"I'll go first." She smiled and blinked purposefully. "I have been married once before." She hesitated as she came up with the other sentences. "I love jewelry, and I make delicious rabbit stew."

"I think the lie is the stew." Carmen Louisa said, smiling like she'd won the lottery.

"Hmm, I think the marriage is a lie," Isabella said, now quite sure she was the right one.

"I think so, too!" Maria added, now feeling more perky and wanting to participate.

The girls each took their turn, but when Isabella's turn came, she said very little about the stone amulet or her family. Amy did learn that her grandmother came from Guadeloupe and that she had a brother who died very young. Amy might further investigate the Guadalupe thing, especially since it involved the grandmother who had gifted her the amulet.

When the game was over, the girls took their usual positions. Amy was kneeling again, pushing up against the peephole, and listening as closely as possible to the pirates' conversations.

They talked of other mates and whores. Ships and towns. Then, one of the invisible pirates (impossible to distinguish) described boarding another ship and taking all they wanted. The marauders took kegs of rum and gunpowder, chains, and chickens. He also describes a few valuables they'd split among them. Things like jewelry and belt buckles, but mainly gold. He stated that the gold originated from Colombia.

They'd stolen it from a ship bound for the Spanish King; only the pirates got to them first. That meant those treasures were with them, and Amy couldn't think of a better way to get even with the damned kidnappers.

She listened for a long time, and when she turned and looked at the others, they were almost asleep. Lying down in the sand, Amy gave up and fell into a dreamless sleep.

The muffled sounds of voices began to rouse them from their rest. Amy lay there silently for a while, but she began to think of how she might use the knowledge of the booty to their advantage, maybe as leverage if they could manage to get out of the shack.

She thought for a moment, then began to panic, understanding that pirates steal and pillage, and would likely try to double-cross Red, the kind man who was supposed to buy them. Her mind raced and skipped, recalling that Isabella said he would be kind to them. Amy hoped that the man would come prepared to bargain with the pirate scum because she knew they couldn’t be trusted.

After trying to slow her scattered thoughts, Amy lay awake for some time, waiting for exhaustion to take over. She sighed deeply, yawned, and soon slipped into a fitful sleep.

19. Histories - 1620

Given that they had nothing but time on their hands right now, Amy pondered over how the four of them ended up here. She knew she had historically been misplaced, but what about the others? *What were their stories?*

She stood motionless, staring out the little window in the door. Outside, there was nothing more than the wild bush, but there was a flow to the landscape. There was very little change from one rolling hill to another, and it looked like waves in the sea, short peaks and valleys in a velvet blanket of green.

As she watched, the bees buzzed, and a few small, colorful birds fluttered about. At that moment, she wasn't a prisoner.

Turning gracefully, she asked Isabella, "Where are you from? Did you travel from somewhere far away to work at the hospital?"

Isabella rested her head against the wall, stroking her long hair with her fingers. "I went to Hispaniola from a little village north of San Juan. Maria did as well. We both have family in Ch'in wasi." She closed her eyes slowly as if to savor the thought of her home.

"What does your family do? Farmers or builders?"

Isabella smiled now, her eyes still closed. "My mother is a gifted seamstress, and my grandmother was a baker. My father is a blacksmith." Amy smiled, thinking that not much had changed throughout the centuries. All those trades still existed.

Maria perked up. "My mother is a midwife, and my father breeds and sells goats."

Amy sat back and nodded her head very slightly. Although she was in the wrong time, she felt she knew these people and that she had been placed here for a purpose. She had yet to figure it out.

She thought about the day she was roused from the depths of darkness with the faces of the girls surrounding her. Shocked about her condition, she tried to assimilate into this group without behaving like someone with far greater knowledge. She, admittedly, was no wiser than any of these women, who had nothing. *The things I could do if we only got out of here.*

"Carmen Louisa, what about you? Where are you from?" Isabella's voice pierced her thoughts, carrying on as if she didn't already know the answer.

"I am from Havana, on the island of Cuba. Our family has a large farm with sugar cane. We all worked in the fields for many years. Helping at the hospital was the only way I could travel anywhere other than Cuba. Now look at me!"

Suddenly overcome by sadness, Carmen Lousia began to cry. The reminiscing brought about memories of things that were now lost to her.

"I can tell you something, all of you, this …" Amy moved her hands, swiping the air all around her. "This is not how we will end. This will end!" She was determined to lift their spirits and share her faith that their captivity would end soon. She only hoped that these bastards would get what they deserved.

"What about you?" Maria gingerly asked the question, trying not to be too blunt, but truly wanted to know.

Amy looked at the others, her eyes scanning theirs, wondering what tale she might weave. "I am from a place called San Antonio." The Spanish name that came to mind, even though it didn't exist in 1620. "My father disappeared when I was young, and my mother was a shopkeeper; she is gone now, too. There is nothing to keep me there." Although she tiptoed around the truth, she didn't lie either. Her father left them when Amy was a baby; her mother was a social butterfly and very organized, but in truth, she was a librarian, and she, too, was gone. After Amy spilled the few facts she was willing to share, she did not want to make eye contact with the others.

This conversation reminded her of Izzy, and the wounds from losing her were still too fresh to take lightly.

Shifting gears, she asked Isabella more questions, knowing she was unwilling to share much about her family. Smiling, she looked at Isabella and said, "My grandmother's name was Isabella. She was named after her grandmother, who was named after her grandmother. It is a strong, important name in my family. Do you know how your name came about?"

Isabella was perplexed about why Amy was interested in her life. At this time in the world, giving away too much information was dangerous. It was easy to say or hint about family members in mixed company that could be exploited. Amy understood completely, but that didn't stop her from trying.

Isabella seemed a bit flustered but began to share her tale slowly. "I was named Isabella because my father wished for me to be protected by the Gods. You see, my father was an Incan, and the Spanish invaders had destroyed their village.
His father," she hesitated, "was a Spaniard." She sat biting her lip and nervously waited for a reaction.

Amy tried hard not to react, knowing that she also had Incan blood running through her. Trying desperately to visualize the family tree she had found, Amy mentally worked to conjure the names at the very bottom.

Amy smiled warmly. "Don't distress, Isabella, for we wouldn't exist without the ancestors who came before us." Amy reached over and touched Isabella's arm. She briefly felt a tingle and smiled. She knew the amulet was responding to Isabella's words and whatever was happening in her heart.

"So, you are both Spanish and Incan? A fine mix of beautiful people, if you ask me." The other girls nodded as Amy forced a reaction from them. Her questions helped her to find a morsel of the information she was looking for. There was Incan blood in Isabella.

They had reached the end of another day, and as she stared out the little window in the door of the hut, Amy saw the clouds building in the distance. Since she'd been in this century, she remembered one very blustery day and another when rain had fallen. It wasn't essential when they were in a cramped black room on a gloomy ship away from it all. But now she could see that the little island camp was in for a storm. In St. Louis, she knew that this time of year, December, could bring rain or snow, and she could easily handle either one. The horizon was dark and ominous, but the change would be welcome, she thought. The alter-reality was nice, aside from being a slave.

As the girls settled down once again, the wind blew, and the clouds drifted like black cotton balls across the moon, leaving silvery trails that danced upon the sand. Amy watched the shadows for a while, and finally, giving in to exhaustion, she resigned her post to gain some rest.

The others were already asleep, so she lay down in the sand, placing her head softly on Isabella's lap, and closed her eyes. The lightning began to flash, and the thunder rumbled, slowly intensifying and rolling on for what seemed like forever.

Amy began to tremble in sync with the rising storm, feeling fear rise within her as the women ran through the brambles and bushes, panting from the effort. The women ducked their heads and hid in a panic. What she saw morphed into the family tree that Izzy left for her. She suddenly saw the name De'Cabrillo clearly. Then, just as suddenly as the vision came, it faded into a fog.

Abruptly sitting up, panting as though she'd just run a mile, she looked at the pile of girls, hoping she hadn't woken them. Staring back at her was Isabella, panicked and panting just as Amy was.

"What did you see?"

Isabella slowly moved her head from side to side, trying to deny the vision she saw. "Running, terrified by what might be behind us."

Amy whispered, "That's what I saw. By touching you, I could see your vision." There was still so much Amy couldn't understand about the inherited amulet, but every day, she learned more of its mystery. "Do you see? Through the connection we share, we can both see the visions. We both will touch the future, which will get us out of here and to a safe place."

Isabella seemed so confused. Scared of the incredible power in the incredible stone that embellished her neckline. "It talks to me. Sometimes it wakes me in the night. Why can I hear it and no one else can?"

Despite the hours of research, she had done to find out why this amulet did what it did, Amy couldn't give Isabella a reason. She didn't know.

Amy pursed her lips together, trying to temper the speed at which the words would flow and contain her excitement. She understood Isabella's fear and shock, just as she had when she first experienced the magic. Isabella didn't understand, and although it was scary, she could do a lot of good with her power.

Amy spoke to Isabella in a controlled whisper. "Where I come from, this is a gift," she said softly. "This gift is a good thing when you know what it can do for you or how you can help good people. Open your heart to it; you won't regret it."

For the next few minutes, neither of the girls talked. Amy was sure that Isabella's dreams would continue despite her fear of what they held, and the magic could help them. She reached over and gently patted her arm, then lay her head down again, secretly smiling about having the amulet on their team.

She closed her eyes and pondered how it got from Isabella to Izzy, then to her. She may never know.

20. Red - (Red Legs Greaves)

It was a blustery morning, with a swift breeze wafting the insignificant odors through the camp. This was the day their new Master would come to lay claim to his new property.

The pirates around the little encampment seemed nervous and jumpy, as if they were ready for a battle rather than a business deal. The women watched them scatter about, ensuring the men had dispersed and standing guard in case the meeting's end turned into a clash.

The women's confinement here was hot and cramped, but the fresh breeze was better than the black cavern any day. Pierre seemed to be the only one to give the girls any attention, ensuring they had water and food, no matter how meager. This day was no exception.

Amy stopped him to ask, "Why are you all so nervous? You look like children awaiting their punishment."

Amy knew what they were nervous about, but wanted to know if this little man taking orders would give in to the pressure of his superiors. She knew that pirates were mostly followers and suspected Pierre of being one of them, not a leader. The leaders wielded the sword.

"We'll ave an important visitor t'day. Mind yer' mouth!"

Amy pulled back, surprised by the gruffness of his words. "I didn't mean anything by it, I was just curious."

"Humph," he said, then walked away with the standard sand-sauntering stagger.

She figured it was the new Master they talked about a week ago, finally showing up to examine the goods. As with all things, change can be unnerving, but Amy reasoned with herself that their future placement couldn't be any worse than their current one.

Maria sat up straight, grooming herself. She ran her fingers through her hair until it lay smoothly, then she twisted it into a braid and tied it with a strip of cloth she tore from the inside hem of her apron. The rest of the girls just watched her. Impressed with her finished look, Isabella followed suit. Carmen Louisa followed Isabella's lead. Since she had wild, red hair, Amy decided to tie her hair back. She was not unhappy with the climate here, but the humidity made her hair frizz uncontrollably, and tying it back at least tamed the unruly locks.

They each took turns taking off their aprons, shaking them out, and turning them around to present a cleaner side. The simple white shifts had yellowed since they hadn't been cleaned in nearly two months. The brown and gray tunics covered the lion's share of the dirtied shifts and had also been flipped to expose the cleaner side. In all their time together, Amy hadn't seen any of them take as much care in their appearances as they did today, but her better sense told her to follow their lead. Amy thought, *maybe a good impression would encourage their buyer to treat them better,* though that didn't put her mind at ease.

Pierre brought them water and a disgusting fish broth soup to share, hoping to tell the buyer they had food and water regularly. Amy was sure the orders came from Wild J, as he seemed to be in charge of this pitiful little island camp. It was his job to get the most money he could from the sale or trade, and that would make him look good in the eyes of the captain in charge.

Despite the unsettled atmosphere, the encampment looked tidy and clean, with no carcasses, bottles, or blankets visible. All the camp's activity could be seen through the crack in the wall. The view from the window in the door gave them no advanced warning of anyone approaching. Carmen Louisa had her eye pressed against the wall, keeping the girls alerted to any changes.

"I see men coming from the beach. It looks like there are five, no, six of them. And they're dressed nicely." She spoke in a whisper to the other girls. They were excited about the exchange and anxious to see something else. Be somewhere else.

The women listened carefully to the words shared between the pirates and the new *Master* and prayed that the man would be kinder to them. After all, they hadn't done anything to deserve this.

The group's apparent leader was the one they called Red. It was a nickname from another time, but it clearly identified the man. He was tall, with a deep voice, a thick Scottish accent, and he wore a clean green jacket. The girls took turns getting a peek at him through the crack, although they remained silent, knowing the way he looked did not decide how he treated people.

Finally, Pierre arrived with Wild J and opened the hut door, binding the girls' hands before inviting them out into the open fire circle. He lined them up between two other pirates and one wayward who came along with the new group. Red stood silent for a moment, then looked directly into the eyes of each of the girls. "You," he pointed at Amy. “Come along with me."

Amy followed the man fifty yards down the path from the gathering place, trembling with fear of what would happen next. She never expected to be separated from the others, and she thought this segregation was quite unusual.

The man they called Red turned to her, looking suspiciously over her shoulder.

"Donna, worry, lassie. I'm not going to hurt ye. Ye' look different than the other girls, and I speak English far better than Spanish." Amy kept looking at his eyes, waiting for something unexpected. She felt a gentle warmth within her, seeing kindness in him. It was something she hadn't witnessed for quite some time.

The man continued. "Listen. I intend to bargain for ye' but not to keep ye' or yer friends. I wish to free ye." Amy had to think about what she'd just heard. "Free us? You want to let us go?"

"Aye. That's what I said."

Amy's eyes began to water, surprised by the emotional upheaval she felt. Sadly, the thought of someone being kind to her or her friends was incomprehensible. Not only had she and the other girls been mistreated, but it seemed respect was not freely given. This man was different.

"Why?" She asked the Scotsman, nearly breathless.

"I kin these heartless bastards. I kin ye' women didna do anything to deserve it. I'm just settin' it right."

Amy smiled through the tears and stepped forward to the tall man with devastatingly blue eyes and mousy brown hair to embrace him. However, she found she couldn't with her bound hands. Instead, he placed his arms around her shoulders and hugged her. All he needed was to know that what he was doing was right.

"I need them to think this is just another business deal, so ye' canna give it away, ye' hear?" He spoke softly, his words filled with tenderness. Amy wiped away a tear with her balled-up fist and nodded her head. "Thank you. Thank you, truly."

Red followed her back to the camp, and Amy stepped back in line with the other girls. Red told the pirates that he'd seen all he needed and would return with the amount they'd settled on.

Crammed back into the hut that had most recently been home, the girls flopped back onto the sand floor, quiet. Amy pushed her head against the crack and watched Pierre and Wild J walk away. Then, she turned to the girls with a smile.

"He's not buying us to enslave us. He's buying us to set us free." She looked at the others, sure they all thought she was lying.

Isabella said, "That's impossible. No one would do that."

"I'm afraid it's not impossible. However, I guess that when our new *Master* comes back, it won't be to pay the settled-upon amount." Amy's face spread with a wry smile as she contemplated what her words truly meant.

She sat back and let the news sink in. Even if her eyes were closed, she would know that this little room had hope where none had existed before.

From the little window, Amy watched as the horizon gradually changed from blue to orange. A wisp of wind tickled the leaves, and the calming rustle brushed away her troubles. A purple hue overtook the sunset sky and enveloped all things; the sun slowly disappeared.

21. Broken Promise - 1620

Another dreadful day passed in the island camp, and nothing changed, except that the girls' outlooks were different, brighter. It was as if they could see the sunlight through the rainstorm when nobody else could. They finally dared to share what they would do when they got home—the things and people they missed.

Amy didn't know what was next in the grand scheme of things. She didn't know how she got to this place and couldn't see a clear path home. At the very least, she would hope to leave here as quickly as she had appeared, not caring about what would be left behind. She wanted to believe that with all her heart.

The gangly crew of pirates was drinking again, and the conversation became louder and raunchier as time went on. Growing up in a big city, Amy had heard just about the worst she could hear long before spending time with these marauders. More sensitive, Maria lay down and covered her ears, sure that what she heard would make her burn in hell. Carmen Louisa only scowled at their harshness, hearing them talk of raping women and gutting a man for stealing a bottle of rum.

"Is there a good bone in their bodies?" She asked, shocked.

Amy responded, "I'm sure there are a few. They're acting tough to make the other men think it's true. Most of this is only a sham."

Isabella looked at her, confused. "What is a sham?"

Amy blushed slightly, unaware that the term was still foreign to them at this time. "A lie is what I mean. It's only a lie."

The girls nodded but remained quiet for a few more minutes. Then Carmen Louisa began to sing, *Arrorro mi' nino.* Amy thought it was her way of drowning out the unpleasant conversation by creating something more beautiful to listen to. She had a lovely voice, and the words were surprisingly comforting.

She had been gently singing the lyrics of one song, and began the melody of another when something hit the side of the hut with a thud, and a loud "shut up!" came from the men circled around the campfire. Carmen Louisa jumped, and the song stopped abruptly.

Isabella smiled and said, "Sing your song. They won't do anything to us. We now belong to Senior Red." And she giggled at the thought. With that, Maria finally sat up, and the four women began to sing loudly together, the song lifting their hearts as they worked together to taunt the unsavory crowd. Four of the six men finally got up and walked toward the beach, leaving the two men of less importance to stand guard over the captive choir.

Another hour had passed, and the girls began to settle down to rest. Amy, as usual, was the last to rest, the shadow of a smile crossing her face. Still, before falling asleep, she listened intently to the pirate's conversation, surprised at the tidbits of information she had discovered.

Almost inaudible, they talked of ways they'd planned to double-cross Red. "Ez well dressed. I think ez got too much already. Wild J is plannin' to loot iz ship when e' comes to get the girls. Ee'll leave with less than e' come with, heh, heh."

"I thinks we should ave one more go at the women before e' gets em'."

"No, the tall scrawny one said to him. "Cap'n says to leave em' be. Day isn't ours, now. I don't want the hell comin' down on our heads!"

There were chuckles and more poking fun at each other going on, but now Amy had helpful information if she could only speak to Red before the trade was made.

***

Rising just as the sun began to lighten the eastern sky, Amy made her way to the little window and poked her face through it as far as she could. There was a light mist that covered the whole island, and when she looked toward the rising sun, she saw a rainbow encircling the trickle of light.

Smiling silently, she was reveling in the peace there on the secluded island. Although they were captives and soon to be slaves to another, she saw, through the depths of darkness, the goodness that prevailed. The girls, the beauty of this place, the silence, and the sunrise were all wonders to behold.

An unexpected clatter of activity abruptly woke the women. It was still quite early when the grunts and quips of several men hauling fistfuls of things from the beach dropped them in piles near the other hut. Isabella was the first to press her head against the wall at the crack and gave step-by-step details. It was obvious to Amy that they'd been plundering; what or who was unknown, but it looked like they'd made a haul.

Isabella recited, "They have a tarp full of weapons, swords, and bows. Then I see a box. It is a hefty box indeed. Armfuls of clothes?" It was more than likely the makings of their usual haul, and their take of items would depend on the type of ship they assaulted.

Amy hoped for food. If they'd taken any, the girls would also be fed. She imagined they would take what they could use or sell and not focus on things that were too heavy or too frivolous.

She shook her head as she thought about how these people could steal for a living. Worse yet, they would steal for someone else. She knew that often, the privateers would steal for the king or queen, thinking they were doing an *honorable* thing in support of the mother country. The most bewildering, Amy thought, was how stealing, killing, plundering, and destroying someone else's property was honorable.

Once all the stolen items were placed either in the second hut or in a stack beside the hut the women were in, the thieves settled down and slept. They were strewn about the fire circle; some would be sleeping off the bottle they'd consumed during the night, and others were exhausted because of all the work it took to drag the plunder up the gradual rise to the camp.

It was another two days before Red showed up, and on that day, the pirate shipmates were unwilling to make a good impression. That meant that the girls would not receive food or water. No one volunteered to take care of the girls, and they were helpless. If the prisoners had asked, they would have been denied, so nothing was said in the hope that someone would show kindness.

Midday, there was a ruckus when one of the crew spotted *the Hector,* Red Greaves' ship, about a mile out.

Suddenly, those insolent pirates livened up, organizing the makeshift camp to receive a guest.

In short order, Carmen Louisa, posted at the crack, recited play-by-play as she watched Red and his crew members approach.

"Tell me when he can see us," Amy told Carmen Louisa anxiously. "I need to get his attention."

A moment later, Carmen Louisa spoke softly to Amy. "He can hear you now."

Amy had removed her apron and was waving it like a flag of surrender out the tiny window to signal him. "Mister Red?" Amy said loudly. The spectacle got his attention, and he approached the hut, walking right past four marauders standing in front of him.

"Can I help you, my dear?" He said politely.

"I must tell you, I overheard two pirate crewmen saying they would loot your boat when you left it. I believe you and your ship are in danger."

Red laughed openly. "Aye. Ye must know it happens every time I make it to port. Dunna worry, lass, we are prepared."

And as if on cue, a commotion could be heard down the path to the beach. "Ye' see?" Red said with a wink. "Now, whattay say we get ye' outta here?"

He took the dagger out of his belt, broke the lock, and then jimmied the door latch. Flinging it open wide, he said, "Now hide yourselves!" Four girls stared at him with the eyes of a deer in the headlights. All at once, Amy grabbed Isabella's arm and darted out the door, the other two following closely.

Amy ran so quickly that the other girls had trouble keeping up. She didn't know where she would go, but looked for the deepest, darkest part of the island she could see and headed there. The shrubs and brambles tore at their clothing and scratched their skin, but they knew this bold move might be life or death for them. Tucking into a thicket, they crouched low, panting and trembling at the daring stunt they had just pulled.

Taking off her apron and burying it in the sand, Amy spoke to the others in a desperate whisper, "This color is easy to see; get rid of it!" The other girls did what they were told, removed their aprons, and pushed layers of sand over the pile.

The sun moved slowly across the sky, changing the shadows that had once hidden the girls, and hours passed as they remained tucked away, hidden from the world.

Maria, who looked like a scared rabbit, finally whispered to Amy, "How can you be so calm? We're running for our lives!"

Amy looked down and watched a tiny ant crawl across the sand mound covering their aprons. "It is because we're running for our lives that I remain calm. I have to keep us safe."

Maria stared at her, lips pursed tightly together. She didn't realize that Amy felt responsible for them.

The women remained quiet so they could listen. Carmen Louisa heard something that no one else did. "Someone is coming!" She mouthed the words in panic.

"Nighean! Lassie! Are ye' there? Ye' can come out; all is well!" It was Red. Relief wafted over them. Amy and Isabella dug up their aprons and stood, focusing on the direction of their new master's voice.

He stood a hundred yards away, scanning the area for movement among the trees and flora. Amy couldn't believe the swell of reassurance she felt when she saw him. Suddenly, her emotions calmed, and deep down, she knew everything would be alright.

He watched as they made their way out of the bushes and brambles they'd dashed through to hide, a subtle smile growing on his face. "Those puppets of Jack Ward are long gone or dead. Ye' got no worries now, lassies."

As Amy came through the final hedge, Red reached for her hand to help her. Once she was out, he did the same with the other girls until they were all standing beside him in a clearing just up the rise from the encampment.

"Are ye' alright?" So contrary to what the women expected from him, his sky-blue eyes twinkled with delight as he inquired after the women's welfare.

"Yes," Amy said, smiling, "I believe we are all fine. Thank you." She was enamored with the tall Scot, still disbelieving they were now free.

He led the women, like a gaggle of geese, down the path and back to the beach, then boarded a yawl that took them to his ship. Before he left the island, he cleaned out the stores of pilfered items and took them for himself and his crew, muttering under his breath, "at'll teach 'em."

Red shook his head as the group was being shuttled to the ship, then hesitantly made eye contact with the women sitting three abreast in the back of the little boat, and Amy beside him. He said, "I've opened a wound for the Cap'n Ward. E'll be comin' back for ye', and soon. We'll get ye somewhere safe before he does." Then he winked, and his contented soul smiled, realizing the enormity of what he had just done.

As the ship prepared to depart, Red lined the women up and told them without fanfare, "You're free to go where you like. If'n ye'd like to stay ere, or go wi' me, it's up to ye."

The statement prompted smiles from all four women. "I'll stay with you if you don't mind," Amy said. The other three nodded, and Isabella asked, "Where are we going?"

22. Running from the Devil - 1620

The crew and guests were now clean and comfortable on Red's boat, the Hector, one of the five merchant ships owned by William Hawkins. Although he and Hawkins did not get along well, Red was grateful to him for his rather dignified position. He was a gifted sailor and a fair captain, greatly loved by his crew.

Red not only took the girls but also the spoils of previous raids from Ward and his men, including, of all things, clothing. He invited the four women to take their pick of anything they liked. Once they each had a new set of clothing, they took turns bathing, being clean for the first time since they jumped into the ocean three weeks ago—and that wasn't even an official bath.

Refreshed and feeling more human now, Amy strode along the upper deck to find Red. He had also donned fresh clothing and had his soft, wavy hair pulled back with a leather lace. He was elegant-looking, and Amy had a hard time pulling her eyes off him.

Smiling as she approached, Red gave her a courteous bow, and she curtsied. "Ye' look lovely, missy. I trust the others have found clothing and have indulged in a proper bath?"

"Yes, thank you. It is all quite nice." She stood beside him as they conversed, speaking of Scotland and San Antonio, lovely dresses, and the open sea.

"Yer eyes are the most beautiful I've seen. They're hard ta' pull away from." Amy blushed. She'd only heard someone mention her eyes once before, and that was a guy in a bar who wanted to get laid. This man was a true gentleman. He graciously put women first, seeing to their needs and comforts.

"And yours are too. I've never seen anyone with eyes that color of blue." She thought this was 17th-century flirting, although she hadn't had any practice.

"Would you dine with me this evening?" Red's words were abrupt and awkward.

Amy knew dining with the captain was quite an honor and said, "Of course, I'd love to." *Hmm, a first date.*

***

It had been three wonderful days since their island escape, and they had since had regular nutritious meals, comfortable beds, and the kindness of strangers. Red saw to that. She and Red spent time together each day, talking, eating, and drinking simply to enjoy each other's company. They did not always converse, but were just there, together. He touched her hand once, and Amy craved more than this tiny brush with fate, although she knew women did not make the first move in this century. If they did, the men would think them a whore.

Just as the sun began to fade harmoniously to the edge of evening, Amy and Red watched the gathering clouds slowly become imposing. He heard from the catwalk above that a ship was heading their way. Red asked for the glass, and after a few moments at the very tip of the bow, he saw it too, not needing to see *who* was coming at them; he already knew.

Red looked at Amy, almost panicked. "Ye' need to hide yerself in a safe place. Take the other girls n' go to my cabin. Ye' can find a place to be hidden thar."

He placed his large hand on the small of her back and gently urged her toward the door that led to the cabins. Finding Maria in the hall, she said, nearly breathless, "We've got to hide. They're coming."

"Who's coming?" Maria asked curiously.

Amy decided she wouldn't be so nervous if Red hadn't looked at her like he did. She was surprised that Maria didn't know that Ward would come after them, and she snapped, "the fucking pirates!"

Maria looked at her with wide, frightened eyes, mouth agape, but turned to follow Amy to the tiny room where they slept. Bursting through the door, Amy looked around, surveying the room before her. She found a comb they had used and stuffed it under a blanket. She threw the pillows in the corner behind two casks, then turned to Isabella and Carmen Louisa with a frenzied look. "The pirates are coming! We must hide! Come with me!"

With startled looks on their faces, the two other women moved quickly and followed Amy, unsure about where she was going. She went to the boat's stern, where the captain's cabin was, thrust open the door, and looked around, scanning the room. "Maria, you hide in there." She pointed to a large chest on the floor. Maria removed a pair of boots and a jacket and crawled in. She was the shortest of the four of them and fit rather well.

Isabella and Carmen Louisa emptied a tall cabinet, stuffing all the items into a desk drawer. They were able to stand crammed together, and Amy shut the door. Before taking her place below the desk, she went out to the main deck to see just how close the other ship was by now. She could see it about a hundred yards away on the port side, packed with men, and the round nose of a cannon pointed right at the *Hector*.

She ran, her feet barely touching the ground, and tucked into her hiding place, preparing to cover her eyes and ears against what she knew would be an awful sound.

Folding herself neatly into a space under the desk, Amy took the captain's velvet green jacket off the bed and covered herself. She felt something under her and went to push it out of the way, only to find a short length of chain that was terribly uncomfortable to sit on.

In a few short minutes, clatters and bangs could be heard. The woman shrank into the darkness and tensed, unsure of what the next few minutes would bring. The biggest fear came when Amy realized that if the pirates won, they would be right back with the bastards, where they started.

There was a ghastly bang against the ship, which rocked the vessel hard to starboard. Amy imagined it was a cannonball that had found its way to the target, and all she could do was hope it struck above the water line.

Suddenly, something that sounded like a bull crashed through the door, and the sound of shoes scraping on the floor could be heard as someone rummaged through the room. The intruder opened the trunk where Maria was hiding, and the women listened to a diabolical laugh. Maria shrieked. Amy couldn't let them haul her away. She was the sweetest and most timid of all of them.

Amy reacted to the mistreatment without thinking, bursting from her concealment to defend her friend. She had the jacket in one hand and the short length of chain in the other. Throwing the coat over Jack Ward's head, it distracted him enough that he let go of Maria. She proceeded to swing the chain as hard as she could toward the man's head in one smooth motion. The sound of it hitting and cracking his skull turned her stomach, the sound followed by a body falling and hitting the ground full force. He let out a huff of air and was out.

"Get back in the trunk," Amy whispered to Maria, and she waited behind the door for another pirate to test her new weapon.

Another half an hour had passed before the commotion quieted down. Even Amy, with the weapon in her hand, couldn't bring herself to go out to the main deck to see the result of the battle.

The door opened again, this time more slowly. Amy brought back her hand with the chain and was ready to swing. Before she did, she saw Red squatting on the ground to assess the damage done to the wicked Captain Ward.

"Red!" she said, and he rose quickly, embracing Amy.

"Ye' alright, lass?"

She nodded. "Is it over?"

"Aye, we've done our damage, and they gave up. Now, what to do wi' him?"

Red could see he was still breathing and kicked him to bring him around. He opened his eyes and closed them again in obvious pain.

"Wa'd ye' do to him?"

Amy held up her hand and showed him the chain. Then he snickered and nodded. "Aye," he said, understanding what kind of damage the heavy chain could do.

They heard a muffled sound, and Amy immediately remembered her friends. She opened the trunk and then went over to open the cabinet door and help the other girls out.

Carmen Louisa asked, "Did we win?"

Amy laughed. "We wouldn't be standing here if we didn't."

The storm that began in the distance with a rumble and a flash was now dumping torrents of rain upon the ship, and the lightning flashes were right on top of them.

The boat bobbed like a cork in a bathtub, and even though they'd spent a month on the ship, the vicious sea made all the girls feel its intensity.

Without a moment's hesitation, Red dragged Captain Ward from his quarters to the deck, just as he began to come around. Red treated him like he'd treated the girls, with no mercy.

"I leave you with yer' life, ye' bastard," Red said to Ward just as if he was chastising a child. With the girls and a couple of other shipmates as witnesses, Red threw the man into the sea.

“Good luck!" He shouted after him and watched the pirate splash and disappear, and his body rose as the foam dissipated into the stormy sea.

23. Daring Affection - 1620

A peaceful absoluteness settled over the ship, and once the storm abated, fairer weather moved in, showing its face in the way of a robin-egg blue sky and a favorable breeze.

Amy was above deck in the open air and, as frequently as Red allowed, accompanied him. He was a pleasant man who always saw the glass as half full. When he spoke of his life's adventures and William Hawkins, the captain who gave the younger Red a home, his eyes sparkled with good-hearted pleasure. It took very little for Amy to admit to herself that she had feelings for the good captain.

This ship had a gentle rhythm; she imagined it was the way of all vessels. But now, she felt safe in the arms of the captain, the crew, and the sea. It paved the way for contentment that Amy couldn't describe. She reflected briefly on the time she came from, and things she missed, like toilets and hot showers. This century had its charms, but it was nothing like 1971.

After her harrowing adventure with the others, this slow, relaxing sway of the ship under Red's protection was a broad contrast to the day she opened her eyes to find women looking down at her. She had been so devastatingly lost.

They'd been living day to day in fear and shame until only a few days ago. Thoughts of Izzy came to her, and she wondered if her grandmother had sanctioned this historical trip for her. The amulet's power spanned centuries, guiding the innocent bearer toward an agenda that was meant for her alone. It was a rare and bewildering experience.

On this ship, there was still only one meal a day, and often, Red would invite her to share it with him. They would talk about his many adventures in the Caribbean. He had a rough upbringing, but he lit up when he spoke of the little island of Nevis, where he lived with his extended family. He wasn't married, but he had a few loyal servants he considered his relations.

When his parents died, he found his way aboard a ship and eventually proved an asset. The good Captain Hawkins put him to work and gradually gave him charge of a vessel in his fleet. His dedication to the group of men was admirable, and they loved him.

She watched him talk, and his voice became almost melancholy; he stared blankly, focusing on nothing, but his mind was elsewhere. He looked up at her and smiled. "How about ye'? Tell me bout yer' family and where yer' from."

Amy hesitated. *How can I piece this one together*? She remembered Izzy's love of adventure and used her life as a blueprint as she began to weave a tale. "My parents have been gone a long time, and my granny raised me. I grew up in a place called San Antonio. I came to the islands here to help sick children. We were kidnapped right out of the hospital, and I thank God that he saw fit to land us here in your hands." She looked at him and smiled warmly; the radiance in her eyes made Red's heart skip a beat.

He reached out and took her hand across the table, looking at it closely. The intricacies of her delicate fingers were uniquely hers, and his fingers brushed them adoringly. Then he gently brought it to his lips and kissed it.

Amy felt the warmth flooding her body as her heartbeat quickened. His touch was gentle and kind, and his lips were warm and welcoming. She wished for more than a delicate kiss to her knuckles.

"I am beginnin' ta ave feelins fer ye', lassie. Yer as sweet as they come, n' if I'm right, ye' has feelings fer me too."

"Yes, you're right. I do," Amy said, blinking her eyes slowly. She surprised herself with the words, biting her lip to keep from saying more. She knew that just feeling anything for someone else broke through the mantle of her commitment to Cam.

He smiled again, then rose, encouraging her to stand. Never letting go of her hand, he tucked it into the loop of his arm and escorted Amy out onto the deck.

The winds had calmed considerably, and the half-moon peeked out from behind the passing clouds. They stood at the rail, listening to the waves splashing up against the hull and the subtle clinking of the pulleys and ropes knocking against each other behind them.

"I think this is the most beautiful evening I've ever experienced." Then Amy turned her head to the wind, suddenly aware of the scent of it that blew across the bow of the ship. It took her somewhere else, making her wonder where the wisps of air came from and where they were going.

Red dropped her hand and wrapped his arm around her waist, now tiny because of the near-starvation conditions she'd endured on the pirate ship. He pulled her close and brought his head closer, taking in her scent.

"This is bout as near ta heaven as I can be." Then he turned her to him, drinking in her beautiful, craving eyes, and kissed her.

Amy would have melted in his arms if it were possible. Their eyes locked, and they both hesitated, seeing the softly painted shadows created by the bright moon. The kiss sparked a flutter within her that she didn't want to stop. She brought her hand to his face, wanting to touch it; she had never done so before he kissed her.

"I'm sorry, lass, I shouldn't av' …"

"No, it's alright. It was a very nice kiss." Amy watched his eyebrows move up and down, trying not to make contact with her twinkling eyes. She stopped him in his tracks and made him look at her, wanting him to see that she was okay with his forwardness. Holding his chin gently in her hands, she brought him to her and kissed him, moving away slowly. Smiling brightly, she said, "See?"

This time, he smiled, content now that he hadn't offended her. He kept his arm around her as they both turned and watched the clouds change shape as the wind pushed them, revealing the moon's remnants that they had been hiding.

Although the powers of attraction worked hard on her tonight, Red was a complete gentleman. He led her back to her room and kissed her hand when he left. He knew this evening would change his life forever.

***

Isabella heard the sound of water sloshing from a bucket and activity all around when she decided to emerge from their cabin. She considered asking the captain for parchment to write a letter to her family, knowing they would soon reach a port where they could get a message to Puerto Rico. She saw the captain near the bow of the boat, talking to his boatswain, and approached him hesitantly.

"G'day to ye' missy. Are ye' farin' well?" He bent slightly in the middle with a subtle bow.

Isabella nodded and offered a gentle curtsy. "Yes, thank you, sir." Red smiled and turned his attention back to his conversation. She smiled at him, still waiting to finish her question. He looked up and realized she was still there, but before he started to speak, she got the word out before he had a chance. "I–I was hoping you might have a piece of parchment that I might write a letter to my father. All of us would like to send messages if possible."

Isabella was the tallest of the four women, standing straight and proud. Her eyes were a deep brown, delicately almond-shaped. The enticing beauty that could swallow a man, and she was in no way intimidated. It was not in her nature to accept defeat, no matter how it presented itself.

Red smiled and nodded, showing her to his cabin, where he pulled out several pieces of parchment, an inkwell, and a quill.

Rather than try to find a flat surface to write on in their shared cabin, the women went to the room where the men ate and drank. It wasn't large, but it provided a smooth plane.

They took turns scratching out letters to their families, each with different messages and an array of emotions on their faces. When it came time for Amy to write, she didn't know who she could write to. She decided to write to herself as she would in a diary, addressing it to Miss B.

Upon the Hector
January 8, 1621

My Dearest Miss B,
I hope this letter finds you well. We have had a harrowing experience on a boat in the West Indies and are now en route to the Island of Nevis for respite.
I have met a wonderful man, Red Greaves, who takes our welfare very seriously. I'm disclosing that I'm very fond of him, as he has treated my friends and me exceptionally well. I will send a message once we reach our destination, but for now, rest assured, I am well and content.

All my Love,
Amy

Folding it neatly and binding it with a string of jute, one of the few materials available on a ship, Amy addressed her letter to A. Bishop, San Antonio. She had no idea where the letter would go, but the ruse was enough to satisfy the others. Carmen Louisa gathered the letters and left them on the desk in the captain's quarters, along with the inkwell and quill.

After a short while, Amy meandered back up on deck, seeking out her recent flame. She was surprised she could turn her emotion toward one man, Cam, into a flame for another, Red. It made her question her commitment to Cam, who was terrific.

Given that the distasteful band of pirates had recklessly abused her and then was subsequently rescued by the brave Captain Red and his crew, how could she not be attracted to this daring captain?

She saw him and stopped, watching his twisted locks of light brown hair whipped by the wind. He pointed at the rigging above his head and discussed something with the first mate. Amy saw the commanding presence he had with the sailor and was flooded with admiration for him, recognizing his skillful handling of the ship and its crew.

She smiled, thinking about the evening before and the soft kiss, wishing she had more. If there were any man worthy of her affection, it was Captain Red Greaves.

Feeling her eyes upon him, he glanced in her direction, then gave a subtle nod of satisfaction and the faintest smile.

"Ye' got the helm, Huggins."

He approached her briskly, his day-old whiskers shining reflectively in the sunlight. "Hello, my dear," Red said, obviously happy to see her face. He took her hand carefully and kissed it, not taking his eyes off of her. She batted her long lashes, briefly looking down, then their gaze met again, and she couldn't look away a second time.

Speaking quietly with a playful smile on her face, Amy smiled warmly and replied. "Captain Greaves, I do believe I'm smitten."

The subtle, pleasant look on his face grew to a happy smile. He put his arm around her waist and escorted Amy to the rail, knowing how she liked to watch the waves in the sea move gracefully and arbitrarily crash into one another.

"Don't the waves remind you of life? It can be so unpredictable," Amy said as she pondered the wake made by the boat.

Red looked out, quiet for a minute, then said, "I've sailed for nearly twenty years, and I've never seen the sea that way. I think I'll never see it any other way again, thanks to you."

He was fascinating. Amy eagerly wanted to draw him in for a long, passionate kiss, but stopped, knowing they were not in the twentieth century. Despite her growing passion for him, Amy was comfortable, relaxed, and quite happy. She was, however, desperately curious about the kismet that ended up placing her where she was right now.

24. Parting Seas - 1620

After nearly two weeks at sea, other islands were finally in sight, and Red told her and the others that they were only a day away from his home, the Isle of Nevis.

Hearing the news that they would soon be on solid ground, the girls were more animated and chirpy. The excitement of getting off the boat was now all they could think of. Without much in the way of toiletries, the girls planned their disembarkment by rummaging through the limited items they could wear, having pulled other dresses from the trunk their host had brought. It was essential to all that they try to look their best, wishing to make the best possible impression as they made port.

Amy was on the deck with the wind in her face as usual. She watched the seagulls intently as they almost always flew above and beside the ship. The islands that were scattered around them now made the view much more enjoyable. There was an occasional small fishing boat with the day's catch lying in the middle, and Amy was happy to greet them, waving vigorously, and the fishermen always returned her salute.

Given the hazards surrounding the *Hector*, the main sail was dropped, and the ship's speed slowed as the first mate skillfully navigated the more difficult passages. Red was busy and distracted, but Amy was driven to watch over his shoulder to be near him. She kept her distance and remained quiet, not wanting to distract the man from his important work.

The other girls joined Amy on the deck, enamored by the view that changed hourly. None of them assumed they were so above their station that the men should go around them. The girls constantly darted out of the way of those hard-working men. All the women on the ship knew there was a superstition about them being on the boat, but their situation was unique, and in less than a day, they would be off the ship and standing on solid ground.

***

Morton's Bay was a charming settlement that seemed to be the center of the universe for the people of this island. The narrow street was dotted with homes made of stone and thatched roofs, and an occasional whitewashed house with a chimney spouting smoke. It was exotic and welcoming. To Amy's surprise, Red conversed lightly with many as they perused the street, fluently speaking English, Spanish, and French.

"You are full of surprises, Red Greaves," Amy said, smiling up at him as she squinted against the sunlight.

"Aye, I expect there ta' be many things at'll surprise ye' here, lass."

His crew members were busy unloading the stolen goods from the ship as he and the women walked down the street to the end of a row of houses, where a wagon, jarvey and all, awaited them.

"Up ye' go!" And Red hoisted each girl into the wagon, giving a wink to Amy as he drew her near. Climbing to the driver's seat, he sat beside the jarvey.

The conveyance began to roll down the road. As the men, women, and miscellaneous goods left the settlement and headed into the jungle, the road climbed slightly, rising from the flatter, sparser area on the island into a dense, green landscape.

The ride took about thirty minutes, and they came to a clearing featuring sugar cane fields on both sides of the road. They approached a carriage house a couple of minutes later, and the main plantation house loomed over it all. It was a tall, whitewashed, regal-looking front entrance, with faded black shutters framing the windows.

After taking in the house, Amy turned toward the settlement and was gifted with the beautiful rolling vistas of the town and the bay behind it. The breathtaking deep azure of the ocean swallowed the sky's blue, becoming one on the endless horizon. She breathed deeply and sighed heavily, wondering if she had somehow crossed into heaven.

Red hopped down from the wagon, immediately assisting the women and saying in a reserved tone, "We're home."

"Oh my, Red, this is beautiful!" Maria observed.

"I'm lucky enough ta av' a few acres to farm, and cane grows well ere." He smiled shyly.

Amy and Isabella stood side by side and noticed two young slave men pulling a cart with huge wheels loaded with cane. "You have slaves?" Amy said, shocked.

"Yes, I do. I canna run a plantation wi'out em'. My workers are good men, and I treat em' well. Donna, worry, my dear." Then he smiled and winked at her, making Amy blush.

He brought them to the main house, graciously swinging the door open to invite them in. The walls were decorated conservatively, but they boasted beautiful candelabras and fluted glasses, finer accents befitting an affluent home.

"Margaret," Red said in a deeper-than-usual tone. A woman of color came bustling into the room from down a hallway.

"Welcome home, Mr. Red. How was your trip?"

Red smiled. It was evident he liked the woman's company. "Fine, just fine. I've brought some visitors who I expect'll be stayin a few days. Would you please bring us some wine and prepare the guest chambers?"

She looked at Red and smiled. "Yes, sir." Then she bustled quickly into the kitchen, emerging a few minutes later with a tray holding a decanter and several glasses for them, scurrying away with a slight curtsy to attend to her other tasks.

"Is she your only housemaid?" Amy asked. Her words seemed a bit cool toward him, as she did not like being served by a slave.

Red pursed his lips together and nodded. Not making eye contact with her. "A fine helper and a good cook." He added.

The five of them stepped out to the long front porch and sat, admiring the view. Amy reluctantly drew a deep breath, helping ease the tension that had built in her neck from weeks of travel. Maria asked, "How many slaves do you have, sir?"

He glanced toward her; then his eyes fell on the sugar cane fields. "I have twenty-four, including Margaret." He paused for a moment, then continued. "I treat my slaves quite well. I ensure they have good food and drink, and I have no overseer. I do my best ta' see ta' their health. These slaves could do a lot worse on another plantation." He concluded.

"If you'll excuse me, I must inquire after my business."

Once Red was gone, the women looked at each other with injured feelings. The subject was personal to them. A gang of pirates held them, nearly starved, repeatedly assaulted, and attempted to sell them. They were within their rights to have personal opinions about slavery.

Hours had passed, and Margaret got to know the girls, taking great care of them. When she entered the kitchen to prepare food, Isabella went with her. Having spent a great deal of time with her grandmother, she'd learned to bake wonderful breads and crisps. Maria and Carmen Louisa followed and watched, helping Margaret set the table for supper.

Amy lingered outdoors, trying desperately to see Red, wishing to catch a glimpse of him. It had been a warm day, but the carriage house and a couple of full-grown Mahogany trees cast shadows that blocked out the severe afternoon sun, making the porch quite lovely. She listened to the sounds of this place, which made it unique in yet another way.

She finally saw Red coming from the carriage house in his sweat-soaked shirt. He wore a straw hat to help shade his face, giving him a very farmer-like look. She smiled at him, thinking how she might get used to this kind of life, possibly with him.

He looked up, catching her looking at him, and smiled. He thought she was lovely and adorned the front of his house nicely.

"Hello there, lassie."

Amy gave a nod and a moderate curtsy. "Hello, sir."

“I'm ready for supper. Has it been prepared yet?"

“I'm sorry. I've not been in the kitchen, I don't know." She shrugged her shoulders slightly. Then he lazily approached her, coming up the front steps. He took off his hat, grabbed her hand, and kissed it.

He said quietly, "I'll go wash." Then, he gently let go of her hand and pushed through the door, walking down the hall to his room.

The dining room was quaint and barely big enough for everyone around the table, but Margaret had dressed it up with beautiful linens and fine China plates. The dishes and utensils were exquisite, and the food was divine. Margaret was indeed a fine cook.

They spoke casually of the island, the crops, and the shippers and merchants that moved the products from Morton's Bay. The conversation morphed from the price of sugar at the market to travel plans as Red told the girls about a ship heading north to Hispaniola in three days. He realized it was a bit soon for them, as a trip like that could be anywhere from one to two weeks long, but it may be another month before an opportunity like this comes to Nevis.

Once supper was complete and the dishes were cleared from the table, Red asked Amy to join him on an evening stroll around the plantation. She was flattered that he asked her and happily obliged, taking his arm as the others were served plum pudding for dessert.

He gently placed his hand on hers, and a swell of warmth flushed her cheeks. Happily, she settled her hand into the crook of his elbow, smiling. She wasn't sure why his eyes focused on her, but she was quite taken with his attention and happy to be right beside him.

"I'd like to know yer' plans, lass. I wish fer ye' to stay as my guest, but there is a place fer ye' on the ship goin' north with the others if ye' like."

Amy didn't say anything at first, carefully choosing her words. She didn't want to sound forward, but she also didn't want to appear disinterested. Turning to him, she tried to focus on his eyes so that he would know what she said was genuine and sincere.

"I don't know if I'm ready to settle here, Red, but I'm not prepared to leave yet. Would you have me for another month?"

His eyes settled upon her again, and the view warmed his heart. "I was hopin' you'd say that. I have so much to show ye'." He smiled and drew her in; his kiss was long and passionate. They both were very slow to draw away, butterflies filling them up just then. She didn't want the kiss—this moment to stop. Amy searched his eyes for an answer he couldn't give her. *Will I ever get back to 1971? Do I even want to?*

They walked, skirting the field, and she listened as Red described his business venture. He showed her how the cane grew, how it was harvested, and what was involved in making the sugar, explaining in the end how it would be sold. He was knowledgeable and understood the market well, but she somehow sensed that his passion lay in the sea.

She could see how he loved the freedom and unpredictability of the wind and waves. He loved being in command, and more than anything, he loved double-crossing men like Jack Ward.

The couple strolled for more than an hour, stopping occasionally, and engaged in pleasant conversation. The sun began to set, and they walked back to the house. Pausing on the porch, the two romantics turned just in time to witness the sunset on the horizon. The scene, with the sky lit up in a brilliant array of oranges and reds, was breathtaking. Admiring the sky as it changed, they stood in awe as the reveal gave an illusion of an orange ball simply dropping into the sea.

***

The three days passed quickly, and the morning came when the girls had to say goodbye. Isabella, Maria, and Carmen Louisa packed their few belongings and slowly prepared to depart on the merchant ship at midday. Maria was emotional, knowing that Amy would stay, and she'd have to bid farewell. The others were subdued and seemed more trepidacious about the trip than they were about the goodbyes.

Just as they had when they arrived at the plantation, Red insisted they accept a ride in his wagon. He loaded a few parcels and the women into the conveyance and headed down the road toward Morton's Bay.

The wagon bumped and swayed along the road, and even though their departure was inevitable, the women made the most of it and enjoyed a beautiful day. None of them was especially talkative, which made Amy uncomfortable. She did not want to leave them all sullen and sad.

"Look," she began. “I know we will all be going our separate ways. It was meant to be that way, but that doesn't mean we won't always be with each other here," she said, holding her hand over her heart. “We can send letters, and someday I will travel to come and see you. We may not be together, but we will be with each other always." She smiled and winked.

The expressions on the three other women seemed to warm with Amy’s words, but they were still having difficulty dealing with the parting alliance as a sea would now be between them.

Before they reached the edge of the settlement, they saw the ship looming at the docks in the tiny port. It was different from Red's ship, *Hector*, taller and more substantial. They watched several men scurry around the pier and across the deck, evidence that the merchant meant business, and Amy was sure her friends were part of that business.

Red and the four women stood in a semi-circle, talking about the trip ahead, and they all wished for easy travel. As they stood at the end of the pier, saying their goodbyes, he handed each of them a heavy pouch filled with coins and trinkets. It was some of the treasure he'd stolen from the pirates' camp on the unnamed island. The bags were heavy, and they knew the gift was generous, something the girls did not expect.

They hugged and shed tears, cutting the strings that had bound them so tightly. However, Amy casually wiped the sweat from her forehead and smiled politely, not feeling that same connection. She felt that her presence in their lives was merely a stop along the way. Many more adventures were lying in wait for them. Her connection to Isabella was undeniably deeper. Before Isabella said goodbye to Red and Amy, she pulled Amy aside for a more private conversation.

Looking Amy square in the eye and holding her hands, she spoke sharply. "I need you to hear what I say." She took a deep breath before she began to speak. "I know you. I've seen you in my dreams. I've seen you in a metal carriage with many other people, and you were hurt. You were in the mountains, and you were looking for truth. The truth about this." She held up the stone amulet and swallowed the lump in her throat.

Amy's eyes grew large, and she held her breath in anticipation. "What can you tell me?" She asked, tears welling up in her eyes.

"It came from the great *Hatun* and was blessed by my great-grandfather, the holy man for his village. Both my parents are Incan. The bloodline lives within you."

For the first time since she met Isabella, Amy was speechless. She knew the stone was unique and that Izzy had investigated its truth but never went far enough. Here she was, with the truth standing right in front of her.

Isabella continued, her voice desperate. "Be assured, I will leave part of me in Ch'in wasi for you." Isabella, her ancestor, held the amulet again, letting her know what part of herself she would leave behind. Then she hugged Amy fiercely and turned to join the other girls, who were walking slowly down the pier to the ship.

25. To the Bitter End - 1620

Amy stood resolute, watching as the ship pulled away from the pier, the name scrawled across the stern: *Victoria*. It seemed remarkably tall and was a good 20 feet longer than the *Hector*, leading her to believe it truly was a cargo ship that moved goods from port to port.

Red gently took Amy's hand, startling her, as the ship disappeared around the bend just out of the harbor. She smiled and looked into his devastatingly beautiful blue eyes, still reeling from Isabella's confession and the emotional rollercoaster it had set in motion. Amy should have known that Isabella was the one who left the legacy for Izzy's mother, and her mother before that. She was empowered by its influence, by its time-piercing ability.

She let Red lead her back to the wagon, and he took her by the waist and lifted her again onto the wagon. This time, she sat on the bench with the jarvey, three abreast, with Red next to her.

She could feel him looking at her, and when she glanced over, he smiled shyly. "You're such a bonny lass." He said softly, then kissed her hand, casually turning his attention to the road ahead.

Amy's eyes looked forward as well, but her mind was elsewhere. Red's affections certainly stirred her passion, but she recalled her eager zeal toward Cam. She remembered how easily she climbed into bed with him and how anxious they were to have each other. Knowing he wasn't himself made her uncomfortable, as she thought of how she had left him. And she was here, in a different century, being doted upon by another passionate man.

The wagon rambled back to the carriage house, and Red helped her down. Giving the nod to Ben, the jarvey, he turned to Amy and asked, "How would ye' like to go for a ride with me, lass? We'll go up the mountain a ways. It's quite beautiful."

Amy nodded. "That would be nice." With her friends gone, she wouldn't have much to do in the big house with only Margaret to keep her company. The lovely housemaid was very social but always busy with something.

After a short while, Red led two horses from behind the carriage house to the main house. He looked up toward the veranda, and Amy appeared almost magically. Among the odd stolen items Red took from Ward, she found a dress that would let her straddle a horse. The fit was not perfect, but close enough and a bit more comfortable than the snug maroon satin she'd been wearing.

He helped her climb on a beautiful chestnut-colored mare while he rode a black mare with a long, flowing mane. The horses almost knew the route by heart, following the road farther north from the house and finally to a trail that took them higher up the side of the mountain.

The forest was dense, and its shade was cool and welcoming. It was a partly cloudy, blustery day, and the dense brush and scrubby trees eventually thinned out, exposing them to the perpetual sunlight, making it almost balmy. The air was heavy with humidity and the smell of wet soil and grasses.

There were long periods of silence between them, and occasionally they would ask each other questions, trying to get to know one another. Red graciously described the island to her, covering its history and how he had happened upon it. The conversation was pleasant as he talked about the reality of his plantation and the little island.

The ride was lovely, and Amy couldn't help but think about how comfortable she was with him. She found him quite debonair and self-assured. He was undoubtedly a kind man and confessed that he was no more than a pirate, robbing other pirates and merchants and splitting the proceeds with his crew.

He was more generous than other people of his trade, as he would share his abundance among the poor on the island. Aside from his aggression toward people like Jack Ward, he had sworn not to hurt innocent people or ravage peaceful villages.

His desire to procure money, jewels, and other wealth was simply that, and not a reason to be cruel.

Amy told him the unembellished truth about her relationship with her grandmother, her cousin, and her aunt, smiling gently as she described her grandmother's death and how the woman was pivotal in keeping the family together. She sighed and said, "I'm afraid there will be little communication between us again."

Red said, "I ave no family to worry me; I was left an orphan. Hawkins found me an' gave me work. The sea is all I know." He looked away just then, and Amy couldn't tell whether he was emotional about it or simply looking to see where they were.

"Ah, here it is." With a few more strides by the horses, they were on top of a rise, with the view of the settlement below them, and the vast open ocean to the north of the island's crop-covered hills.

"Oh, it goes on forever!" Amy said, soaking up all she could of the breathtaking view. In the distance, she could see a small grouping of unnamed islands dotting the field of blue and a ship a great distance away. It was tiny now, but she thought it was the Victoria. The vast expanse of the open ocean was indescribable.

They dismounted and found a large, flat-topped boulder just beyond the clearing where they could sit. "I'm sorry, I dinna bring anything along for refreshment."

Oh, that's all right, Red. I'm fine." She reached over and touched his hand, and he took hold of it with his own.

Without speaking, he locked eyes with her, and they kissed. The soft symbol of affection graced her lips, and the butterflies in her stomach fluttered as he placed his arm around her waist. Amy loved his touch. She loved being the focus of all his attention, but deep within her, she felt like she was betraying Cam.

"I've grown very fond of ye' lassie. In time, I hope ye' might like to have a life wi' me."

Amy held her breath for a moment. Even though she didn't belong in this time, she was so drawn to him, unwilling to deny it, and unsure if she ever desired to go home. The thought occurred to her that someday, when her guard was down, she would disappear and end up back in 1971. Wouldn't she? Was she here forever? The thought of it nipped away at her self-assurance, but she was so happy to be here now, with Red.

"I'm very fond of you, too." She felt a *but* wanting to interrupt her words and was suddenly terrified to say more.

They sat and talked of other things, admiring the captivating view. After a short while, Red stood, assisting her to her feet and drawing her closer to him. He kissed her gently and smiled, making his eyes twinkle delightedly.

He spoke softly and said, "We best be getting back ta' the house. Margaret'll have supper ready." Amy smiled, allowing him to lead her back to the horses and lift her again into the saddle.

***

After a delicious meal, Red and Amy sat together by the fire and played chess. Before long, it became too dark to see easily, and Amy politely excused herself, retiring to her room for the night. She needed some time alone to contemplate her sticky situation.

Red stood and kissed her hand tenderly, sure to make eye contact before she took her leave. Her knees felt weakened by his devastatingly stunning blue eyes. *How does he do that?* she thought. Then he smiled warmly. "G'night te ye' lassie."

She lay awake for hours, considering this place, these people, this time, and most of all, Red. The decision to stay or go was hers, wasn't it? But right now, she didn't have the amulet; Isabella did, and no matter what happened here, her presence or absence would be left to fate.

She realized that in this century, she had no one but Red, and he, except for his workers, had no one but her. T*his may be my destiny*, she thought, letting the corner of her mouth curl into a subtle grin. Finally, she closed her eyes and drifted off to sleep, knowing that Red lay in his own bed, only one room away.

She thought she was dreaming, hearing an urgent voice that kept shaking her. Gradually opening her eyes, she realized it was still dark when Margaret woke her, panic in her eyes.

"Mistress, you must get up and dress. We must go!"

"What?" She said, her voice filled with shock. "Why?"

Margaret scurried around in the dark room, finding Amy's clothes. "It be Cap'n Ward. He wants ya' back."

Her heart stopped, shocked with fear of what Ward would do to her if he caught her.

Although he hadn't made it to the plantation yet, the unwelcome arrival of the pirates caused chaos in Morton's Bay. Even with the distance from the house to the village, the shouts and musket shots could be heard echoing up the hillside.

She threw her clothes on as quickly as she could. Margaret shuffled behind her, following the orders given her to keep the mistress safe. Ben met the women just outside the carriage house. With fear in their eyes, the two plantation workers led her away from the house toward the settlement, then detoured along the outer edge of the property toward a neighboring plantation. Ben knew the overseer there and urgently asked him for help.

"Da' mistress need to be kept in a safe place. The mad pirate is after her. Do you have somewhere ta' hide er?"

Ben looked anxious, imploring this tall, thin man servant to agree to help. "It'll cost yeh, " the man, Anthony, said to him. Ben nodded, and Anthony led her to a root cellar behind the other house by fifty yards. "You'll be safe here." He showed her the pit, which had two adjoining doors and round iron pulls. She could see a ladder sticking out of the darkness, right up to the opening. Ben locked eyes with her and nodded.

Once down in the cellar, Anthony handed her two candles, unsure how long she needed to stay there. The dark, damp air was close and claustrophobic, but she had to stay low and quiet if she planned to be alive the next day.

The doors closed, and a bolt slid into place, locking her in the crypt out of sight. One of the candles had been lit before they'd left her, and she stared for a long time at the dainty flicker of the light and the movement of the air around it. It was a comfort to her that this flow of air was familiar, spanning the centuries, never wavering.

As she listened intently, a random musket shot could be heard, but the shouts had gradually died to silence. Not hearing was almost worse than hearing, and she felt that danger existed all around her.

***

Red had gone to Morton's Bay with ten of his workers to

head off the clan of pirates, meeting up with nine others who lived in town. Although the group had only three guns, many had swords and spears, and the island residents wielded them confidently.

A dull glow grew with intensity between the cracks of the doors to the cellar, and Amy realized it was likely the first light of dawn. Taking stock, she realized she'd been there the remainder of the night. Amy heard voices whispering, as if they were hiding from someone. A few moments later, the bolt slid back, making a grinding metallic sound. Amy stood, expecting Ben to retrieve her from the pit and tell her the coast was clear. Instead, she saw Anthony, who gave her a nod and said, "G'day ta' ya, mistress."

He held out a hand to help her up the ladder. Amy was so grateful to be exiting the darkness. It had been a harrowing night; not knowing the turn of events and running to hide in the darkness was mind-boggling. She was more than anxious to bring herself out into the light.

As she stepped onto the solid ground, Anthony took her wrist, holding it too tightly. She looked at him and realized the other body standing back away from the door wasn't Ben. It was Wild J. She looked at Anthony in shock, thinking he had betrayed Ben, Margaret, and herself by giving her up to the pirates. Wild J roped her by the wrists and elbows while

Anthony held her. Wild J dug into his pocket, pulled out two shillings, and handed them to Anthony.

The neighboring slave turned to her and said, "The pirates pay better." Then smiled, waved, and headed back toward the other plantation house.

Wild J pushed her and grabbed handfuls of hair, guiding her roughly down a path toward town. He stayed in the flora without a path, and Amy stumbled and staggered toward the settlement, finally coming through a cane field right onto a street a hundred yards from the pier.

Once they'd returned to civilization, Amy screamed, "HELP! Help me!" Wild J slapped the side of her head, but that didn't deter her from continuing the banter on the path to the ship.

The familiar band of pirates met her as she was dragged onto the top deck, greeted by Jack Ward himself. "Ello miss …" bowing and expecting her to give him her name.

Instead, she said, "You bastard. You will pay. I promise you."

"Be careful about promises, miss. They're not always easy to keep." The good captain flicked his hand, shooing them away, and Wild J and another whose name she didn't know took her below and shoved her into the tiny, dark, dank room she'd spent the better part of a month in—only this time, she was utterly alone.

Amy could feel the ship moving away from the pier and screamed as loudly as she could toward the tiny porthole. Her screams dissipated, as she had no more voice left, and she fell into the corner and cried.

***

It was a day and a night before anybody opened the door or even spoke to her. Pierre and Wild J opened the door and laid a bowl of broth on the floor, along with a flask of water. She didn't realize just how thirsty she was until she began to drink, forcing herself to leave enough for the next day.

She had a vague idea of how often she would be fed, expecting the same experience she had previously with them. It was early afternoon when the two servers returned to the room and took her to see the captain. He was dressed well, though his fancy clothes were dirty, and his hair had been flattened by the tricorn hat he wore constantly.

Captain Ward didn't speak. Instead, he struck Amy's face. A slap smacked her cheek, then a punch in the stomach. He slapped her again as he spoke slowly and controlled.

"That was just in case you didn't know who was in charge."

Amy didn't speak. She had tried to double over to protect herself, but nothing seemed to work correctly. She took a second and then gasped, catching her breath.

"You are a miserable bastard." She spoke to him in an even tone.

"Cap'n." A ginger-haired man popped his head into the room, interrupting. "We got company."

He turned to leave, but not before he showed her a guarded smile. "I'm not done with you yet."

The guards returned her to the dark room and locked her in again. The ache from the punches and slaps began to fade gradually, but it brought back memories. She remembered the torturing bastards, swearing that foremost in her mind, she would make him pay. How could she so quickly forget her previous captivity?

Amy listened as the activity on the ship picked up pace, and men scurried around like scared rabbits. She heard shouting, and the ship lurched as it had suddenly been rammed by another boat.

She smiled, knowing Red had come to save her. The only thing that was bigger than his heart was his determination. Wanting to see the battle firsthand, Amy jumped up and grabbed the edge of the porthole. It seemed the attack came from the other side of the ship, and just as she was ready to let go, she watched a man get tossed over the ship's rail. Unable to hold herself any longer, she dropped back into the room.

26. Smoke on the Wind - 1621

Amy could see the changing hue of the trickle of light from the tiny porthole and knew that the evening was approaching. She could still hear muffled voices and shouts, interrupted by an occasional thump, but the sound comforted her. She had friends with her on the vessel now.

She thought briefly about harm coming to Red or any of his people. It made her heart beat frantically, and she nervously began to chew on the nail of her pinky finger. Amy understood that Ward was a slimy snip of a man and couldn't fathom what he might have up his sleeve. Although she knew Red was also a pirate and could anticipate the evil Captain's next move, she feared for him. Her fate and future hung in the balance between good and evil.

She squished in the corner, as far away from the door as she could. Her eyes were directed down, but occasionally glanced up at the opening, envisioning her savior, Red, as the first to show himself.

As the noise above her quieted, she looked at the portal more often, merely guessing the battle's outcome on the above deck. Her mind was fearful about the fallout, and she suddenly closed her eyes tightly, uttering a short prayer.

She heard rummaging in other rooms and along the hall just outside the door. A rattle at the latch made her jump as she slumped in the corner of the dungeon. Her heart jumped, so frightened now at what the miserable bastards had in store for her.

A dark face appeared around the edge of the door. It was Moses, a man who worked for Red. He slowly entered the room, his face barely discernible in the darkness, but his teeth shone as he smiled. "Mistress?" Amy couldn't believe her ears. She couldn't speak and wished for words, finally pushing out a response with great effort, still weak with disbelief. "I'm here, Moses."

He took her hand and patted it, feeling her trembling. Moses opened the door and looked both ways, then quietly led her out of the darkness onto the main deck. The sight was a slaughter; blood pooled around the bodies of several pirates. She caught sight of two other men from Morton's Bay, and all eyes were looking desperately for Red.

Moses went immediately to the rail and searched for someone to paddle the yawl up to the ship to get Amy and himself off. Others from Morton's Bay were still aboard, and aside from killing every last one of the pirates or throwing them over the rail, they were stuck there without a way off.

The transport wasn't there, and he looked back, seeing Amy with a short rigging knife fighting off one of Ward's associates. Moving as if the scene in front of him was in slow motion, he leaped toward the marauder, but he was too late. He watched a patch of crimson begin to grow just below the mistress's ribcage. The pirate bastard had stabbed Amy with a knife.

His reaction was explosive. He took the sword of a dead pirate that lay on the deck closest to him, its sharp edge smudged with blood and angrily drove the tip of it into every other pirate he saw on the deck that had shown any life. In his anger, he single-handedly killed the last three pirates on board.

Moses dramatically dropped the sword, and he was on his knees at Amy's side, sliding off his shirt and pressing the wound to stop the bleeding. A tear let loose from the corner of his eye and trickled down his cheek, gently falling from his whisker-pocked face. He looked up when he saw Red come over the rail; the sadness in his eyes revealed the facts of the attack.

Red was overcome. Panic struck him as the reality of what had happened to Amy became clear. He ran to her side, kneeling to be close to her. "Ach, lass, what'd they do ta ye'?

She smiled a strained smile, writhing in pain. She grabbed at his hand and held it, squeezing tightly when a wave of acute pain swept over her. "I'm so sorry, Red. I wasn't careful. It was stupid of me."

He shook his head and kissed her bloodied hand, then swept his arms underneath her and carried her to the captain's quarters. Red gently laid her on the straw bed and asked Moses to bring water. "I had a mind ta'ask ye to marry me, my sweet. Please, donnah leave me."

Amy's consciousness faded slowly, and when it did, her body faded too. It was as if she'd turned into vapor and reappeared, leaving Red bewildered. He wanted nothing more than to take her home with him. She was more to him than any being ever was, and suddenly, an overwhelming loneliness swept over him, dreaming of her sweet face and delicate manner.

He did not leave her side for hours, weeping over the loss. Finally, when her life's light withered away, she disappeared, just as smoke does in the breeze. Red's prayers went unanswered, and he felt abandoned. The reaction he had to her disappearance was anger and pain. He knew she was magical, leaving his world the way she did, but it was more about how she'd touched his life that made him know her existence was a gift.

***

Red sat alone on the veranda in the dark, admiring the

vivid contrast between the stars and the deep darkness of the endless sky. It was a curious thing to him. The sky was the same vast, unexplored territory as the sea, only unreachable. It comforted him to think of Amy as one of the stars up there looking down on him. He stared up for the longest time with drunken eyes, imagining what his life might have been like had they been able to finish what they had started. He blinked hard, then smiled.

Sighing deeply and slowly, he poured another shot of rum into the heavy glass and swigged it down. Mindlessly, he pulled the shard of a stone out of his pocket and tossed it. Once he let go of it, he shook his head, thinking that it had always brought him good luck, but now he was unsure. It seemed to him just then that the best thing he'd ever had in life just disappeared. It wasn't lucky at all.

Feeling the pressure of his constant bouts of misery, Red tried hard to kill the pain with liquor, finally pouring the last few drops from the bottle and into his glass. He rose from the chair with a stagger, his head hung low. He wandered back into the lonely house with heavy steps, softly closing the door as he went off to bed.

27. More than an Average Loss (Isabella- 1621)

The murky gray sky deepened as the waves grew more restless. There was no telling if the storm would hit them head-on or if they'd merely skirt the edge of it, but there was no doubt the atmosphere on the ship was more intense because of it.

Isabella stood on the threshold of the doorway, watching the men scurry around, picking up the pace to keep up with the intensifying winds. She watched them lower the mainsail and the foresail, leaving only the smaller storm sail and a jib deployed for navigation.

She turned and went to the cabin she shared with the other women. Opening the door, she saw that Carmen Louisa was an odd shade of green. The rough sea was especially difficult for her as she and the other girls had been crammed in a dark cabin. Consulting with her sensitive stomach, she suddenly wished she weren't on a ship in the water.

"The ship is encountering a storm. We should all stay here and hang on until the storm passes." The words she spoke were about something the other girls already knew, but as she tried to reassure Maria and Carmen Louisa, she honestly reassured herself. She was fortunate to have traveled safely by sea before, but she'd seen the wreckage of many who hadn't.

Closing her eyes tightly, she uttered a prayer, and her stomach wrenched with tension. Her eyes fluttered open as if on cue, and the amulet began to warm. Feeling the spirit of the stone, she was immediately comforted. The tension that had clutched her before had suddenly let go. She loosened her hands from the grasp her fingers held, bringing her hand up to the amulet around her neck. *It is a blessing,* she thought, wanting to tell everyone of its magic but knowing they'd all mistake it for a witch's evil.

The storm raged on for hours, and not only were they forced to listen to the shouts of the men above, but they also heard the panic in their voices when the ship had lost its rudder. They would soon crash into the rocky outcropping of a nearby island.

Isabella suddenly took charge, having the girls gather their few belongings and secure them to themselves by whatever means they could find. Without warning, the ship lurched violently, tossing the women to the floor. They looked at each other, terrified; then Isabella urged them to get up and follow her.

The three of them wandered into the hall, heading toward the door that led out onto the main deck, where they heard the cracking of wood and the crashing of waves as debris began to scatter across it. The scene on the deck was chaotic; some men had been injured, and others were looking about, trying desperately to hang on and save themselves.

They held on as the ship began to split apart, knowing they would have to swim to shore if the current didn't take them elsewhere. The ship listed sharply, now crushed between the waves and the rocks it had struck. The deck was disappearing beneath the waves, and Isabella grabbed the hands of her friends as they were suddenly swept away in the current.

Maria pointed to the beach she could see through the driving rain and wind, and they began to swim in that direction. Two men had been injured, and the girls watched them struggle in the surf, losing sight of them among the debris that was floating all around them.

Isabella battled to keep her head above water, finding a section of the main mast and using it as a floating device. She whipped her head around, searching for her friends, but could not see them. Helpless to do anything other than hold on, she began to cry, praying that her friends would survive the devil that had taken control.

She heard a sharp *crack* and turned in time to watch the front half of the ship snap off, breaking away from the crag it had been resting on and falling abruptly into the sea. The action produced a massive wave that rolled toward Isabella like a tsunami, tossing her abruptly into a pair of barrels that had been roped together. She recovered and held onto the rope, choking and spitting, but still alive. She saw Maria's blue dress on the other side of the barrels. "Maria!" She shouted, unsure how much could be heard amid the waves that crashed against the rocks.

Fortunately, the surf had them, and Isabella and Maria could feel it driving them toward the sandy beach. Neither one saw Carmen Louisa until they could stand. She was lying face down about twenty yards away. They ran down the shoreline to her with whatever little energy they could muster. Maria flipped her over, moving her shoulders abruptly, trying to get her to come to.

Carmen Louisa was so pale. It was fearsome looking at her, but Maria didn't give up. "Carmen Louisa, wake up!" Isabella slapped her cheek, and suddenly, Carmen Louisa began to choke and spit, gasping for air. Maria began to cry, reeling from the terrifying event, and so glad she didn't have to say goodbye to her friend.

The storm raged on for another hour, then slowly subsided as the girls surveyed the damage. Two men had made it to shore, but the other ten had met their fate on the unforgiving rocks, just as the ship had.

One of the men was injured, having been rammed in the ribs by a cross-tree, and although there were no protruding bones or open wounds, there was significant internal damage and bruising. There was no telling what might happen to the poor man.

They moved farther up the beach, away from the surf, and gathered any useful supplies they could salvage. Isabella thought it would be a good idea to get away from the weather and closer to the wall of rock and dirt behind them, making it a suitable place to set up camp.

Howard and Alex joined the girls up the beach, away from the surf. Howard could pitch in, but Alex was in a bad way. None of them were equipped to help him, and aside from a few miscellaneous bottles of wine and liquor, nothing could dull the pain.

Once the rain stopped, the girls and Howard gathered dry kindling and started a fire using dry foliage from under the trees and bushes. Although it was quite warm most of the time in the islands, they had been wet for almost an entire day, and the dry heat from the fire was welcome.

***

Those first days on the beach passed quickly. The survivors were in shock, feeling the fear and isolation creeping in around them as they lost hope of a rescue. On the third day,

Alex succumbed to his injury and died in the night. Digging a grave in the sand was easy, and each said a prayer. "I'm sorry I couldn't do more," Maria whispered as she made a cross of sticks to mark the grave. Once the sand was smoothed over the resting place, there was very little sign that a man had been buried there.

One of the items they pulled from the debris was a satchel containing paper, a book, and a quill. Isabella laid the items out so the breeze and sunlight could dry the pages, along with a blanket and a spare jacket from what they assumed were the captain's quarters.

After the refugees emptied a couple of bottles of wine, Howard journeyed inland in search of a source of fresh water to refill them. It was some time before he returned with the bottles full. Isabella and Carmen Louisa dug for clams in the sand, rinsing them in the waves, and had them ready to cook.

Wrapping the crustaceans in palm fronds, they cooked them in the hot coals. It was not much of a meal, but it helped to fill their empty stomachs.

More than a week later, Isabella had given up hope, deciding that it was time to get a message out to someone—anyone. She drafted a note on some of the paper using charcoal from the fire. When the message was complete, she rolled it up and put it in one of the empty bottles, sealing it with a cork dipped in tree sap to prevent it from absorbing water.

She walked upon the rocks as far out into the sea as she could go, thrusting it hard toward the waves. Then, as the sun began to set, she watched it for nearly an hour as it bobbed and dipped, finally disappearing out in the current.

From her new vantage point, she felt free. A salty mist rising from the sea was pushed by the brisk breeze that always seemed to accompany the ocean. She observed how the waves continuously forced themselves against the sand. She realized that, in this fantasy world, these two things were nothing more than dance partners.

Although they were free from the clutches of the pirates and the briny sea, this beach began to feel like the dark, dank room in which she had been held captive almost a month before. That time seemed so far away, but the oppressive feeling remained. She walked the beach as far as she could, first in one direction and then the next, seeing nothing and finding nothing. They existed, but this was not life; it was a living hell.

28. Reality - Isabella, 1621

The terrain on the miserable little island was rough, rocky, and unforgiving. The days ran together, and if it weren't for Carmen Louisa scratching hash marks on a rock at the base of a cliff, they would never have known they'd been there 21 days.

Isabella had worked it out in her mind over and over and decided that at low tide, she would try to make it along the shoreline around the island, thinking there may be a better place they could either stay or make a fire that could be seen by a passing ship. Attracting attention was not always wise, but getting off the island would never happen without help, and getting out of here, even with pirates, was better than just surviving this hell.

She described her plan to her friends, who were more afraid of being carried away by the tide than dying of lack of food or water. However, their feelings were the same, as they all agreed it was time to leave.

Two hours later, the four misfits trekked over rocks and under cliffs, heading north and east from the beach they'd been stranded on. It was difficult to travel, but with determination and bearing scrapes and cuts, they'd made it to a wide, flat area that could accommodate them for the night.

Howard had filled two bottles with water and carried them in the jacket they pulled from the sea, bound by a piece of rope. They had no food, but they were able to catch a few rock crabs and cook them on sticks over the fire he started after scavenging for dry wood deeper in the jungle.

As she lay still pretending to sleep, Isabella grabbed at her stomach; the ache and grumbling never stopped. A tear trickled down her cheek, falling into the sand and disappearing as if it splashed on a hot rock. Her stout demeanor collapsed, feeling the vulnerability of hopelessness. Trying to stay strong for the others was a herculean feat. She felt as though she was dying on the inside. The nagging in her brain kept arguing with her heart, even as something told her there was a happy ending and that this hell would soon be over.

Isabella closed her eyes, trying to force herself to sleep, when her mind suddenly blurred, and a vision of her and the other girls came to her. They were huddled together on a boat. A dirty little boat, looking up at a larger ship before them. That vision faded softly, turning smoky, and then Amy appeared. She was walking on a beach wearing practically nothing. The place was unfamiliar, but she was getting used to that feeling.

Still semi-conscious, Isabella felt like she was teetering between asleep and awake when, finally, her eyes fluttered open, and she heard the water on the beach again. The little glimmer of happiness replaced the feeling of dread, and she allowed a half smile to appear. She knew the amulet was the driving force that kept her from giving up. For some reason, she felt it was her responsibility to save them all from a certain death.

As she lay awake for some time, Isabella was uncomfortable, but not altogether unhappy. Her mind took her back to the path she'd traveled since receiving the letter from the hospital in Hispaniola, dragging her through all the things she'd seen and done in the past two months. Although there were some horrible memories, there were also some wonderful ones. She remembered the trip that took them from San Juan to Hispaniola, recalling the friendships she'd made and the fine food she'd eaten there. She glanced at Maria and Carmen Louisa, who remained cuddled together beside her, nestled in the sand.

None of the gangly group slept well that night, unsure whether their move had put them in a more precarious position than before, but at the very least, they felt they were doing something.

On the new beach, the sun rose quickly and warmed the sand around them almost immediately. Waiting for signs of the incoming tide, Isabella explored their new location, finding a place where a fire had been built not so long ago. Knowing that a human had visited here before them gave her hope.

Abandoning the beach, the small group began trekking and repeatedly encountered more evidence of human occupation as the easterly direction turned more north. Howard spotted a faraway ship, the first they'd seen in all their time in this place, but it was merely a speck on the horizon.

Turning to look behind them, Isabella saw that the previous location would soon be underwater. They continued walking, eventually finding an overgrown trail that led them up a rise away from the sea. Soon, the trail led them to a view of the water above the rocks and surf.

It was windy there, but Isabella hoped they could make a fire to signal a passing fishing boat or ship. Maria wandered around the bluff, searching for dry wood and leaves, hoping to gather enough to make a fire and keep it going. As she bent and pulled at the dead leaves, she stood and caught a whiff on the wind of something familiar. It was food being cooked over an open fire.

"Isabella! Come quickly!"

Isabella was afraid she'd injured herself, in which case they had absolutely nothing that would work as a treatment, not even a bandage. She approached Maria and saw her pointing. "Look!" When Isabella reached the bluff's edge, she fell to her knees with sudden relief. Below them was a village. It was small, with only a few cottages and fishing boats, but it was a gratifying sight. She sat still in the tall grass and cried, so exhausted her body wouldn't let her move.

Maria waved to the others, and they moved toward the two girls, first walking and then running, anxious to see what the commotion was about. The women smiled and hugged each other at the sight of a small community.

The foursome paused momentarily at the possibility that the people might be aggressive or unwilling to help them, but the decision to continue and take a chance was unanimous. One after the other, they picked their way down the hill, leaving the bluff behind, and made their way toward the village. Once on a path that led them to the settlement, they'd been spotted, and a child and a dog came running toward them. The child rambled excitedly in a language that the girls were unfamiliar with. However, Howard recognized the language as Dutch.

It was obvious that they were friendly, yet relatively poor, and the gathering crowd was mostly made up of fishermen. More than twenty people came to greet them, the strangers patting their arms and backs, offering fresh water and a place to rest. All four wanderers wept tears of joy, realizing how the twist of fate saved their lives. Isabella stroked the amulet, knowing it was responsible for the turnabout of events that brought them to this place.

During their discussion with a few villagers, it became apparent that one particular gentleman was in charge. He understood them, speaking bits and pieces of several languages, and stated that bigger ships seldom made it to their bay. Their solution was that fishing boats often met larger vessels out in the passage, and they were confident they could find meandering ships a short distance from the island. They could make contact with a ship that might take their visitors to a larger, busier port.

29. Endeavor - Isabella - 1621

In a few short days, the three women and one man were shuttled on a fishing boat and escorted to meet a merchant vessel, taking a chance that today would be the day.

Maria had learned a few words of Dutch and could communicate roughly with the villagers. She proudly spoke what she knew to the older man, who was undoubtedly in charge of the boat.

The Spanish girl had discovered that a local merchant frequently visited the small island group and often took travelers to larger ports. It was a chance to find civilization again, and no one questioned where they'd come from, or where they wanted to go.

Once on board, the women received nothing but dirty looks from the crew members, who believed that having a woman on a ship brought bad luck. Howard was quite cheerful and talked openly to the men, but he knew very little Dutch, and his words were also met with sideways glances and unapproving headshakes.

The misfits settled into the middle of the boat out of the way of the men who worked to cast out nets and long lines as the vessel moved along slowly. The course was set to meet other ships beyond the channel between two unidentified islands.

It had been three or four hours since they'd left the fishing village, and the fishermen had brought in and recast the nets several times, filling the boat to capacity. Only one sail was deployed, keeping the vessel moving forward slowly so the men could cast out and retract the nets without trouble.

Isabella looked up and saw the captain pointing north. "Ship! Ship Ahoy!" The girls were amazed that the words he'd said were understandable. When it was spotted, no one knew what kind of ship it was, but as the two drew closer together, the captain muttered, "It's English." It was not the merchant he would usually meet, but they would try their luck at getting the travelers aboard.

Moments later, the crew of the tiny fishing boat hoisted a white flag to attract the attention of the passing ship. Another man in a striped shirt began to ding the bell as loudly as possible, encouraging the passerby to stop.

The large merchant ship's mainsail came down, which most likely meant they would pull up alongside to investigate the cause of the trouble.

The fisherman in the striped shirt spoke English very clearly. He cupped his hand around his mouth as he spoke, ascertaining if the ship could transport four people to San Juan or a larger port.

"This boat is from Meads Point, and we don't have large ships that come to our shores. Can you take on these travelers?" He gave his head a quick jerk in the direction of the girls. "Where are you headed?"

A dark-haired man with a hearty mustache nodded. "San Juan." He threw down a rope alongside the rope ladder, willing to hoist the women or their baggage onto the ship. It was welcome news to all parties as Howard and the girls pawed their way up the rope ladder.

They were greeted politely, but when Captain William Abrams addressed them, he merely nodded curtly. Looking them up and down before speaking, he said under his breath, "I hope you're willing to work for your supper." Given that they had been eating so little, fetching firewood, picking burnt bird bones off the carcasses, and sleeping in the sand, Maria, Isabella, and Carmen Louisa brightened, anxious to do their part for a regular meal.

None of them balked at work or the distasteful captain, and they were earning their suppers in no time. Several days had passed before they saw anything resembling civilization, and the ship was now skirting an island that was another day's distance from San Juan. Isabella tugged on the sleeve of a man manning the mainsail, asking him, "What port is this?"

The man scowled at her and said, "Ponce."

She knew Ponce was another settlement on the island of Puerto Rico, and she suddenly flushed with relief. Then another thought came to her, and she swallowed hard. She asked, "Will we still be going to San Juan?"

The same man was tugging on a rope and did not make eye contact with her, but growled, "aye."

She turned and stumbled back to the others. "It appears we'll be making a stop before continuing to San Juan." The other women remained quiet, expecting as much.

Although Isabella and Maria were going home, Carmen Louisa still had a distance to go to hers, and traveling on such a ship was dangerous for a woman by herself. Discussing this dilemma, the girls agreed that she would stay with them in San Juan until they were sure they could safely return her to Cuba.

As for Howard, he had secured himself a position on the merchant ship after consulting with the captain. None of the girls had asked him where he was from, but he seemed happy to sail. Several sailors who spoke Spanish were on board, and on more than one occasion, he and the captain conversed successfully. He seemed quite at home.

The next day, the ship approached Ponce late in the afternoon. It was a busy port, and several ships were at the piers, doing much the same thing: exchanging crates and supplies and loading and unloading their goods. Isabella, Maria, and Carmen

Louisa stood and watched the activity, keeping out of the workers' way. Seeing the busy port was exciting, and the women's anticipation at arriving in San Juan was palpable.

In less than a full day, they would be at the port of San Juan and only a few hours from home.

After the ship was underway again, the cook fixed up a meal of chicken and potatoes, having picked up the supplies in Ponce. A lovely port wine was served, bringing smiles to the crew members for the rest of the evening.

Maria and Isabella stood at the rail after the meal. They watched the sky's colors change once the sun began to set. Maria touched her hand. "One more day," she said and smiled blissfully.

Finally, the mainsail came down, and the vessel began to slow. The crew was busy preparing to dock at the long, busy pier. Although the three women didn't want to hinder their work, they couldn't help but want to see the city and port as they docked. The excitement was almost more than they could bear, waiting impatiently at the rail again.

Howard was gracious as he said his goodbyes, wishing them well and thanking them for their help with Alex, a loss still felt by the sailor. As they disembarked one at a time, they repeated goodbyes, disappeared over the rail, and descended the rope ladder.

***

Because they'd made port so late in the day, Isabella reminded them that the trek to Ch'in wasi was hours away, and she didn't fancy being on the road in the dark. They agreed to find a place to stay and wait until morning before making the final journey home.

Isabella carefully pulled out the bag of coins that Red had given her, extracting one coin and keeping the rest concealed. "This should be enough for a room and a meal." She stood tall and confident on her home turf, glancing up and down the narrow street for an Inn.

She led the others to a corner pub and inquired about a room. A pleasant-looking woman obliged, leading them up a narrow stairway to a tidy little room with two beds. The girls looked at each other and shrugged, accepting the space offered. The woman gave a short nod and left the room, closing the door behind her.

They looked shabby and unkempt, but none of the clothing they had with them was clean. Brushing and fixing their hair neatly, they smoothed out the wrinkles in their dresses and washed their faces in the basin, ready to see about a meal.

The pub began filling at sundown, and the girls finished their plates of overcooked chicken and stale bread, retiring gratefully to a room with a floor that didn't move below their feet. Since Isabella was the largest of the three, they agreed she could have a bed. The other girls shared the other; one rested at the foot and the other at the head of the glorious padded surface, sharing the blanket.

During the night, Isabella stirred restlessly, disturbed by another vision. The very realistic dream showed Amy with blood covering her body, and she suddenly disappeared. She woke up gasping and abruptly covered her mouth so as not to wake the others.

She wept, knowing that the injury to her friend surely meant the end of her. Knowing she was from another world, Isabella couldn't tell whether Amy had returned to her rightful place or was gone for good. She may never know and would certainly not share this dream with the others.

The room slowly began to lighten as the morning sun's glow filtered through the tiny window. Carmen Louisa was first to stir, anxious to get out of the shared bed and relieve herself at the chamber pot. The others did the same, pulling on the disheveled dresses for one more day. They gathered their belongings and made their way down the stairs and out the door of the inn.

Maria stopped at a street vendor selling bread and bought a loaf, splitting it between them.

It wasn't long before they were out of the town and on the quiet road north to Ch'in wasi. There were scattered clouds and a stiff breeze, so the heat was not bothersome. After a couple of hours, they'd come to Glory Rock Plantation, a place they were wary of, and kept their eyes down until they passed.

"It's a beautiful place, here, below the big rock, but ugly because there are so many enslaved." It broke Maria's heart to see how enslaved people were treated, knowing that none of the dark-skinned men and women chose this life. Today, it was quiet, but more than once, the girls had witnessed whippings and other beatings. The plantations were often so appalling.

When the young women reached the village, it was mid-afternoon. Tika saw Isabella first and ran, nearly tripping on her skirt. The screeches and laughter caught the attention of many, and moments later, Maria's brother was there, along with the rest of her family.

It was a grand reunion, and everyone stopped to greet the wayward girls. Carmen Louisa was accepted by Maria's mother, Lucia, who was excited to show her famous hospitality to an outsider.

Cayo was the last to see his daughter as he had been out hunting seabirds for dinner. He heard her voice first, thinking he was imagining it, and rounded the corner to see her standing and laughing, inches taller than the other women who bustled around her.

"Issa!" He said as he hustled closer, dropping the birds as he caught her eye. "Taytay!" Isabella exclaimed as she pushed past the other women to embrace her father.

"What? How is it you've come home?"

Isabella was known to the villagers as Issa, and although she thought she would outgrow the nickname, she couldn't be anyone else here. "It's a long story, but I hope to tell you about it soon. How is everyone? You look well." She knew if she filled her father in on all the sordid details, he would never let her out of the village again. Now was not the time, though; when the time came, she decided it would be best to leave some parts out.

It was a blur of conversation and laughs as the girls refamiliarized themselves with the news and updates in the little, close-knit community. Amos shouted, "Feast!" and several other men seemed to agree. With little coaxing, the families came together for a celebratory feast.

***

For the next five hours, they witnessed a whirl of activity. Issa and her friends eventually pulled themselves away from the food and drinks. Maria and Carmen Louisa toddled off with broad smiles and droopy eyes, as did Issa, increasingly happy to have an undisturbed night in her waiting bed. The three women crawled into bed, absolutely exhausted.

In the morning, well past sunrise, Tika woke her daughter with the promise of a bath in warm, fragrant water. Issa let a broad smile fill her expression as the bath was something she'd dreamt about on the unnamed island. Her mother had crushed hibiscus flowers to release the scented oils into the water, leaving a few to float haphazardly on top. Issa soaked in it until the water began to cool, repeatedly washing her hair in the wooden barrel, finally ridding herself of many weeks of filth.

Stepping out of the barrel and into the warm sunshine, she wrung her hair and twisted it into a long braid hanging down her back. Her mother had brought her a clean dress from the trunk that held most of her belongings. It was a deep green color with simple lines and no petticoats. She was more than happy to go without one because the weather was often warm and muggy, making a petticoat too uncomfortable to wear.

She was content to go barefoot and sit at a table with her parents, eating guava and flatbread and enjoying the peaceful morning. The simple meal was incredibly delicious, and she experienced the comfort of home as she ate. Once the meal was cleared, she went to her sleeping place and pulled the box out from under her bed. She took a precious piece of paper from it and began to write about her adventures. This process became her go-to activity when she reflected on her most recent adventures. It was her way of sending messages to those she met and didn't want to forget. The words she wrote were filled with memories and love. Lots of love.

30. Stamp of History - 1971

The pounding headache was more than Amy could bear, and she kept her eyes closed, wishing it away. She heard muffled voices nearby and took a long time trying to catch a glimpse of who it was. Through mere slits, Amy opened her eyes just enough to see a woman with dull brown hair, a white dress, and a funny little nurse's cap. She closed her eyes again, and a moment later, the woman held her hand, massaging it and patting her face, trying to make her come to.

She lay in bed, unable to move her limbs. They were so heavy. *Why were they so heavy?* Slowly opening her eyes again, she watched herself move her arm. It was like watching a slow-motion movie, only she felt she couldn't operate her body. Closing her eyes again tightly, she tried to erase the fogginess. The woman spoke loudly to her, trying to rouse her.

She said, "Hello, Amy. I am Sofia."

Blinking several times and working hard to focus, Amy decided the woman had a kind face and a terrible dye job.

"Hi." Amy pushed the word out, but her voice sounded hoarse and raspy.

"You've had quite a bump on your head. You've been out for days."

Amy blinked and paused momentarily, trying to remember where and why she was there. Nothing she tried to recall made sense.

Sophia shook her head and wrung out the washcloth with cool water, placing it again on Amy's head. "You know you were one of six people brought into the hospital because of the accident. You were a lucky one. We've waited quite some time for you to wake up." Then she smiled, trying to comfort the American woman lying in a hospital bed in a foreign country.

"How long?" Amy asked with a raspy voice.

"Oh, today would be day six."

She closed her eyes and tried to imagine where she was, but the only things that came to mind were Isabella's desperate words on the pier and Red's beautiful blue eyes, sparking when they met her gaze. She opened them again, and another nurse was staring at her. "You were talking. I think you said Red."

Amy fluttered her eyelids. "I did?"

***

For the next three days, Amy recovered. She ate and drank a ton of water, and walked the halls, indoors and out. Now, feeling much more like herself, she was ready to leave this depressing place with only one TV on each floor and nothing but lumpy quinoa for breakfast.

During the days she spent recovering, Amy tried to reconcile the adjustment from one century to another. Her heart hurt, having left Red the way she did. She craved his touch and the twinkle in his eye. A tear materialized in the corner of her eye as she recalled how her mind and her body withered away and returned to her body here. *It was so ethereal, yet so brilliant.*

Although the days seemed to drag on, the time finally came when she was released, having received a clean bill of health from the doctor who treated her. She rummaged through her backpack for the map, camera, and notebook, pleased that everything she had brought remained in her bag. Grabbing at her neck, she found the stone still where it was before the accident. For some reason, she didn't expect it to be there, but was glad of it.

Amy had never been in the hospital in Peru before, but naturally compared it to the hospitals in the US, which would take *everything* off and put it in a bag labeled with your name.

The staff and nurses in this strange place refrained from touching it, making her feel more at ease. There were so many unknowns here, in the country of her ancestors, and was precisely the reason she had to complete what Izzy started.

Amy called the airline about her previous reservation, scheduled to depart four days ago for Pointe-à-Pitre,

Guadeloupe, and explained that she had been in an accident. They charged her a convenience fee and then rescheduled her booking to depart at 4:30 am the following day. She boarded the train back to Lima and awaited the next leg of her big adventure.

Although she had been released because of her smooth recovery, she ached after more than half a day of travel. She stopped, bought tamales from a street vendor, and checked into a hotel. Amy needed a hot bath and a nice glass of wine to soothe her before climbing into bed. She knew it would be an incredibly early start the following day. Besides, she had completed her mission here, having obtained the answers to the questions she came to find.

***

The flight itself was normal, and the view was spectacular. Amy's mind wandered suddenly to Cam. She wondered about his condition but was hesitant to call, since he was in such a sour mood when she left him. Since he was out of sorts the day before she left, Amy thought leaving for a few days would be good.

In the next thought, her mind drifted to Izzy's trip to the Caribbean. *Was she taking the same steps? Where did Izzy find out about the stone?* These questions floated around in her head until they began to blend together. She sighed heavily, then asked the stewardess for a drink.

The plane landed in Caracas, Venezuela. Amy's next connecting flight would be on a puddle-jumper to Point-a-Pintre, Guadeloupe, which didn't depart for another two hours. Once on the island, she would spend the night, then rent a car and explore the day after.

Tossing and turning, Amy woke abruptly, only to see people in her dreams. She felt the mighty, gusting wind in her face, and she remembered the blood staining the deck of a ship. Moses. She saw Moses mourning her. *What happened?* Then she remembered Red's tear-stained face, and he kissed her hand. *Oh, my God. I was there! I died there!*

The reality of the dream slapped her, and before she was aware, Amy began wiping the tears that poured out of her. This vision made her feel empty because Red was the one absolute she held onto. He was her reason to be there. She shook now as the realness of it soaked in. The steadfast love in her life was alive and well in 1621.

Sadly, the young woman mourned her loss alone in the dark of the strange hotel, crying in a way she never had before. It was such a bizarre twist of fate. *How does this happen to people? To me?* she thought, remembering that what she had experienced had to be very rare. At that moment, Amy felt as though she was left all alone on the face of the earth.

When Amy looked at the clock, it read 4:10 am, and she was wide awake. She didn't try to go back to sleep, and her mind sought the distraction of her mission. She pulled out the map Izzy had left her and her notebook and laid them on the bed in front of her.

The main town on the map was Basse-Terre. She pulled the modern-day map of Guadeloupe from her backpack and found Basse-Terre, now a thriving city. The markers with notes showed a path between Basse-Terre and Boulliante. Amy closed her eyes and tried to envision it. The markings said simply, "Black stone, cliff edge, flat rock, and an arrow pointing north." She looked at the modern-day map and shook her head. *Would it all be gone? Lost to development?*

She had a short list of things she'd need to do, and now she added permission to cross private property. She may need to navigate properties to find what she was looking for.

When Amy was ready to leave, it was nearly 6:00 am, but she knew she'd have to wait one more hour before getting a car. Down in the lobby, she found coffee and sugar but no cream. Adding cream to coffee was probably a distinctly American thing.

Happy about the coffee, she poured a cup and sat in the lobby, which was peaceful at this time of day. Cam popped into her head. After her middle-of-the-night revelation about Red, how could she return to Cam and *pretend* she loved him? She did care about him, but this trip changed everything about what she thought she knew.

Driving to Basse-Terre was not much different from driving in Pensacola, except that the street signs were mainly in French. It didn't matter. She knew where she was going, at least until she made it to Basse-Terre. Finding the trail and the markers might be more complex than managing a few street signs.

Most of the drive was along a winding two-lane road flanked by a rocky coastline. Just outside the city, she pulled into a turnout that opened to a vista that stopped her heart. She could see a lively port just below, and little shops dotted the beachfront, but they dwindled to nothing, ending when the sand took over. A few sailing vessels were parading out in the bay, and beyond that was nothing but a blue ocean which met the sky in a smoky line on the horizon. It was hard to know where the sea ended, and the sky began. She wanted to be there. Be out where there is nothingness and get lost in the enigma.

Aiming her camera, she took several shots, but she knew this feeling it gave her could not be duplicated. Breathing deeply, Amy stood there for what felt like a long time, relishing the warm sun, and the breeze, fresh and virgin. It was a place she might like to stay.

The next thought brought her back to reality, making her realize that a place like this might be better to visit. Seeing the spectacular view every day would force her to take it all for granted.

She'd made a note about a museum that might have historical information about the area. Looking at the city map, she realized that almost everything had French names. It took her longer than expected, but she found the location on the map, and, jumping back into her car, headed in that direction.

Amy admitted she was slightly intimidated by the museum's grand entry. Walking slowly up a broad staircase, she looked up in awe at the massive marble pillars and imposing red brick walls. She never expected something this elegant to appear in the middle of what used to be a fishing village.

Taking a brochure and any other pamphlet she could find, Amy hoped something would offer a hint of the old settlement. Browsing through cases in the front hall, she saw artifacts of Spanish origin, along with many pieces of pottery and leatherwork typical of the Carib people, who established a significant presence hundreds of years ago.

One display featured a ceremonial rug or blanket used by the Quechuan people of Peru. The description stated that it was a floor covering upon which the bride and groom knelt while sharing their wedding vows.

Amy was ecstatic to learn that many people from Colombia and Peru made their way to this island to escape the torment and slavery and the Spanish invaders. Among some relics, she saw a ship's manifest with the names of several people who'd traveled either to or from this island. The names represented a variety of nationalities, and as she scanned the list, one name stood out: De'Cabrillo. That was Isabella's last name, and suddenly, the Isabella in her dream became very real again.

Her brief time in the Caribbean of the past came flooding back to her in a wave of emotion. She read as quickly as she could, wiping away her tears with the back of her hand. Amy lowered her gaze and scanned the placard, doing her best to conceal her blatant display of emotion.

She was relieved that she'd brought a notebook, in which she wrote down the names, places, and ship's name that carried the De'Cabrillos. The manifest's date was September 22, 1561.

Amy shook her head, awestruck. She was amazed at how the voice from the past resonated with her so undeniably since she'd been in South America. Her dream had revealed facts, morsels for her to follow.

It was mid-afternoon when Amy left, finally satisfied with all she had learned from the museum. It was time to get on with the search she'd started nearly a month ago.

Standing beside her rental car, she took a minute to understand the terrain from her vantage point. Flopping the large sheet of parchment down on the car's hood, she pored over the map again. Amy matched it as best she could to the landscape by moving it around until she thought she understood where the trail began.

Getting back into her car, she hastily headed to a geographical point in the city that she'd located on the map. Approaching what she thought was the beginning of the trail, Amy found a city park and a long, paved strip that skirted the length of it.

She turned off her car and sat for a minute, taking in the picturesque scene: a view of the Caribbean Sea and a busy port on one side; a dense green tropical forest on the other. The two views were split in the middle by the park she now faced.

Taking hold of her backpack, she got out of the car and closed the door gently. Locking it, Amy walked along the green velvet lawn and tastefully groomed landscape, her eyes scanning the grounds, looking for historical markers. Her mission was to seek out some morsel of the area's history.

There were fragments of the information she hoped to find freely offered on an occasional historical placard throughout the park, most of which she already knew. Historical data indicate that Basse-Terre was originally a fishing village, and on more than one occasion, the villagers had to defend themselves against Spanish invaders. Aside from a brief stint under British rule, the French consistently retained control of the island.

Scanning this peaceful place, she caught sight of an older man on a park bench. From her point of view, he seemed to be a lifelong resident and may know a few things himself, perhaps something of the history of this place.

"Excuse me, sir. Do you speak Spanish?"

The fellow smiled up at her. He wore a shabby straw hat with a black scarf tied around it. He was missing a few teeth but had kind eyes and welcomed the conversation.

He gave a subtle nod and said, "Yes, good day, madam." Amy smiled. She had never been called madam before.

"I was wondering if you could tell me about a trail around here that locals may have used a long time ago."

He glanced over his shoulder with a slight movement, signaling behind her. "Enchantée' chemin."

Amy looked where he was looking, but saw nothing. "Is it marked?"

He smiled again, and his look softened. With a twinkle in his eye, the man's voice went low and quiet, like he was keeping a secret. "Your feet will know where to go if the path is what you seek."

Thought wrinkles marked her forehead, as she hesitated a moment and looked at him intently. It was almost as though he was reading her thoughts. A chill ran through her, and she nodded, taking a second to savor his words.

Smiling slightly, Amy said, "Thank you." Hoisting her backpack up to her shoulder again, she began to walk in the direction the elderly fella had indicated.

31. Footsteps - 1971

As Amy walked along the path, she looked intently at the terrain, trying to match the map's landmarks to what she could see in the expansive green landscape. Walking east toward the end of the park, she read a sign that said *LA SOUFRIERE.* Her heart skipped a beat as she recognized the mountain's name from the hand-drawn map.

Pulling it out of her bag again, she faced the direction the sign pointed and sojourned on.

The hiking trail was clearly marked, and a historical placard mentioned an ancient trail from the 1500s used to spot Spanish ships on their way to harass the little island and its people.

Amy started up the trail adjacent to the ancient one. She thought about staying on the trail and just keeping an eye on the old path, but then she understood that she wanted to be on the other trail, not this one. She walked another 20 yards, crossed a boundary, and found the overgrown path that hadn't been walked in many years, now guiding her along the ancient route to the named mountain.

She'd hiked for what she thought was a mile, then took out the map and began comparing it to the landmarks she'd seen.

On the right, the hillside fell abruptly to a cliff front, just like on the map. *I must be on the right track.* Hiking further, she knew she'd found another feature on the map her grandmother had left for her. It said *flat rock.* Amy stared at it and squatted down to take a closer look. Pushing aside a rather large bush, she approached it, and her conscience told her to sit. Feeling a little weird, she sat on the rock, and only then took a minute to look around.

From her vantage point, she could see Basse-Terre below her right on the bay, and to the east, nothing but the blue of the endless Atlantic Ocean. Tiny islands dotted the field of azure, and they remained unnamed on the map she held.

Closing her eyes, she savored the cleanness of the air and the rich blueness of the sky. Amy felt a sudden heaviness, experiencing a pull from the rock she sat on. She thought the best way to describe it was magnetic. It was as if the stone itself pulled her closer to it. Bewildered, she suddenly felt a deep connection to the stone upon which she sat.

Realizing the amulet was modestly vibrating, she sat very still and quiet, straining to hear or feel what it was trying to say. A vision appeared, showing her an “+” on a map. It was her map! She concluded that Izzy's map from the safe deposit box was attuned to the amulet. Excitedly, Amy’s breath quickened as she understood now that the amulet truly had a place here. It made the map make sense, as the sitting stone, the map, and the amulet came to life upon this spot.

The elation she felt at that moment was overwhelming. Amy stood up and danced, throwing her arms into the air. This reaction was exactly what she had hoped for.

Settling down and now standing upon the stone, she saw birds just a few steps farther up the trail floating on the wind currents, their wings outspread and entirely still. Quietly watching them, a surreal feeling she got from this place stilled her heart, and she smiled.

Pulling open the flap of her backpack, she took out the map and unfolded it. Concentrating, she found the tiny + along the trail. She wasn't sure what it marked, but it must have been important if the stone had indicated its presence. Glancing over her shoulder, still in awe, she descended from the stony perch and focused on finding the special mark.

She came to a place where the old trail split, and rather than take the branch that headed toward Basse-Terre, she took the other, which traveled more north. The trail was overgrown and full of what seemed to be obstacles, but she forged on, keeping her eye on the trail that was thankfully still visible.

There was a clearing off to the right. Amy stepped out of the brambles and leaves and found ground that looked level, with a ring of rocks partially buried by decomposing trees, bushes, and leaves. Using her foot, she pushed vines and dead leaves aside to see it, and the two large stones suggested a campfire. It was a wide, flat opening that had not been used for a long time and was now part of the jungle.

She compared this place to the + on the map. There were words on the graph at one time, but they'd faded and had become unreadable. It looked like this wasn't the right place, but she was close. Rolling up the map again, she continued on the overgrown trail. Out of nowhere, a rather large lizard scurried past, giving her a start. The gangly gray creature made her aware that she probably wasn't the only thing roaming around in the wilderness on this tropical island.

Amy poked her way through the leaves, logs, and tropical flora, and the thought struck her that her ancestors likely had traveled this same path. *What were they like? What would it be like to be them?*

She walked a short distance farther and guessed this was the closest point to the + and it was time to leave the trail in search of it. Amy climbed an incline that rose above the trail, offering another view of the bay, thanks to a fallen tree that had opened up the space. "How cool," she whispered to herself. Taking the map out, she laid it over the fallen tree and compared it to the landmarks. The scale was nowhere near the proper size, but from what she could tell, the + was west of the last clearing. Now, in a dense forest, she feared she might never find the mark on the map. She tripped as she pushed through the massed vegetation and nearly fell, stubbing her toe on a cairn. She suddenly broke into a broad smile, astonished by this unbelievable find. *Was this the + on the map?*

She tugged and pulled away the vines and branches hiding it, finding another smaller cairn right beside it. After clearing the brush, she took out her camera and photographed the two stacks of rocks from all angles.

A glimmer of something caught her eye. It was strange because there was no sun here to reflect anything, but it was a glimmer, no doubt.

Putting her camera down to further investigate, she brushed away the dirt and moss that hid it and found a gold coin tucked in between the rocks about halfway up the side of the cairn. Working it loose, Amy saw the same Spanish Escudo currency she had a stack of back home. Collapsing beside the pile of rocks, she was utterly gobsmacked. She found the + on the map. This spot marks the burial site of an ancestor. "Izzy, I found it," Amy said in a whisper, laughing and crying simultaneously. She had gone through so much to get here.

She sat for a long time right there, wondering whose remains it was. She didn't know them but loved them and wished she could see the world as it was through their eyes, those many years ago. The contemplation led her to remember that they migrated because of the Spanish invasion by the Conquistadors, like so many others, and she curiously speculated if the Spanish had finally caught up with them – here.

Slowly, after being satisfied that she had found what she was looking for, her trip back to the rented car was dismal. The anticipation and excitement she'd repeatedly experienced had now dwindled to a mere flicker. The investigation into the stone's history kept her constantly searching, never knowing what was around the next corner. She wrapped her fingers around the amulet, which warmed gracefully. She knew this kinship was uniquely hers, and that thought brought her a swell of happiness.

Amy's outlook on her future had changed dramatically as she picked her way down the side of the mountain. She was determined to change directions, make her life count for something.

Aside from a trip to close out things in St. Louis, her next goal was to create a home in her new house in Pensacola. Amy's new life in the coastal city would begin now, bringing change with her the moment she returned.

With two more days before flying back to Florida, she spent them exploring the island. That evening, she drove to Boulliante to have a seafood dish in a quaint French cafe near the wharf. Amy sat alone in a booth that looked over the sea, sipping her wine. The windows and doors were open, and she experienced a fascinating blend of the smell of fish and the cheerful sound of live music on the veranda.

On the following day, Amy visited parks, museums, and courtyards with brightly colored tile floors and huge green tropical plants. The atmosphere of this island was inviting, and for a short while, she forgot the complications of the life that awaited her return. Although it was temporary, she loved the fantasy-like pretend life she had here on this Caribbean island.

The day came to board the plane and head back to reality. The hours-long flight gave her time to savor all she'd learned and to think about Cam and their now-unsettled relationship. That thought drifted gradually into the not-so-real relationship with Red. Her stomach knotted when she thought of him and how natural their interconnection had felt—like it was meant to be. Only, how could it? He was a figment of her imagination, right?

In less than two months, she had become deeply, emotionally attached to two men and was now here alone without either of them. Her peculiar relationship with Red wasn't real, but it made her think the one she had with Cam wasn't either. The waves of emotion Amy felt led her to doubt the closeness they once shared.

These invasive thoughts shook her confidence and exposed her weaknesses. Wanting too badly to feel love in someone's arms made her rush like the waves along the shore, and now, she retracted, just as the remnant of the wave did, back into the sea.

32. Splitting Loyalties - 1971

The flight and the layovers took most of the day, but it was just about supper time when Amy landed in Florida. She'd traveled light, with only her carry-on, which let her slip through the ominous front doors of the airport and hail a taxi in minutes.

She had paid weeks in advance for the hotel room, needing a private space for all her research and a quiet place to wait for the renovation that would take a couple more weeks to complete. Although it was only a hotel room, she was pleased to be there and glad the extended trip was over.

Amy wanted to call Cam, but more than anything, she needed to jump in the shower on a mission to wash off a little Caribbean dust. She pondered all she'd seen and done, wanting to tell him; there were so many things to talk about.

As she massaged shampoo into her hair, the thoughts of her trip played like a movie reel in her mind. Once the truth of the map was discovered and her expedition had been completed, Amy felt the wind in her sail suddenly stop, leaving her abandoned, as if adrift at sea. Content with what she found, it seemed she wanted nothing more than to continue her adventure.

The thought of Red's blue eyes never left her. As Amy stood there dripping wet, she imagined sitting beside him on the flat stone, admiring the view from the plateau. She recalled his gentle touch, a poignant reminder that he cared for her. He was so polite, so tender. A true gentleman. She admittedly missed him, feeling an empty place that his countenance occupied. His demeanor was unlike anything Amy had ever known. Most guys want to rip your clothes off on the first date, but not him. He *courted* her.

Finally done primping, she was ready and picked up the phone to call Cam. It rang repeatedly, but he didn't answer. She knew he used to play darts at the pub just down the street from his house. Maybe he started up again.

Slightly frustrated and anxious to see him, she got into her car and drove directly to his house. She glanced at herself in the rearview mirror, her thick, wavy hair pulled back neatly. She dabbed some pink lip gloss on her lips at a stop sign, then checked herself and smiled. *He can't resist this*, she thought, pleased with her reflection.

She slowed down and looked for his truck around the pub parking lot and on the adjacent street, but didn't see it. Then she drove to his house and saw his vehicle in the driveway. She parked on the street and got out, wondering why he wouldn't answer if he were at home.

Walking up on the front deck, she looked into his window, seeing only the kitchen light on and no other activity. She knocked on his door, but there was no response. Knocking again, she struck the door harder in case he was sleeping. She shook her head gently, made her way to the car, and retreated to the hotel, stopping at the liquor store for a bottle of wine.

Amy felt odd, like something was wrong, but she just couldn't put her finger on it. After letting those thoughts interfere with her otherwise pleasant mood, she slammed the car door and walked up the back hotel stairway to her room.

***

After drinking half the bottle of Chardonnay, Amy woke the following morning with a headache from hell. She went down to the lobby for her morning coffee and asked at the desk if they had any aspirin. Securing the pain reliever, she took her time getting ready for the day, thinking it was time to visit the recent renovations on her soon-to-be home.

Caden watched as she pulled up, tugging at the drop cloth draped over the front entryway. Amy smiled at the subtle changes he'd made to the exterior: a new roof and sidewalk greeted her, along with a larger, improved front porch.

He smiled. "What do ya' think?"

She took a minute to respond, taking in the changes. "I like it." The new porch was twice the size, featuring a deck large enough to accommodate a table and chairs. He opened the new front door, showcasing the exquisite tile floor in the entry and a brighter color scheme on the walls.

"Wow, it's really coming along. How about giving me a tour?"

Caden led her around, pointing out the features updated at her request, and tallying the few remaining items on the list. "All in all, if the inspections happen on time, we should be out of here in about ten days."

"That's perfect," Amy said, realizing that the trip to Saint Louis to pack up and move would take her about ten days. As he talked, her mind gently wandered back to St. Louis. She didn't look forward to moving.

They walked past the room with the attic access, and she noted it was still untouched, just as she wanted. It would take her a while to figure out what to do with that room, so far keeping her gold coins a secret. She was willing to part with some, but they would most likely be part of her legacy, something she could leave for someone else to find, just as Izzy did.

Leaving her new home, she thought she would stop by the warehouse and see if Cam could meet her for lunch.

Pulling up in front of the place, she found the lot empty. *How strange*, she thought. It's *the middle of the day and the middle of the week. Where is he?*

She drove to his house again and found that nothing had changed. It was as if he had disappeared. She shook her head, getting agitated now, and descended the steps, almost running into the neighbor from across the street.

"He's gone, miss. They done took him away."

"Took him away? Who took him?" Her voice had changed, becoming one she didn't recognize. She was almost pleading with the man.

"The cops. They came an' got him almost a week ago. Anita over there told me he was caught with drugs."

Amy pulled back, shocked. "Cam? No, that must be a mistake. He doesn't do drugs." The man shook his head and continued down the sidewalk. Realizing she was staring at him, stunned, Amy pulled back. She thought she would take a chance and stop by Nick's house. Maybe he knew more about it.

Although it was the middle of the day, she found Nick eating the lunch he had forgotten to pack when he left for work that morning. Smiling, he watched her exit the car and approach the door, opening it before she had a chance to knock.

"Let me guess," he said. "You're wondering where Cam is." Amy smiled politely. She didn't know him well but could sense he was intuitive enough to notice the distress on her face.

"Yes. I've been trying to track him down."

"Well, you can stop looking. Cam's sitting in county lock-up on a possession with intent to sell charge." Amy just stared at him, speechless. He continued. "The drug shipments he tried to blame on Rick and Danny were all his doing. The three of them were working together, but he wanted to eliminate the others to keep all the profits for himself. Dickhead."

What had happened while she was away? Would she have been a victim of his scheme had she been here? Amy suddenly felt there had been a wall that shot up just then between her and Cam. She took a deep breath and huffed it out. "What was he thinking? Man, just when you thought you knew someone, then this …" Her voice trailed off, unable to finish her thought.

"I'm really sorry to have to be the one to tell you. I think it'd be best if you just stayed away."

Amy let a half-smile show on her face. "Thanks, Nick. I'm sorry to just stop by, but I'm glad I did." She turned and walked away, then smoothly got into her car. Turning the key, she revved the motor and slowly drove away.

Amy turned the corner from his house and pulled the car to the curb, bursting into tears. She felt bad that she wasn't here with him to support him and angry that he could be such an asshole. Deep down, she was glad she hadn't remained there to bear witness. She sat and sobbed in the car for almost fifteen minutes before she cried all she wanted to, then pulled away. Telling herself it was the sign she needed, this arrest reminded her it was time to let him go.

Ever since her experience with Red, she hadn't felt the same about Cam. Her heart told her the amulet had led her away at the right time and brought her back at the right time, keeping her out of harm's way. She shivered slightly, thinking about how this whole debacle might have turned out.

33. Settling In - 1971

Checking out of the hotel, Amy loaded all the bits and pieces of her belongings into the van and headed back to St. Louis, ready to turn the page in her life and start fresh. She was saddened by her many losses: Izzy, Cam, Red, Isabella, Maria, and Carmen Lousia. She felt disconnected from the people who meant the most to her. However, she retained a great deal: the amulet, the trip to Peru and Guadeloupe, the house, the inheritance, and a lifetime of experiences. It had been a whirlwind, realizing two months had passed since she was last home.

As she planned the chaos of the looming move, Amy thought it prudent to visit her employer first. Then, the next stop would be the post office since she now had an address to forward her mail. She also had to visit U-Haul to secure a moving truck to transport everything. Planning all of this reminded her that change was on the horizon, and it made her feel alive and refreshed.

Amy reflected on all the late nights she'd spent researching and decided she loved it. She pondered recklessly over an article she'd like to write about the Caribbean, pirates, and the path of destruction they usually left in their wake. She didn't have to work at all, not anymore. She knew there was enough to live on, and likely her children would as well, but she enjoyed working, and perhaps now she would have the opportunity to do some freelancing.

***

Amy pulled in front of the three-story apartment and looked up, seeing her flat on the second floor facing the road. She smiled modestly, glad to get out of the car and stretch. Candice and Dan were walking down the sidewalk a block away when they caught sight of her. They both jogged in her direction, capturing Amy's attention.

"Well, hello! Where have you been?" Candice reached over and gave her neighbor a quick hug.

"Hey! Well, you know I drove down to Pensacola for my grandma's funeral. I was also the executor of her will, and my cousin and I had to pack up the house and a few other things. Turns out I've got a house waiting for me in Pensacola, so I'm moving there."

"Wow! That's not what I expected you to say!" Candice said, with surprise in her voice and an unhappy expression on her face. "When?"

"As soon as I get things packed up."

Candice retracted a bit. "So, you're leaving St. Louis?"

Amy nodded, her eyes diverting to the ground in front of her. "I'm afraid so. She left me an inheritance as well. I think I'll work on that dream job." Then she winked at Candice.

Now, her friend's eyes redirected, looking down at the ground. "I'm gonna miss you."

"I'll miss you too," and she added more cheerfully, "at least now you have someone to come and visit in Pensacola!" The comment made her smile.

“I can help you pack if you want."

Amy's eyes now showed a bit more enthusiasm. "I would love that!" The two agreed to begin collecting the tokens of Amy's life and put them all in boxes on Friday.

Beginning on Friday morning and through the weekend, Amy and Candice worked to fit the menagerie of items in boxes and bags. They shared the recent local gossip and drank plenty of wine, toasting her old life and granting good wishes to the new. Although Amy and Cammie hadn’t been incredibly close friends, they truly enjoyed each other's company, and the chit-chat made the task less ominous.

Before she knew it, a week had passed, and Amy’s life was now bundled in muted brown boxes, each distinctly marked with black ink. She checked off the notice to her employer and the post office. The night before her departure, she met with her friends and co-workers for one last goodbye. It was hard to acknowledge that the visit was so final.

Now that she had much more financial freedom, making a trip to see them all once a year was definitely possible and likely in the cards.

Amy was up early after a late night out and a very uncomfortable night's sleep on the living room carpet. She gathered the final handful of things in a paper bag and closed the apartment door for the last time.

Unable to let herself relax until she took the onramp to I-55, Amy guided her U-Haul out of the city. She didn't mind being alone on the road; in fact, her mind was busy with her recent adventures and imagining what her daily life would be like in Florida.

It was a strange feeling when she realized that she was facing the unknown. What used to make her hesitate now excited her. Amy was ready to meet the unknown head-on and embrace it. The near future may be murky waters, but her path was more straightforward now, with a purpose. Amy was free to do what she wanted, and the thought of it made her smile gratefully.

Two days later, the young ex-St. Louis woman passed a road sign that said she was five miles out and could smell the Gulf of Mexico before she even saw it. She wasn’t aware of it at the time, but this was a rare comfort to her, as, down deep, this place truly did feel like home.

Before she left St. Louis, she spoke with Caden, who assured her that the house was ready. It had received the final inspection but not her final approval, so after giving her an update, he agreed to meet her there when she got back.

One more night in a hotel, she told herself, needing a shower and a glass of wine more than she wanted to be settled into her new house. By the time she'd checked in, it was about 3:00 pm, and she called Caden to have him meet her the next day.

"If I pay you and your workers for their time, could I ask you to help me unload? I know very few people here." Caden laughed. He'd never been asked a thing like that before.

"Sure, I got some strapping young men who'd love to help. See you tomorrow at ten."

Amy was satisfied with herself. If they were unwilling, she would have asked Irene, Izzy's neighbor, if her son would help. Although Amy was capable of doing a lot, she surely couldn't do it alone.

Popping the cork on the bottle of wine, Amy showered, and without a choice, she drank the deep red liquid from the water glass provided by the hotel. It might not have been fancy, but the wine tasted the same, as long as she didn't have to drink it from a shoe.

One of the things that went back and forth with her to Florida and St. Louis was her typewriter, now safely nestled in the van's front seat. Setting it up on the half-moon table supplied by the hotel, she began to type. She had nothing specific to write about, but the words and feelings poured out of her like water over a cliff.

Before she knew it, she'd filled twelve white pages. Most of it wouldn't have made sense to anyone but her, though it felt good to get it out. Since Izzy was gone and she'd left her friends behind in St. Louis, there was no one with whom she could share her feelings, and writing it down now felt natural to her.

Reviewing the synopsis, she realized it was more about people and her emotions than the places or things she'd seen. It was as if she were writing it in her diary, speaking her heart, all along knowing the result was for her eyes only.

Peeking out from behind the heavy olive-green curtain was a stream of light from a pole that hung over a busy intersection. The view was misty, as the light reflected the microscopic droplets of moisture in the air. Given this city's proximity to the ocean, a nearly invisible layer of thick, moist air would often consume everything it touched. Amy liked it because it was different. It made her see things from a sharper angle; not good or bad, just with a bit more contrast.

Ten o'clock rolled around awfully fast, and Amy rushed out the door to meet her contractor. Glancing around the room again for forgotten items, she gently closed the door behind her, jumped into the U-Haul, and headed for Elm Street.

The crew was waiting by the curb in front of her house, smiling to greet her. Aside from the fresh paint on the porch, the outside looked the same as it did when she stopped by two weeks ago. Mainly knowing what to expect, Amy followed Caden into the house and let him cover the details while she mentally checked them off the list.

The knobs on the kitchen cabinets were wrong, but what he did pick out seemed to fit well with the design. The fixture that would hover above the dining room table was on backorder, and he promised to come and install it once it arrived. The details were complete, and Amy couldn't help but smile.

She signed off, and within minutes, the two workers began hauling the larger items from the U-Haul into the house, while Amy pointed out where each piece would go.

The truck was empty in under an hour, and piles of brown boxes surrounded Amy on the floor of her living room. Over the next few days, she worked to find a place for everything, making more than one trip to the local mercantile to purchase items such as curtains, plants, and picture hangers.

In one of the rooms, she set up an office and proudly placed her typewriter in the middle of her desk. The pale pink curtains cast a warm glow in the afternoon light, and she decided she liked this room very much. Given its inviting aura, she privately hoped that many good things would come from it. This workspace was perfect for her.

***

Several months after her final move, Amy sat and sipped her morning tea as she watched the local news run continuous coverage of Cam's trial over his drug charges. They had uncovered evidence that the transporting of the illegal substances had gone on for some time, and initially, Cam had brought on two more to help him expand his business. Greed seemingly got the best of him, and the ruse he attempted was meant to kill both of his helpers. However, the single survivor squawked like a laying hen when offered leniency for his testimony.

Amy watched the news and saw flashes of Cam on the screen. What she saw was not the guy she fell for, and she decided the romance was a ruse, too. When they met, she was admittedly vulnerable. She was grieving for her loss and swept up in the aftermath of tying up loose ends for her beloved grandmother. Not only was he so handsome, but he always said all the right things at the right time. He wasn't kind and loving; he was clever and conniving. After all, that's what criminals do.

It had been determined that over the most recent two years, Cam had moved more than a ton of cocaine and heroin in and out of the country, using his auction house as a front. He held auctions and shipped the remnants of people's lives across the country and overseas, but that wasn't the business that made him money.

Amy watched and listened, still wavering about how she ended up with him in the first place. Seeing his face did not make her miss him or want him; now, she felt disgusted when she saw his image on the screen. It turned her stomach, knowing he was the one she chose to be so intimate with. The man she had known before her trip and the one standing trial now were not the same man. And truth be told, the whole thing spoiled the way she'd ever felt about him.

The trial was complete, but the sentencing would happen at a later date, so the amount of time he'd spend in prison was still unknown. *No bother,* she said to herself. It had been a while since she'd even given Cam a thought, as Red Greaves currently occupied her emotional mindset. Real or imaginary, he held her heart.

Clicking off the television, Amy let out a heavy sigh. Here she was, in a beautiful place, in a beautifully renovated house, with a lot of money in the bank, yet still drowning in melancholy.

34. Indifferent - 1971

It was December now, and the leaves had fallen from the trees and shrubs that shed them, leaving the spindly branches exposed to time and weather. The sun rested at a lower arc in the sky, yet remained ever-present. Even during the worst days in Florida, it was warmer and more inviting than St. Louis ever was.

Sitting at her typewriter for hours each day, Amy typed, tore out the paper, crinkled it up, and started over. She could afford to be particular, keeping only the pages she was honestly pleased with.

The sun peeked out from behind one cloud, warming her shoulder and back for a moment, then ducked behind another, hiding once again. The aura of this room was pleasing, and it was a decidedly good place for her office. She blinked long and slow, soaking in the warmth of it.

Quite completely alone, she was not unhappy. The house was a warm and wonderful place. She felt the spirits of those who lived there before her, and the thought comforted her. She found work freelancing and researching, now focusing on a project for Melissa Armstrong, a woman who loved her work and hired her to do an article about extinct sea creatures. Melissa had become Amy's friend, meeting for coffee at least once a week and occasionally inviting her to dinner with her family. Amy had become like an aunt to Melissa's children, always bringing little treats when she visited.

Melissa and her family were great fun, but Amy still spent much of her time alone. She wasn't lonely for company; she was lonely for someone to share her life with. After all, her biological clock was ticking, and she hadn't found Mr. Right, or at least, a Mr. Right in this century.

She blamed her apprehension on Cam, or perhaps she would never be satisfied because of Red. The pain of separation was still a sharp, rough cut. Feeling that she was at a standstill, Amy knew healing had to take place before getting on with her life.

Keeping busy, she wrote and found pleasure in refinishing furniture. For the room with the attic access, she decided to paint the ceiling a pastel peach and finish it off with antique furniture; something one might expect in a house over a hundred years old. She had gone to a second-hand store and found a wooden rocking chair in great shape, along with a small side table to hold a lamp.

Amy’s days were spent writing, and evenings and weekends were spent working on a few special pieces. She wallpapered the room in subtle shades and laid a bright rug in the middle to add a pop of color. She never understood the profound satisfaction that came from physical work and skillfully transforming items into works of art.

These things occupied her hands and mind, allowing her to avoid the emotions that seemed to engulf her otherwise. She would detail her car, visit the library, and conduct follow-up research for her articles, all on a weekly basis, but there was a gaping hole that occupied her heart.

Adding a little spice to her limited outside contact, the neighbor, David, would come by to chat when he caught her outside; however, the rest of the neighbors kept to themselves. It was a delightful little street, just the perfect distance from the gas station, the store, and the bank.

All was well. Nothing was ever too exciting, but things were never really dull, either. Her whole life was just indifferent. She worried that careless, negative thoughts would influence her mind, turning her into an old spinster. She didn't want that.

Amy would frequently drive to the beach, park, and take long walks along the shore. The sea air always seemed to bring her fresh ideas, and she found that the wind in her hair and the whisper of the waves did a good job of clearing her mind of the clutter that trapped it.

Today, on the beach, among the seagulls and sand dollars, she found the peace necessary to consult the amulet. The semi-precious stone would frequently warm when she touched it, but it hadn't shown her any visions recently.

Not speaking out loud, Amy consulted its magic about Red or Isabella, and also, in silence, the stone would answer. It was almost as if that door had closed. She refused to believe it, sure that there was something in her heart or mind that interfered with the telepathy of it. She thought it silly, but perhaps she contracted a virus or illness that disrupted the connection.

Mindlessly, Amy searched for joy, but no matter what came to her, it wasn't quite what she needed. Flopping down in the soft, white sand, she slowly filtered the grains through her fingers. The warm sunshine distracted her, taking her mind to other places; sparking memories, both good and bad. Somehow, feeling provoked, she was suddenly driven to build a sandcastle.

Slipping off her tennis shoe, she ran to the water's edge and filled it several times, wetting the sand she planned to work with. She began with a moat and then built a castle wall for protection. She did a drawbridge and four towers, two in front and two in back. Going back and forth to the water, she wetted more sand. Watching her shape the sand, several people began to gather, and one fellow gave her a to-go cup he had in his car for the water.

Finally, after almost two hours, she had built a huge sandcastle standing monolithically on the beach. She had done an admirable job. Standing back, now teeming with pride, she smiled. *Now, why can't life be that simple?*

Amy sat nearby, watching as curious onlookers happened by to admire the work. Sitting quietly, she observed the tide. In the last fifteen minutes, it came in, inching its way toward her masterpiece.

She knew that when she built it, the water would erase her work, but she still had to do it. *Maybe this is the stone talking to me,* Amy thought, reacting to the sudden energy that had taken over. Its voice wasn't loud or obvious, but the way it guided her hands wasn't something she would have done on her own, and certainly, not to simply watch it wash away.

Smiling to herself, all she could do was watch as the water finally reached the moat and began to wash away the drawbridge. Sighing deeply, Amy stood, took her wet shoes in her hand, and made her way back to the parking lot.

Immensely satisfied with her afternoon's work, she climbed back into her car barefoot and drove home, feeling much better than when she arrived at the beach. The wind on this day was brisk but warm, and the clean, uncluttered air did much to ease her melancholy.

When she pulled up outside her adorable little house, she smiled. *A place of my own,* she thought, never having felt that she belonged anywhere more than she did here, now. Dropping her wet, sandy shoes by the door, she went directly to the kitchen and made tea, pouring a loose-leaf Earl Grey into her favorite teacup.

Casually walking into her living room, she sat gently on the couch and placed the tea on the table. A soft stream of sunlight painted the sofa's arm right where she sat. Caden had done the short wall in this room with a lovely bookcase, and Amy had almost filled it with her collection of books and manuals.

The books caught her attention, and as she scanned the titles, the two newer additions caught her eye. Pulling out one of the books that Izzy wrote, she smiled broadly. She envisioned Izzy swooning after some French Captain when she thought of her grandmother writing the book *ROMANCING CAPTAIN JACQUE*. It sounded intriguing, and she was in the mood for a cozy romance.

Opening the book, she began reading, not stopping for two hours. The book was interesting and nearly a carbon copy of Amy's experience in 1620. Still in awe of the period's accuracy, the book followed a young lady and her romantic involvement with a French Captain who constantly battled with a vicious band of pirates. Her heart gently throbbed as her mind induced a vision of the elaborate dresses from the trunk and the roughness of the seafarers. She felt the overwhelming tug at her heartstrings when she thought about Red at the supper table, ripping apart a crust of bread. Amy swallowed hard. *Had Izzy's experience with the stone been the same?* It was likely, but Amy never thought it was possible. She never thought her trip was possible. *Was it?*

***

She sat and contemplated for a long time before finally getting up and moving to her typewriter, decisively spilling the whole memory of her adventure onto the wonderful white pages. Amy didn't stop until she noticed the sun was going down, and she hadn't eaten all day.

Pulling out the last sheet of paper and placing the cover over her typewriter, she left the room, fulfilled. She was delighted with her ability to recall her visit to the past. It was so awful in many ways, and so wonderful in others.

35. An Unrelenting Force - 1972

Amy woke abruptly for the third time in a week. The dream was so real. She was panting, and her heartbeat wildly, snapping like a snare drum. She rubbed her eyes, seeing Red appear, smiling. His hair was much longer now, and the soft curls flicked in his face, encouraged by the wind. Her heart leaped at the sight of him, close and so real to her.

She touched her face, feeling a tear trickle down her cheek. Wiping it away with her knuckle, Amy was suddenly saddened. It was apparent to her now that the amulet was trying to tell her something.

She stood and pushed the curtain back, revealing a nearly full moon. It was beautiful, and the sky was softly painted, highlighting the wisps of clouds that crept slowly past. She went into the bathroom and took a long drink of cool water, splashing a little on her face to wash away the tear stains.

Climbing back into her bed, she curled up and grasped the amulet, wishing for the comfort it brought her. After a while, she drifted back to sleep, praying for more than a dream to hold her.

***

Slamming the door of the Volkswagen van, she slipped her shoes off before she even approached the sand. It took her more than one scrubbing to get the granules out of the car's carpet and the cracks of the seat from her last trip.

Finding a reason to go to the beach again, Amy decided to go shell hunting. She'd seen a pencil drawing of a sand dollar on the wall in the Dime Store on Main and wanted to try to duplicate it. The small woven basket she brought with her was one Izzy had used for many years, and she fondly recalled herself and Jennie accompanying her granny to the beach for the same activity.

The sun was bright and cheerful, much warmer now that spring was here. Feeling the warmth of the sun-soaked sand and the wind whipping through her wild red locks made her feel free. Drinking in the wind, the gentle sound of splashing waves, and the sun's reflection off the water lifted her spirits. The life around her consumed her soul with a heartwarming delight.

She poked, tugged, and tossed shells, some broken and some intact, looking for the right one to add to her basket for her project. The sun was most certainly bright and reflected sharply off the water as if it were crystals being pushed ashore by the tide.

Making the turn and circling back toward her car, she saw someone walking along doing much the same thing she was, but the figure was too far away to see clearly. Everything around the distant shape was a blur, and Amy thought she'd fallen into another dream; however, this time, the figure got closer and didn't disappear. A few steps later, she was able to focus and realized she knew him. The man had dusty brown curls and a Rolling Stones T-shirt, making large strides toward her. He had an off-colored beard that changed when the sun hit it. Recognizing his eyes as he approached, Amy gasped. It was Red!

Overwhelmed with the sensation of deja vu, Amy saw the more-than-real dream from the night before come alive right here in front of her. Dropping the basket, Amy ran to him. Tears flooded their faces as they wrapped in an embrace that neither of them relinquished for a long time. When Amy finally pulled back, a bewildered look flushed her expression. "How?" she said, realizing he was not supposed to be there with her in 1972.

Without a word, he loosened his grip on her long enough to pull a shard of a bright blue stone from his pocket and show it to her. She gasped in disbelief. Their eyes met, and she said, "You too?"

He nodded and smiled, but remained captivated by the depth of her deep brown eyes. "It was given to me by my grandfather, who received it from his grandfather and so on, throughout our family's history. I just knew you had the same fate when you disappeared, right in front of my eyes." He did not hesitate for one more minute, pulling her to him and kissing her long, as if savoring a beautiful sunset. She gracefully gave in to his touch, something she'd waited for since the day she faded away, losing him in the past.

"Did you come from 1971?" Amy began to inquire, curious if their journeys were the same.

"No, I left in 1969. I was stuck and didn't know how to return. I believe it was my love for you that brought me back." He reached down and kissed her again, almost as disbelieving as Amy. He still had a Scottish accent, but his words were much more Americanized than they were in 1620.

"I knew you were from a different time when you spoke of San Antonio. It didn't even exist in 1621." He gave a subtle wink and smiled. Her eyes grew big with surprise. She'd forgotten about that conversation.

He held the shard of the magical stone in his hand, and she took hold of it, pulling back his fingers to get a clear look. The piece was a narrow, broken chunk—a morsel about two inches long, now smooth-edged because of the years and experiences it'd seen.

"Did you leave from here?" He couldn't take his gaze from her as her appearance was nothing less than a miracle to him.

Still disbelieving, Red shook his head. “I was on a train in Egypt on assignment for Lively Magazine. I'm a photographer."

Amy's expression intensified. "How did you find me?" She said softly, her deep brown eyes twinkling as they met his baby blues.

This time, Red smiled shyly. "I didn't have to. The stone brought me here. In the past two weeks, it has shown you to me dozens of times. I went to the airport in Egypt to book a flight, not even knowing where to go, until I opened my mouth and the word 'Pensacola' came out. Then I knew you were here."

Amy's heart was whole again. After all this time, she had found what she had been looking for, the piece of her that she thought she’d left in the past: the irreplaceable love of her life.

"And … I'm not Red. My name is Hector. Hector Greaves."

Amy smiled and whispered, "Clever," as she recalled the name of his ship. "I don't care what your name is." Then she reached up, bringing his head to hers, and kissed him, absorbing all she could of him where they stood together as one on the beach.

Retrieving the basket, they strolled hand-in-hand, pacing themselves on the way back to the parking lot, exchanging snippets of each other's real lives before 1620. Amy pummeled Hector with questions about his family, how he died, or if he did. She learned about his work, personal interests, and preferences. Hector did the same, as he knew less of her than she did of him. She told him of her endeavor to uncover the mysterious protected identity of the amulet Izzy left her, and of her pilgrimage to Peru in search of knowledge. She didn't tell him about the gold, but she shared details of her inheritance with him, which prompted her move from St. Louis to Pensacola.

Making it to her van, they jumped in with renewed energy. Amy maneuvered the van to her house, a never-ending smile remaining on her face.

They reminisced about the plantation, Margaret, and Ben. Amy spoke of Isabella, Maria, and Carmen Louisa, her voice laced with sadness. She missed them and had hoped for a beautiful, prosperous future for her friends. She knew their world was gone and had been for nearly three hundred and fifty years.

"Isabella possessed the stone back then. She was my ten times great-grandmother, or something like that. She knew it; she knew I was from the future. She told me that day before she boarded the Victoria for her voyage home."

Hector nodded, still reeling from his emotions. "To be honest, the day after you disappeared, I went back to the plantation, gathered my things, and boarded my ship in search of you, and I never made it back to the plantation again. I expect

Margaret and Ben would have kept it going for as long as they could. I think Margaret knew I couldn't live without you."

"She's a sweet woman." Amy stopped. "Was a sweet woman." The reality of the two different worlds made her hesitate. "It's too bad you couldn't bring them with you."

Hector reached over and grabbed her hand. "I can't believe I found you." He brought her hand to his lips, kissing it softly. Amy remembered the beautiful evening on the ship where he had done much the same thing. The thought stirred her emotions with notes of love.

They stopped in the short driveway in front of Amy's house. Climbing out of the van and surveying the newly remodeled house, Hector said, "it's you."

She smiled. "Well, it's still pretty new to me, but the renovations are exactly like me. Come on in. I'll show you around."

He was impressed by the number of books she had and loved the porch, a private place to enjoy the quiet neighborhood.

"I'm a writer. Lately, I've written articles for several different magazines, and I'm fortunate that I have a great workplace." She waved her hand, inviting him to see her office.

Hector wandered around the room with one hand in his pocket, the other pulling back the curtains and touching things that belonged to her. He breathed deeply and sighed, walking over to the stack of paper by the typewriter. Amy started to speak, then stopped as he picked up the top page and began to read. The words flowed elegantly, depicting specific things she remembered on board the ship: buttons on clothing, the beeswax candles, and the twinkle in Red's eye. He set the paper down and looked up at her, his eyes full of emotion. "I don't expect a reaction when I tell you this, but I must say it. It is a burden I've carried since you disappeared, and your hand turned to a puff of mist. I love you. There will never be another in the world, this world, or the next that I will love."

Stepping toward her, he kissed her long and hard, pulling her so close he could feel her heartbeat. The warmth of a tear touched his bristly face, and he realized it was hers.

"I love you too. I have been like a leaf floating on the wind with no place to land. Just floating. Until I saw you, there was no one else for me either." Her words left her lips in a whisper.

***

They talked and touched for hours, catching up and filling each other in on their real lives, not the ones they lived when they met. The shadows began to lengthen, and the sky turned orange, signaling the end of another day.

Amy ordered Chinese takeout, and they went together to pick it up. They ate the food on the front porch in lawn chairs, savoring a couple of beers and watching the sunset.

"You'll stay with me, won't you?" Amy said gently. He shook his head, not believing his good fortune.

"I can't be without you. I just can't. Yes, I will stay." Amy smiled at that. She couldn't imagine saying goodbye to him, even if it was for only a few hours.

Picking up the containers and empty beer bottles, she went in the door, holding it open for Hector, then closed it after him, clicking the lock.

They climbed into Amy's bed, peeling off their clothes, and kissed long and passionately; neither was ready to do more than hold one another, almost afraid to let go. Now that they were finally together, touching, holding, and kissing, they slept like the dead. Finally, they both felt their lives were complete after having found what they'd been looking for: the missing piece.

36. Bound Heart and Soul

It was in Pensacola that Amy and Hector's courtship began, their relationship rooted in the enigma of the past. The two lovers knew there was still so much they didn't know about each other. The discoveries unfolded over several weeks, as the time together was filled with questions about the past and present. Reality soon became a flood of re-education for Hector, as he tried to catch up with politics, the war in Vietnam, and the cost of coffee at the grocery store.

Hector came with nothing, and everything he'd had was gone. To the best of his knowledge, he'd disappeared. He had no idea what was said about him, but knew that disappearances of Americans in foreign countries happened more often than most people knew.

Amy led Hector to the library and back to the research section, hoping to find something about a photographer's disappearance among the microfiche records of regional newspapers. Given that he'd disappeared while abroad, it was a long shot. Unfortunately, they came up empty-handed, but it wasn't for lack of trying.

Because of his reappearance, Hector began to obsess about his most recent realization: he would now be eligible for the draft. He could have avoided it if he didn't announce his return, but if he was discovered, being pulled into active duty was the least he could expect.

After talking to Amy about it, he began to ruminate frequently about his mother and baby sister, knowing he had a life before landing squarely in 1619. What had become of them?

One afternoon, as they strolled on the beach, Hector brought up these concerns to her and was determined to do the right thing. Amy stopped and wrapped her arms around him, holding on so tightly it scared him. "What's this?" He pushed back to look at her straight on.

"I've only just found you, and if you go–if you get called to war, it will be like losing you all over again."

"If I don't, and they find me, it would mean war for sure or possibly prison." Shaking his head, he said, "It's not a place I want to be." He had registered before his disappearance and avoided being called to duty because he had been out of the country more often than in it.

Later that day, Hector called Lively Magazine and talked to the editor. He explained that he'd taken a hit to the head and had amnesia and had only come around recently, returning as soon as he did.

His next call, dutifully, was to his mother, and he told her the same thing. The poor woman was weeping and laughing so loudly on the phone that Amy could hear her.

"Now what?" Amy asked him with pleading eyes.

"Nothing, unless they call."

Over the next week, Hector did his due diligence, becoming an American again and announcing his reappearance. Amy accompanied him with every appointment and every errand, grateful that this special man was in her life again.

Hector planned to go to Atlanta to see his family. It was important to him to introduce Amy to his mother and sister, as she was the world to him and the reason for his return. They had hours in the car during which Hector talked about his family, confessing that he had an uncle with whom his relatives had lost contact years ago. His father had two brothers; one died a few years before Hector's disappearance. The other was in Florida, as far as he knew, but since his father was gone, few from his mother's side of the family would reach out. He didn't know if that had changed since his extended absence.

Meeting Hector's mother was much like embracing her own. Helen Greaves had deep brown hair laced with gray, reminiscent of Amy's mother's. She was portly and had loving eyes, just as a mother should have.

His sister, Elsie, now a young woman, had ginger hair and eyes similar to Hector's. His coloring appeared to be a mix of his sister's and his mother's.

It was complicated explaining Amy's presence, but he said she had been with him when he disappeared. Amy smiled, thinking randomly about the lovely sunset she and Hector had watched from the veranda of his plantation home.

His mother said, "Why Pensacola? Why not here?"

Hector nodded, astute enough to know his mother thought he and his sister should never leave home.

Before Hector could answer, Helen continued. "I think your uncle Tino is in Pensacola. You should look him up." The words grabbed Amy's attention as if her hand had been stuck in a trap. It was a rare enough name that she doubted there could be another. She realized then that if he had been part of Hector's family, he would have, of course, been familiar with the stone.

They enjoyed the time with Hector's family, staying the night, and catching up on the years he had been away. Helen and Elsie were kind and silly, making the visit pleasant in every way.

Their sleeping arrangements put them in Hector's childhood bedroom, which had been casually renovated to a standard guest room. The bed was smaller than they were used to, but comfortable, and when they retired to it, they snuggled contentedly beneath the sheets.

His large, warm hands stroked her as he admired the shape of the swells of her breasts and the roundness of her hips. "Oh, my God, you are so perfect."

"Am I?" She asked teasingly, then kissed his cheek and tugged lightly at his ear with her teeth, further arousing him. They instantly clashed together; the pleasure of their connection was all hers, and Hector had to muffle her moans with his hand.

Hearts beating rapidly, the passion subsided, leaving them smiling and fulfilled. It was as if they had been possessed, the strange surroundings somehow encouraging their animal-like behavior.

Hector whispered in her ear, "I've been wanting to do that to you since you told me you were smitten."

Amy's eyes pulled open wide, and she giggled. "I wanted to do that to you since I first saw the sparkle in your eyes," and she suddenly recalled how her heart throbbed with merely a glance.

The following morning, they left Helen and Elsie with a promise to visit again and stay the weekend.

During the drive back to Pensacola, the couple seemed to be on a different plane than the one they occupied before, their souls having reached a place that neither had ever shared with anyone.

Having time for a more serious conversation, the two discussed Hector's family.

"I think I know your Uncle Tino," Amy confessed. He was at my grandmother's funeral and knew about the stone's magic. I know where he lives, too."

Hector was shocked, staring at her with his mouth ajar. "Then, we will try to find him." He smiled gently, looking at her longingly. He delicately moved her hair away from her face and whispered, "kuyasquay."

"Hmm, what does that mean?" Amy asked in a deep, throaty voice.

"Something my father used to call my mother. It's a pet name passed down from the Incan side of the family. It means "my love."

She smiled, then took his hand and kissed it. She remembered her mother calling her father "mi querida," bringing warm thoughts of her family to mind. It had been a long time since any such vision of their tenderness had surfaced.

The landscape passed by the car windows in a flurry of green overgrowth and gold underbrush as the two talked about their future, making it more of a game than a real-life decision. Hector was ready to get back to work, and Amy recommended that he get some equipment. Once he had the tools, he could inquire at local newspapers and television stations about freelance photography work. He was brilliant and had many other skills, but photography was his passion.

During one of their intimate late-night talks, surrounded by candlelight and wine, they reminisced about 1621—the people and the crops, not forgetting the fiendish Jack Ward and Isabella's secret.

"She was intent on telling me that she would leave something of herself for me in Ch'in wasi." Amy's expression intensified with the thought of that conversation. "How would you feel about taking a trip?" She hesitated for a moment. "To Puerto Rico."

Hector looked at her with curiosity. "You really mean that? You want me to go, too?"

Amy smiled wryly. "Get used to it."

Hector's excited expression morphed into a broad smile. "Of course. It'll be fun, like a lover's getaway." He pushed her down on the couch, kissing her deeply. He loved being here with her, soaking up every minute together.

Amy laughed, thinking that having an adventure with him would be fun. "I'll make arrangements tomorrow. Do you want to go back to Nevis?"

Hector was silent for a moment. He hadn't thought of it since the day he set off to find Amy. She could see the friction her question caused. " I-I'm sorry, Hector. We don't have to."

"No." He gave an ever-so-slight nod, holding up his hand as if it would stop his thought. "I think it would be good to go. Closure, you know."

She nodded and kissed him again gently. He responded suddenly, turning ravenous with his need for her. Picking her up, he carried her into the bedroom and undressed her carefully, as if she were a porcelain doll. They made love and lay silently together for a long time. Amy got up quietly, blew out the candles, and then climbed back into bed, wrapping her arm around him as she drifted off to sleep with a smile.

***

The travel agency was busy, but they'd secured their seats on a twin-prop commuter to San Juan, leaving on Friday afternoon. Neither of them was planning a vacation; it was more of an exploration, so packing was light, with mostly necessary items that fit into a backpack.

Amy had once again pulled out the family tree Izzy had made, writing notes regarding the ancestors recorded in Puerto Rico. Finding evidence about Ch'in wasi would be challenging, but since San Juan had been there since the 1500s, the area's records might still be available.

As they boarded the plane, the only extra carry-on item the couple brought was the camera Amy insisted Hector bring. The case was bulky but loaded with all the tools of his trade. Anxious to put his honed skills to use, he looked forward to creating an evidence trail that might lead to a book featuring full-color photographs on every other page. Finding their seats in the coach section, Amy took the window seat, excited for the adventure that lay ahead.

The flight was remarkably short, and the couple landed in San Juan at dusk, enjoying a cocktail and a light dinner before settling down to rest and ready themselves for the busy day ahead. They strolled back to the hotel, arm in arm, taking in the menagerie of buildings, some old sprinkled among the new. Laughter and conversations filled the air as the voices of others echoed, drifting alongside them in the evening breeze. Even here, the warm ocean breeze and the simple sounds brought them back to a place and time long ago.

Taking their time over morning coffee, Amy closely examined a map, pointing out where she thought the village was located. She'd found a reference to a large plantation nearby called Glory Rock, a place named after a huge cliff-like overhang. "That should be easy to find," Amy stated cheerfully, but she really had no idea what they would find or if they would even get close.

Starting at the courthouse, neither Amy nor Hector could find a record referencing Ch'in wasi. Finding little else but landowners of the larger parcels, she reasoned that it would not likely be on a map or in the courthouse if it were a settlement of refugees. She assumed they would have to find it themselves.

Amy suggested they visit the library. A city as old as San Juan must have some documentation concerning immigrants and related settlements. By asking a few people on the street, she discovered that Biblioteca Carnegie was most likely home to the oldest books on the island.

Making their way hand in hand, through the strange, tangled streets, they found the building, which she realized was hard to miss. It was a looming whitewashed building with pillars across the front and a grand entrance with an ornate door. "This architecture is beautiful," Amy stated, running her hand along the marble pillar, which led to a portico featuring white and gray marble tiles. Realizing Hector hadn't responded, she turned and watched him as he moved across the lawn, taking pictures from different angles. She smiled, understanding this was his canvas, and she and the building were his subjects.

Speaking to a receptionist at the front desk, Amy inquired about local history books or documents. The woman pointed to a long staircase and said, "The special collections are up the stairs."

Amy's heart was beating faster as she climbed the stairs. She was anticipating finding something, anything, that might give them the evidence they sought.

She found that the oldest collection of books and documents was easily accessible. Among them were hundreds of years of documents, along with a book of plat maps covering hundreds of square miles. She opened the simple folder and laid several diagrams on the table. The library was built well after the maps were created, but the main road through the city remained in the same location. Hector helped her find North and South, then matched them to her incomplete map.

It was just a guess, but recognizing etchings on the map with nothing identifying them made Amy dig deeper. What was it marking? Pouring over the faded yellow pages, they spent an hour cross-referencing Izzy's map with the library's map and found that the conclusion was the same. Ch'in wasi was not marked on any map or plat.

"It must be there. Isabella just didn't make it up."

Hector nodded, but it was still not clear why it wouldn't be there. He pored over the maps and other documentation, looking for connections.

He found a letter among the plat maps that spoke of times of war in Florida, when local native tribes hid deep in the Everglades, but didn't see any reference to treasure, people, or the amulet.

Digging in just about every book on the subject, they found bits and pieces, but nothing that clearly linked the map to any city or mark consistent with both the map and the historic register.

Relinquishing the win to the library, Hector and Amy left, no wiser than when they arrived, but impressed with the well-kept and organized volumes of ancient documents.

37. Whispers from Beyond

Paying the fare for an excursion on a bus, the two lovers melded into several other tourists and were on their way to a tobacco plantation. The guide led people to the remains of several outbuildings, explaining the realities of life on a large working plantation. The information hut featured maps of the area, restrooms, and a fountain for filling thermoses with water.

A handful of artifacts were found from the farm and the surrounding area, some labeled Incan, some Dutch, but most were specific to Spanish culture.

Amy studied the artifacts in the glass cases lining the walls with intense interest, obviously looking for something specific. Some of the relics were from a woman's bedroom dressing table, including a metal hair comb and a decorative hair bob similar to the one Isabella wore.

Having absorbed all they could from the plantation, they continued up the road, keeping the immense cliff front of Glory Rock in sight. It was hot in the sun, and precious few trees to find shade. Spotting one tall tree right next to the road offered a perfect place to stop.

"I was hoping to find some trace of the world we left behind," Amy said in a somber tone, searching Hector's eyes for encouragement.

Hector took her hand and squeezed it lightly. "I have mixed feelings. Many things I miss from the 17th century, but I felt like I was a prisoner there." Amy looked at him, quietly digesting the emotion she saw in his eyes. She blinked hard, remembering her captivity and understanding just what he meant.

She reached over and kissed him gently. "I just gotta know."

She stood and walked in a small circle, seeing a rise just beyond the big tree, and climbed it to take in the view. Just beyond the big tree was a large, round boulder. She put her hand on it to boost herself up, finding an indentation with her fingers. Looking more closely, she saw that the indentation was part of an X with a circle around it etched into the stone.

"Hector, come look at this."

He jumped to his feet and walked toward her quickly, hearing the question in her voice. She pushed back a bush that half hid the symbol, and he followed her eyes, concentrating on the marking she found. He said, "People from that time would often mark trails like this. Kind of like an address."

Amy looked at him, surprised. "Do you think …?" Then she scoured the area around the rock, and although the overgrown, bristly bushes hid it well, she could see an ancient trail beginning right there from the marked rock. It was invisible from the road, hidden by shrubs and sparse trees, but the ground beside it was well-worn and travel-bare. Her eyes opened wide with excitement. "You know we have to follow it, don't you?"

Hector smiled. He knew her well enough to recognize that her curiosity was far more significant and overpowering than her common sense. Agreeing that there was some faint trail to follow, he nodded and held out his hand. "Lead the way."

The hike was challenging because of the overgrowth. The shrubbery was stiff-branched brambles that scratched their arms and legs. Once they'd passed over a knoll, the landscape dropped gradually, and taller trees took over. The couple hiked for nearly an hour before coming to a secluded lake. Even though there hadn't been people in this place for a very long time, an area on the south side of the lake had been trampled, and very little grass grew. Amy thought it was likely due to wildlife but trekked in that direction anyway to make travel easier.

They saw a rough trail continue past the small lake and followed it, finally coming to a clearing where discernible activity had once taken place. Drawing closer, the two found a firepit–a ring of rocks where there was proof of fire activity. There were huts—piles of rubble broken down and weathered, edging back into the trees, barely discernible.

Amy turned to Hector again and said, "This must be it. Ch'in wasi!" Hector was a bit more skeptical, as it could have been any village, hundreds of years old.

Amy went to several piles that were now ruins, moving logs and decomposing clusters of grass and leaves, revealing the inhabitants' homes below the wreckage. She found a section of rug in what might have been a bright red-and-black woven pattern but had faded to nothing more than shades of brown and gray. Moving to another, she found a bed made of straw on logs still together and covered with the filth of the forest.

She scoured as many homes as she could find, each one uncovering evidence of the previous inhabitants while Hector photographed it all. Each item was logged in history, a time and place long forgotten by the world, but not forgotten by Amy.

Coming to a more extensive rock foundation, Amy was sure this place belonged to people who were better off. Just outside was an iron wash basin, against what would have been an outer wall. The iron was full of holes and rusted beyond recognition, but it was a basin of some kind. She moved the part of the roof that had fallen in on top of a bed, finding nothing more than a frame, but her eyes caught the corner of a box that was visible beneath it.

She pulled it out and found it was in remarkably good shape, obviously sheltered from the weather underneath the layers of wood and grass. She found a spot to kneel with the wooden box, pulled off the top, and slowly revealed the contents. It was a book. It had a piece of wood bark on the top and bottom, and a leather lace held it together. The pages within it were uneven and yellow, brittle with age. She gently pulled back the cover and found what looked like a diary, a record of letters hidden for safekeeping.

Reading the first page, Amy discovered the writer mentioned someone named Maria and her betrothal. There was a message about her grandmother's passing as she moved to the next page. She leafed through a few more pages and found one that said *Dearest Amy* across the top. Slapping her hand over her mouth, she was flabbergasted and realized this was the part of herself Isabella had left for Amy to find in Ch'in Wasi. She looked up at Hector, tears forming in her eyes. She said in almost a whisper, "This is it."

Amy combed through each page. Nine of the yellowed pages started with *"Dearest Amy."* Tears streamed down her face in a torrent, and all Hector could do was watch. She had been assaulted and physically abused, marked as a whore, and meant to be sold as a slave, yet she was overcome with the pain of separation and departure from that miserable world. He didn't understand. He couldn't.

As she pored over the pages of the simple journal, Hector photographed her, amazed at her compassion and the beautiful being she was. He knew then it wasn't only that they fell in love 350 years ago; she was the one he'd always looked for. It was as if the enchanted stones pulled them together. The words kindred spirits came to him. The connection so intense that they couldn't be whole unless they were with each other. He felt the connection, and the emotion brought a tear to his eye. In his soul, he felt the depth of her sorrow. But was it sorrow? Maybe it was joy, knowing her friend made it back to her home and lived a full life.

She'd looked at every page and word written and discovered that the *Victoria* had been wrecked in a storm, and her three friends and one man had been stranded for weeks. They were eventually rescued and escorted home, and she lived in Ch'in wasi or San Juan for the rest of her days on earth.

Isabella had dreamed of Amy and Red, repeatedly mentioning them, knowing their lives would be one. She spoke of the amulet's power and protection, sharing that she couldn't be happier to know that Amy ended up with it. She wrote about her son, Juan Pedro, and great-granddaughter, Rosa Maria, who had been born with deep red, curly hair, just like Amy had. She knew it was a connection shared with the amulet, Amy, and the earth.

Closing the book, she held it tight as a flush of emotion swept over her. Wiping away the tears that streaked her face, her eyes met Hector's. She stood and let him hold her for a long time. "You found it," he softly whispered as she sobbed, glad that the events of this journey had brought her full circle. Hector was pleased that he was there to offer her the comfort she needed, seeing this new fragile version of Amy.

Holding the book up, Amy looked at Hector with puffy red eyes. "This is why you need to go to Nevis," she said, seeking his secrets in the depths of his eyes. He gradually nodded his agreement.

***

After taking a tour boat from one island to the next, they arrived in Charlestown by dinnertime. The trip took 24 hours, but it was relaxing, the drinks were good, and the company was subdued and comfortable.

Hector seemed nervous the closer they got, as it roused his sense of direction, having traveled these waters more often than he traveled the road to his plantation. They stayed at a hostel and ate in a pub, trying to get their bearings before setting out to the plantation the next day.

The quiet island environment piqued Amy's curiosity, and her eyes darted around, searching for something familiar. She had only spent a short time there but knew that the memories would come flooding back in a rush of familiarity.

***

In the wee hours of the morning, Amy raised her head off the pillow to see Hector sitting in the straight-backed chair with his head out the window, staring at the beam of moonlight reflecting on the water in the bay. Amy rose and knelt next to him on the chair and put her arm around his waist. She kissed his shoulder softly, then rested her head against it, adoring him silently.

He turned to her; his eyes filled with deep memories and a glimmer of desire. "It's the same moon," he whispered, then turned toward her, kissing her passionately. He gently lifted Amy, his eyes locked with hers and carried her to the very cozy full-sized bed. They made love passionately, the moon looking down on them, filling the space with a milky white glow.

Left breathless, neither had felt a love so deeply as that they felt for each other, being connected in a way that was so immersive it was impossible to understand.

"I wanted you for so long. I spent long nights on the veranda thinking about the evenings we spent together strolling the plantation. I was so in love with you."

Amy's eyes glazed over as she reminisced. She smiled as he kissed her breast, petting her softly. "I was, too," she said, then lifted his chin and kissed him lavishly with her soft lips.

***

As the sun rose, the pink hue of the sunrise began to paint the wall through the narrow crack between the shutters. Amy woke suddenly and yawned, remembering where she was. She reached over for Hector, but he wasn't there. Instead, he sat in the chair by the tiny table along the wall. She rose onto her elbow. "Good morning, babe. Couldn't sleep?" Hector gave a nod. He had been cleaning the lens of his camera equipment and placed the piece gently back in its padded container.

"I've been watching you sleep. You make funny faces when you dream." He stood and approached the bed, close enough for her to pull him to her. She kissed his head and held him.

"It's gonna be fine. Perhaps the place is now owned by someone else. Or maybe it is a ghost town. Either way, we're gonna see it today and be done with it." She did her best to let him know she was right there with him.

They lay together in the morning's quiet, dozing lightly and snuggling. It was nice. Amy's vision began to blur as she drifted lightly on the edge of asleep and awake. She was abruptly whisked away into a violent dream where pirates killed two men to get to a box of treasure or something. It was violent and sad. One of the men pleaded with the sword-bearing man, asking him to spare his life because of his family. The sword swung anyway.

Suddenly jolted, Amy emerged from the dream with her heart pounding, terrorized by the dark side of humanity. She looked at Hector, who was staring at her with the same panic in his expression, taking in breath short and quick. "What?" Amy said, half knowing the answer.

"I just saw something. A dream, maybe."

Amy sat up and focused on him. "What did you see?"

Hector sat up then and told her of a pirate hacking up two men. "It was awful."

Amy began to smile, making Hector sit back in wonder. She excitedly grabbed his hand and said, "We shared a vision!" Hector shook his head in relief, disbelieving that the vision of butchery made her happy.

Curiously, he asked her, "I thought the stones only showed us the future. Does this mean we go back?"

Amy could see the fear in his eyes, but didn't know why the stones showed them the bloody murders. "I don't know,"

Hector responded hesitantly. "I'm not ready for that."

They were too shaken up to settle down and sleep again, so they prepared for the day, packed up the few items they brought, and walked to a street cafe for coffee and a rosquet.

The village had now become a thriving city and was quite different from the layout they remembered from centuries ago. Heading up the gradually rising lane, they stopped and looked back at the square below. Hector was a step in front of

Amy and headed in the general direction of the old plantation, strolling down the narrow lane. They hadn't walked for very long before the number of houses began to thin out, and the rise in the road gradually leveled, making the walk less strenuous.

Hector took a moment to turn and look at the city behind him, trying to recall how it had been. He mentally placed things in the spaces now occupied by houses and shops, then smiled gently. "I know why we had that vision." His voice took on a different tone, and Amy gave him her full attention.

"The hostel we stayed in is where the square used to be, and over the years, the invaders would do public executions there. The spirits of the executed moved us."

She shook her head. "That's never happened before. Why now?"

"Have you ever slept where public executions took place before?"

He took the stone from his pocket and held it to her amulet. The stones began to warm in their hands, and Hector said with astonishment, "Because they're together." Then he smiled, much more relaxed. Moving to her, he kissed her cheek gently, tickling her jaw. "Maybe they're good for something else, too," he said, kissing her again more aggressively.

She smiled in response. "We'll have to give that a try."

Hand-in-hand, they walked up the road away from the town and out toward the plantation. Some areas had not been developed, but everything else was different, except for the shape of the landscape, which remained. A grove of trees still existed where he thought they should, but it was markedly different. Homes lined the road closer to town, thinning out the farther they went.

There was an elderly man in his yard pulling weeds in his garden, and Hector approached him. "Hello, sir, good day. Could you tell me if there is still a plantation at the end of this road?"

The man shook his head. "It's being farmed, but there's no plantation there. I don't know anything about that." He huffed and went back to his garden duty.

Fifteen minutes later, the two stood where the old carriage house used to be. The foundation rock stacks remained, but the stones were in unorganized piles covered by vines and other flora. The carriage house, the main house, and the outbuildings were gone.

Amy's face was saddened. "It's all gone."

Hector shook his head, disturbed by seeing such a beautiful home disappear into dust. Although it was his home, where he flourished, it was not where his heart found its greatest happiness. He wanted to be home in 1969, and in this place, he had been trapped, nothing more than a prisoner.

"Well, not everything is gone. I was a pirate, after all." He looked at Amy mischievously, giving her a wry smile.

Retaking her hand, they began to walk up the trail, the same one they'd taken with the horses for the afternoon ride. Pondering for just a minute, Amy reflected, and her expression changed; that was the day she fell in love with Hector.

The fields they'd passed that used to be sugar cane were now corn and tobacco. The stalks painted the landscape in colorful patches and were beautifully healthy and thriving. Different greens and golds changed the panorama, giving it a fairytale-like appearance. It was indeed breathtaking.

The road continued much the same as it had all those years ago, but as the hill climbed and the crops thinned out, the remaining trail became more rugged and unkept.

Hector had his camera ready and snapped many shots of the colorful fields and the expansive view as they finished the climb. Although Amy was curious about why they were making the trip up the hill, she knew it had to be a stash that nobody knew was there. She watched his expressions with wonder. It made her happy to think this place was special to both of them.

They reached the crest, panting and catching their breath. The view was just as she remembered; the town below on one side and the vast open sea on the other.

The wind wafted through their hair, and they both smiled broadly, remembering the day they'd spent together, with this view and each other.

Hector brought her to him and kissed her, smiling again. His expression was playful and fun-loving, just as if he were a sixteen-year-old boy. When their eyes met, they clung to the others like nectar to a flower. She could see that the loss of the house and the change in crops didn't affect him. He was content in so many other ways, knowing he was free and had found a love he'd been missing all those years.

Hector's smile suddenly vanished when he thought of why he had made this climb. Handing Amy his camera, he walked to the lee side of the flat, weathered stone that had sat on the knoll for centuries. He found another stone with a sharp edge, scraped away all the grass and moss from the location, and began to dig.

Twenty minutes later, Hector had a hole about a foot deep. He found something, but the soil was so tightly packed around it that his progress slowed. Working diligently, his effort was rewarded with the soil loosening from its edges. The box, or what was left of it, was finally free, and he pulled it out of the shallow pit.

Looking up at Amy, he gave her a wink, satisfied that he'd found what he was looking for. The box crumbled as he pulled a black canvas bag from it. The rope that bound the bag was in remarkably good shape, and with a few tries, he pulled it loose, opening the bag to reveal its contents.

There was a beautiful diamond necklace with several diamonds that were over a carat. It was set in silver, slightly tarnished but shining dramatically in the sun, quite unscathed by the years beneath the earth.

Next, he pulled out a set of silver serving utensils, also relatively untouched by the years beneath the soil. These were nothing like the knives and forks of the 20th century. They were quite heavy and appeared to be hand-tooled, featuring a unique fleur-de-lis pattern on the handle. It was fine silverware meant for royalty.

He then took the bag and dumped the remainder of its contents. It was a mosh of silver and gold coins. They were of Spanish and English origin and are now hundreds of years old. These items were priceless, and there were as many of these coins as Izzy had left for Amy.

He looked at her with satisfaction. "See, I told you they didn't take it all." He jumped up and hugged her. The joy he felt wasn't from the riches; it was because the riches survived, just like he had--just like Amy had.

Amy had her grandmother's fortune, which had been handed down to Izzy and then to her. A fortune. Hector had his fortune, which he'd worked for, stealing from thieves. A fortune. Getting the coins valued would be a challenge, but neither of them would ever have guessed the unbelievable good luck they had, all of it coming about when they found each other.

38. Once is Enough - Pensacola 1972

Content and now quite satisfied with their findings, Amy felt that the mystery of the amulet and the gold Spanish coins was solved, at least to her satisfaction. She observed Hector and could see how the trip had unburdened him, more relaxed now as he embraced hope in a way she'd never seen him do.

After opening a fine bottle of wine and toasting to their return, the lovers sat on the front porch together. Lying back in the lawn chairs as far as they could, Amy and Hector watched the clouds. Gracefully, slowly, the clouds thickened and thinned. Their features faded quickly as the evening sky slowly faded to lavender, then to indigo, as the sun disappeared beyond the horizon.

"Remember the evening we sat on the veranda at the plantation and watched the sunset? It was the exact same sun." Hector smiled nonchalantly, thinking about how romantic the comment was.

Amy smiled lazily, then watched as a light breeze moved his shoulder-length hair, twisting it in the wafting air. His hair did this anyway, but the breeze teased it. "I love that you think of things like that. When we were up on the knoll in Nevis, I thought about the sitting stone and how you made me feel when we sat there silently together. I love you." Hector reached over for her hand and brought it to his lips, kissing her knuckles gently.

"Ah, lass, you're my miracle. My magic." Then he winked a sparkling eye at her.

***

In the weeks after their return from the Caribbean, Amy and Hector’s relationship bloomed. Amy told Hector about Cam, the drug bust, and the trial, sharing her embarrassment about their relationship and how clueless she was.

Hector confessed that he had a girlfriend before he left for Egypt, but she left him while he was out of the country for a crop duster pilot. He heard from his sister that she had moved to Indiana. He also confessed that he'd paid for whores in the 17th century, finding the women there shallow and inconvenient.

"Until you, I never knew what love was." He shook his head, looking down in a way that Amy couldn't read his expression. "My God, the way I'm drawn to you is magnetic. Why is that?"

This topic frequently sparked their conversations, and the best explanation either of them could come up with was that the stone and the enchanted amulet knew the outcome before either of them did.

Amy held up the amulet and looked at it intently. "Why do you think I woke on that ship as a captive and sold *to you* as a slave? Why do you think the one person in the entire universe I was put there with was my ten times great-grandmother? The amulet simply had to bring us together. The universe knew you were there. Maybe it also knew I would come and made you wait till I did. It is a very utopian thought, isn't it?"

He laughed loudly. "I've never put the idea to task, but now that you mention it, the whole thing is more than coincidental."

The full moon began to rise when the sun disappeared, changing the light on the front porch of Amy's newly remodeled house. Amy and Hector were reluctant to move from the lawn chairs, but they made their way into the house, locking the door behind them. Hector took her empty wine glass from her, brushing her arm when he did. He set the glasses down on the counter and then pulled her to him, kissing her with ardor.

Easing back just enough to look into her eyes, he whispered, "I'm never going to let you go." He wrapped his arms around her and held her close to him for a few minutes, drinking up the scent of her.

The house with the two of them in it felt as natural as warmth did when the sun shone. Finally feeling complete and happy to be home, they snuggled and fell to sleep only moments after sliding into the bed.

The next several days were spent trying to determine the value of their precious coins. Hector pulled a handful out of his stash, keeping a few relics for those times a person might need them.

Amy confessed that she had only sold a few coins to cover the cost of the trip to Peru. It was time to do the grown-up thing with them. She sold some for cash, just as Hector did, and kept a few for keepsakes, or possibly college tuition for a son or daughter.

When Amy sold her coins for the trip, she wandered into the nearest pawn shop and took what they offered, which was about half their value. It was exhausting to go from one exchange to the other, where they could get the coins valued, and to the coin shops and dealers to see what they could sell. The entire process took the better part of a day.

"This is the perfect time to celebrate," Hector confessed, wanting to go out on the town for a nice meal. Amy was happy about that, finally having an occasion to wear a dress and some jewelry.

Amy bought Hector clothing since he arrived from 1621 with nothing. The clothing he did have was sensible. None of it was fancy for a date night, but he found something new, clean, and that fit him nicely. The dress-up game was complete, and they looked the part. Reflecting at them in the mirror were images of a nearly perfect couple.

Hector went to the dresser and revealed the black canvas bag that held the few coins and silver pieces he'd recovered from Nevis. Removing the amulet from around her neck, he pulled out the dashing diamond necklace and draped it on Amy's neck. "Perfect," he whispered into her ear.

She secretly tucked the amulet in her pocket, not quite ready to be without it. Then, smiling, she slowly turned to Hector, wrapped her arms around his shoulders, and kissed him passionately. She flashed a provocative smile, a twinkle in her eye, and said, "I'll pay you for that later." He kissed her playfully, unable to resist at the moment. She smiled and turned to get her purse, feeling like she had her cake and got to eat it, too.

They wined and dined and had a lovely evening together. Neither was quite ready to go home, so they decided an evening stroll on the beach would be a wonderfully romantic way to wrap up the rest of the day. Hector removed his shoes and rolled up his pant legs so the surf wouldn't ruin them. Amy took off her shoes and carried them in one hand, her arm draped around Hector's waist with the other.

They sauntered the beach arm-in-arm as the moon rose, painting everything it touched with a dreamy, soft glow. They talked about the twist of fate that brought them together, and

Amy said, half-teasing, "What would happen if we got rid of them?" She pulled the magical amulet from her pocket, held up the precious stone and continued. "It has done a lot for us, but I almost feel reliant on it." She looked hard at the amazing blue amulet, seriously contemplating the thought that ran through her mind.

Hector looked at her, momentarily silent, and then nodded in agreement. "You're right. It's time for us to stop looking to the stones for help." He took her by the shoulders and turned her so he could look directly into her eyes. "There is nothing that would change the way I feel about you."

"But what if our love were to change without the stones?" Amy voiced her biggest fear, unsure if they would feel the same outside of the magic that had brought them together.

"These things brought us together, but they don't make us feel the way we do. They only created a gateway. The rest is up to us."

Walking a few more steps in silence, Amy stopped and stared longingly out into the unending blackness of the sea before her. Dropping her shoes, she slowly reached into her pocket and pulled out the amulet, holding it tightly with both hands. Then she walked out into the bay until she stood knee-deep in the water and threw the amulet with all her might, watching it splash into the sea.

Hector smiled as he pulled his piece of stone from his pocket, joining her in the water and doing the same thing. They stepped back slowly, watched the place where the stones disappeared, and then turned to each other, laughing.

"The beginning." Hector's voice pierced the peaceful sound of the waves crashing against the sand. He looked at her, savoring the view.

Amy nodded. "The beginning." She took his hand, and they walked back toward the car slowly, free in a way they hadn't been since their discovery of the stones.

Epilogue

"Nick!" Jesse called out to his brother, pissed off because the winch jammed again and the trawl net was still half in the water. "The damn winch is stuck again!"

Nick and Jesse had been running one of their father's shrimp boats in the Gulf for nearly six years, and the trawler seemed to always have the same issue on the days when the catch was the biggest. Nick approached the winch with a rubber mallet, giving the fittings a whack, then another, and the wheels began to turn again. Jesse got the grease gun and gave the pulleys a quick shot, lubricating them enough to roll through the rest of the day.

After finally pulling in the last net and dumping the load onto the deck, the boat headed back in to get a spot in line for the processing plant buyers, who stop buying once they've hit their daily limit. It had been a long day, but the season was in full swing, and there was bound to be a few more long days before the boys' lives settled down again.

Scooping up the shrimp to unload, Jesse caught sight of something still lying on the deck underneath the writhing critters. He reached his fingers just enough to catch the leather lace and pluck it from the slime left after the last of the shrimp were lifted off the floor of the trawler. It was a necklace with a leather lace and some ornamental knots.

It was a brilliant blue stone, attached to a fitting by a hole pierced through it, held by leather that had been worn smooth. "Look at this." Jesse held the stone up, a bit surprised at the catch. It wasn't something they brought up very often. Most of the time, it was a beer can or a piece of clothing. Never jewelry.

"Well, I'll be," Nick stated with curiosity. He moved closer to his brother to get a look at the unusual find. It was an interesting treasure, for sure, but he took very little interest in things that were not shrimp related.

Jesse rinsed it off thoroughly and tucked it into his pocket. He would figure out what to do with it later. If it were worth anything, it would likely end up going to a pawn shop. Jesse had very little need for a necklace but would surely take a couple of bucks for it.

On weekends, the brothers would head into New Orleans for drinks and a few laughs, meeting their friends at the pool hall. There were a couple of places that would buy something like what Jesse was selling, and they would stop there after completing the list of things their mama wanted done.

Duties done, and forty minutes away from meeting the guys, Jesse and Nick stopped by Jack's to see if he would buy the blue stone necklace. They might get just enough to have a couple of beers and a round of billiards, courtesy of the stone and string.

"Hey, Shauna," Nick said as he pushed open the door of the shop. The smiling blonde salesgirl met them and asked how the shrimpin' was. "Is Jack around? I got something to sell."

"I think so. Let me get him."

The woman went into the back room and, a moment later, reappeared through the curtain, followed by an older gentleman. "Well, if it isn't the Simpson boys. Hello there." The portly man spoke loudly with a billowing voice, and his friendly expression softened his otherwise boisterous manner.

Nick stepped up to shake his hand, and Jesse took off his baseball hat in his presence. "Hello, Jack. Good to see you," Nick said as he grasped the man's hand. "Jesse here found something he thinks might be sellable. It's just no use to us."

Jesse reached into his pocket and pulled out an item wrapped in a handkerchief and laid it on the glass countertop. "We pulled this out of the ocean," he said blankly. Jack unfolded the cloth, revealing the brilliant blue necklace.

"Huh, now ain't that somethin'." He picked it up and examined the article from all sides. "It is a rare find; I'll give you that. It might go nicely in this display case right here." He pointed to a section with a variety of other necklaces and oddball jewelry. "This leather could stand to be replaced, but otherwise

. . ." Both Nick and Jesse's eyes followed the man, waiting for a number.

"How about ten bucks?" Jesse looked at him as if he were joking.

"Aw, it's easily worth double that. You said it yourself; it was rare. How about twenty-five?" He bantered right back. Jack ran his hand across his face, and the four people in the little shop could hear the raspy sound of his day-old stubble against the palm of his hand.

"I'll give you twenty, and not a penny more."

Jesse and Nick looked at each other, then back at Jack. Jesse gave a subtle nod and held out his hand. "Deal," he said, smiling.

A moment later, the two boys left the shop with no more than a wave over their shoulders, on their way to the pool hall. Once they were out of earshot, Jack looked at Shauna and said, "Let's get this cleaned up and put a fresh lace on it. I think we did good on this one." The man turned to leave, heading back behind the curtain where he hid for the rest of the day in his office.

Acknowledgements

I'm forever grateful to God for giving me the imagination and curiosity required to complete a historical fiction novel. It has become, before most of my passions and hobbies, my absolute favorite thing to do.

Digging into facts of a period, often little known truths about battles and hardships fuels me. It seems that the more I know, I'm enthusiastically motivated to try to *up* the last book. It is challenging and fulfilling. Who could ask for more?

As Amy set out to find the truth about the mysterious amulet, I saw myself, for I possess that ever-present curiosity about things, especially those places and things of our past. I wanted her to find trouble, as we know it's not unusual to find trouble when digging in the back of closets.

When Amy was going through her grandmother's closet, I found myself envisioning my grandmother's bedroom, the dresser, the jewelry box, the closet, and the dusty boxes shoved to the back. Thank you, Nona.

I used to work for a newspaper, and to visualize the layout of Cam's warehouse, I would imagine the newspaper production floor and garage. Among other strange recollections, it brought me back to the smell of the "hot off the press" paper and ink of the production floor, too. Funny, how these things creep up after so many years.

The strength of the love between Amy and Hector was difficult to describe, but I wanted it to be so much greater than what humans might feel in a normal relationship. Their love is something that supersedes worldly things, and it makes me smile to think of the two of them locked in their neverending happiness.

I have carried the group of friends with me by shoving the draft in their faces and anxiously waited to hear what they say about this new cluster of ideas and adventures. I thank you all (Kathy A., Marie, Ruth, and Kathy O.) from the bottom of my heart. Even though none of you want to express dislike, I can tell if you like it or not. (wink, wink) It is the push to perfection I need.

Thank you to my family for sharing my posts and helping me to get the word out about my books. I'm proud of them, and my gratitude for your help is over-the-top. Thank you for never giving up on me, and as always, thank you to those people I encounter every day, for the inspiration and interactions that keep my creative juices flowing.

Consider leaving a Review

If you've enjoyed reading *Whispers of Secrets Past*, please consider picking up the other books in the series:

Dream Keeper

Guardian, the Origin of the Amulet

Shadows of Defiance

If you have read any of the books in the Amulet series, I would appreciate it if you could leave a review on Amazon, as that is the only way, besides word of mouth, to encourage others to purchase them. Thank you for your continued support and enjoy the read!

www.ingramcontent.com/pod-product-compliance
Lightning Source LLC
LaVergne TN
LVHW020654110826
845149LV00012B/1997

* 9 7 9 8 9 9 6 1 7 5 4 0 6 *